"Arcadia"

…and the long road to get there

Sidney Krogh Political Thriller - Series III

Copyright 2024, Stanley K. Michelsen, Jr.

ISBN: 9798879422924 *with* Amazon/Kindle Books

and

Sea Dunes Books
seadunesbooks@gmail.com

Correspondence:
Stanley Michelsen Jr.
stancd305@gmail.com

D1713496

This book is a work of fiction.

1

Dedication

In loving memory of:
Stanley Michelsen, Sr.
Dorthy Jean Michelsen
Karen Michelsen Williams

To my family: Marlene, Sean, Kellie, Piper,
Parker, Kendall, Caitlin, Dustin, Reid, Miles,
Stacy, Cole, Drake, Lesley
Jordan, Cash and Liv

Preface

Just two winters ago, I started having these peculiar dreams. They were a continuing story and very creepy at first! I could never imagine me, or anyone else, having dreams with a storyline. My sleep patterns were interrupted for most of my adult life when my nose was shattered while serving in the United States Army. Back in the late 60s, the Vietnam War was in full swing and I invited myself to participate. During one mission my Army PSYOP team was embedded with the 3rd Marine Division in that narrow band of terrain just south of the 17th parallel called the DMZ. The NVA (North Vietnamese Army) had dissenting views about us being there so they began lobbing Soviet made (OF-841) HE mortar rounds in our direction. One of these rounds detonated in a tree high above us.

These are called tree bursts and they sent limbs and other lignocellulosic fibrous material plummeting straight down upon us. A large piece of this pulp found my face and shattered my nose. When I woke up, I was told I'd need to wait at least a week for the swelling to go down before my nose could be reset. I didn't know this meant it had to be rebroken and reset. When the first resetting didn't work, it had to be rebroken a second time and reset again...and yet again...no joy! You get the picture, numerous rebreaks and resets until they got it right. Except for the fact they never did get it right.

No one knew about sleep apnea back then and if they did, it didn't have a name or a machine to strap to your face and to sleep with every night. When such a device was finally invented, it was called a CPAP machine. It included a hose connected to a mask to deliver a constant and steady air pressure to help you breathe while you slept.

When I returned from Vietnam, I moved back to Key Largo, but I could no longer dive. I could not clear my ears

3

because of my nose problem. Diving was my ultimate passion growing up in the Keys. Watching Flipper on TV and pretending I was Sandy or Bud Ricks with our mega smart dolphin, Flipper, was like living in a dreamworld.

I had other problems acquired while in Vietnam, one being an explosion which sent me into a tree injuring my lower back. The VA called it a "single catastrophic event," which has dogged me my entire life. I stayed away from the VA system for many years after dealing with my spinal problems as well as the hassles and hoops one had to go through in order to prove the obvious. Many years later, I finally went back to the Miami VA Hospital to be tested for my sleep disorder. During the evaluation, I had to sleep overnight while they monitored my breathing and other bodily functions. It's called nocturnal polysomnography (or PSG) and during these tests, I was hooked up to equipment that monitored my heart, lungs, brain activity, breathing patterns, arm and leg movements and my blood oxygen levels.

To make a long story short, I had sleep apnea. My right nostril was so blocked that only .2% of oxygen was allowed in. A week later, I was on the operating table at the Miami VA and my nose problem was fixed. Or, was it? I was told my brain would never believe that my oxygen supply would be normal while I was sleeping. For the rest of my life, this brain of mine would open my mouth and have me snore in all the oxygen it could find. That was unless I could go to bed with my CPAP strapped on. The only good to come of this was that I could clear my ears and dive again.

I could also dream once more...YES! I had forgotten that most of your dreaming occurs during REM sleep and I hadn't enjoyed that privilege in so many years that I didn't remember what it was.

However, now that I'm dreaming again, there is a certain baggage which has accompanied these dreams into my life...a

4

precognitive phenomenon, if you will. I know I'm no psychic and there's no accepted scientific evidence that precognition exists, so how the hell do I keep seeing or becoming directly aware of events in the future?

I had left the beautiful Florida Keys and headed west/ northwest to Alaska. "Why?"…you ask! Good question...I got divorced and went looking for a new adventure. I wanted to expand...go somewhere to start anew where no one knew me. I had no idea about the extremely harsh winters.

Just twelve short months ago, it started...these continuing dreams. It was like they had a storyline. Winters in Alaska bring more hours of darkness than you could ever imagine. During these months, I'm always tired and sleepy, always having what we've come to call dream/nightmares. When I say, "We," I'm speaking of Marty, the love of my life and my best friend and me. I met her in Alaska while she was taking part in a marathon in and around Anchorage that raised money for the Leukemia Society. She now shares this journey with me and has to put up with all my quirks.

Last winter, a dream/nightmare became reality when three Russian Antonov An-24s landed at an airstrip in Nuiqsut, Alaska. These are Soviet tactical transport planes. They had entered the United States with a MK-54 SADM or Special Atomic Demolition Munition. Their mission: to blow up the Alaskan Pipeline at Prudhoe Bay, Alaska.

Aboard these aircraft were Saudi Arabian Special Forces and members of Putin's private military called The Wagner Group, also known as PMC Wagner (private military contractors). A battle ensued and all Wagner Group members as well as all Saudi Special Forces were killed that day. Only the aircraft's pilots and crew survived, along with some ISIS terrorists they had brought along to make it look as though the destruction of the Alaskan Pipeline was a terrorist attack. The

5

only other two members who survived were a Pakistani nuclear physicist named Dr. Pavez Ahmad and his Saudi handler, none other than Ahmad Asiri, who was supposed to be in custody in Saudi Arabia. Mr. Asiri was the leader of the Saudi henchmen (working directly for Saudi Prince Mohammad bin Salman) who killed and dismembered journalist Jamal Khashoggi inside the Saudi Arabian Embassy in Turkey in the fall of 2018. Ahmad Asiri is now housed inside a Supermax cell in the United States of America due to his involvement that day in Nuiqsut. (1)

To add a little more spice to this ongoing dream/nightmare, Ahmad Asiri has a son named Mustafa Asiri who is a member of the Saudi Arabian Special Forces and quite a marksman.

He set out on an unsanctioned mission to assassinate me (Sidney Krogh) a number of months ago while I was in the town of Scammon Bay, Alaska, to receive the tribal name of Inua (meaning "the spirits" in the language of Inuinnaqtun).

This was an honor being bestowed upon me by the Copper Inuit clan. It was their belief that I was responsible for the deaths of the men who entered their sacred land in northern Alaska (Nuiqsut and Prudhoe Bay) to destroy everything they held sacred, namely the private military contractors known as Wagner Group.

To me, their premise was flawed because I was there with six other men, one of whom was Milton Coley. Milton was the one who actually figured out the Russian plot to blow up the Alaskan Pipeline and he deserved all the credit. My old PSYOP team from Vietnam consisting of Whoman, Pistol Pete, Hulk and Big Al – plus Sheriff Wayne from Whittier, Alaska, were there to lend Milton a hand. Also, Milton Coley died that day from a single high-velocity round fired by one of the Wagner Group (PMC),

(1) Book Series I - *Hypersomnolence*

better known as Putin's private army. That assassin died immediately from an arrow to the back of his head and one to his throat, shot by a young hunter belonging to the Copper Inuit clan.

Mustafa Asiri never got the chance to put a bullet in me due to the fact that he also took an arrow to his forehead and one to his throat. You can guess whose bow fired those two arrows. The demise of Mustafa Asiri happened while I was with Marty and others in the town of Scammon Bay, Alaska, at the honorary naming ceremony with the Copper Inuit.

If you think for one minute that my problems ended there... think again. Another dream/nightmare happened soon after the Nuiqsut, Prudhoe Bay incident. My godson, John Musselman, Jr., was assassinated in Orlando, Florida. He was the head of the ATF (The Bureau of Alcohol, Tobacco, Firearms and Explosives) for that area. The hit on my godson was to bring me to Orlando where it was believed Wagner Group Commander, Dimitri Smirnov, wanted to put a bullet into me. It appeared he lost his son in Nuiqsut last winter as he was participating in the plot to blow up the pipeline. Father and son, who both belong to Wagner Group PMC, were both private military contractors working for Putin. This was to be payback for losing his son. (2)

Well, the good news is...I'm still alive! The bad news is...my latest dream/nightmare. It was so real...I was inside the Kremlin listening to a conversation between Vladislav Surkov (Gray Cardinal) who is Putin's predecessor and Dmitry Utkin who is the founder of Wagner Group. President Putin was killed by a small group of Saudi assassins sent by King Abdullah bin Abdulaziz Al Saud. This was in retaliation for the Russian assassination of Crown Prince Mohammad bin Salman in Morocco (even though it was CIA sniper Dolph Coley who took

(2) Book Series II - *Bedlamites*

him out — right in front of the Russian commandos). Utkin served in the GRU (Glavnoye Razvedyvatelnoye Upravlenie) Soviet military intelligence organization. He also commanded a Spetsnaz unit (special purpose military units) reaching the rank of lieutenant colonel. They're discussing payback...not just payback, but retaliation, retribution and revenge!

While they're enjoying shots of Billionaire Vodka – Vladislav asks, "Is it true this vodka is poured through diamonds as it's bottled?"

Dmitry replies, "Yes, this is true! It is said that this gives the educated palate the true vodka experience with its quintessentially smooth and vivacious opulence," as he hands Vladislav his refill. They clink their glasses together and in unison say, "Na Zdorovie!"

Dmitry continues, "This cyka (bitch) they call President is becoming much too popular. She spent a week in Brussels meeting with Belgium King Philippe Leopold Louis Marie and Minister-President Rudi Vervoort. Other world leaders from NATO joined them. We had eyes and ears at those meetings, but we already knew their agenda...tightening their stranglehold on Mother Russia and China.

Gray Cardinal says, "She is very good at playing this game and she has shown herself to be a worthy opponent. That being said, I believe it's time for us to make a statement of our own."

Dmitry asks, "What do you have in mind Vladislav?"

Gray Cardinal continues, "That PSYOP team...we got one of them in New Orleans, the one named Whoman. We also took out Milton Coley in Nuiqsut, Alaska, last winter. Milton's son is the CIA sniper who put down Crown Prince Mohammed bin

8

Salman in Tangier, Morocco, right in front of our commandos. Take him out along with Sidney Krogh and the rest of his team — I want them all dead! That cyber czar at the Alaskan pipeline, Ross Brown — dead! And...I want the head of security at the Port of New Orleans, Chucci...dead. Give this mission to your best men and tell them there is no such thing as collateral damage...kill them all!"

* * *

"Sidney! Sidney! Wake up," Marty says, as she's shaking me.

I look at her with fear in my eyes while I try to explain, "Marty, it's not over..."

She asks, "What do you mean it's not over Sidney?"

I sit up in bed as I try to piece together what just happened. How do I best elucidate this dream? I guess I'll just have to lay it all out there so I say, "Marty, while I was in my hotel room back at Disney's Art of Animation Resort in Orlando for John Musselman Jr.'s funeral, I had a very bizarre dream. I just experienced it again. There's no sugarcoating it...they're coming after us all!"

As I pause Marty asks, "Who's coming after us all?"

"Gray Cardinal and the founder of Wagner Group, Dmitry Utkin! They're coming to kill us all!"

Now to me, that sounds pretty clear. All of these dream/nightmares are very vivid and some are a bit frightening. Why would they want to kill us, you ask? What could Madam President possibly do to evoke such disdain from two world leaders? Well, like the motto from the TV show Survivor, she outwitted, outplayed and hopefully will outlast them both.

9

President Xi Jinping of China has been keeping a low profile ever since the Covid worldwide outbreak, which was spread intentionally by Xi and his Russian counterpart. This led to Madam President lobbing a few rockets into China's airspace taking out the Wuhan Institute of Virology, CSA, which was vaporized. At the same time, she had a few more missiles deposited on top of Honker Union Group. This group is known for its hacktivism against United States government websites and the APT41 state-sponsored hackers as well as the Hafnium Hackers.

President Surkov of Russia wasn't happy either, especially knowing an Ohio-class SSBN ballistic missile submarine was not only sitting off his coast, but it had also taken out Evgeniy Bogachev – the most wanted cybercriminal in the world, along with his entire network. There was nothing either world leader could do about it because POTUS had them by the cojones. (3)

(3) Book Series II - *Bedlamites*

*   *   *

"ARCADIA"
...and the long road to get there

Chapter 1

Back in Whittier, Alaska, Marty and I have packed our travel bags and our "Go Bags" each containing plenty of cash, Walther PPK semi-automatic pistols, passports and other assorted goodies. I've got my handy CPAP machine and we are both in an FBI van headed for Anchorage. Special Agent-in-Charge Goggin is in the driver's seat while Special Agent Cope is riding shotgun. Marty and I are in the second row while two more agents are in the vehicle's third row carrying automatic weapons and wearing body armor.

The FBI armored SWAT van is anything but low profile. It's well-armored including perimeter armoring that withstands high power 7.62x51 mm rifle rounds even with the simultaneous detonation of two DM-51 hand grenades. The engine bay and fuel tank are protected using INKAS unique lightweight armor materials. A high-performance gun port enables the crew to protect themselves from the inside of the vehicle and a ballistic steel escape hatch, which can only be opened from within, was designed for all emergencies that obstruct the escape of the passengers from all usual exits. To top it off, this vehicle has push bumpers for clearing objects without damaging internal components while offering maximum protection for the chassis under the most severe conditions — not to mention safeguarding us! We will soon be exiting the fortress as we are pulling into a bastion on the outskirts of Anchorage.

This "Giant Manor" is located on 14.55 acres of land less than a mile from Joint Base Elmendorf-Richardson (JBER). The installation hosts the headquarters for the United States Alaskan Command, 11th Air Force, U.S. Army Alaska and the Alaskan North

American Aerospace Defense Command – plus the 381st Intelligence Squadron, "The Mastodons," Air Force Intelligence, Surveillance and Reconnaissance Wing.

We are quickly escorted inside by Agents Goggin and Cope and introduced to our chef. This all seems like overkill to me, but I'm not privy to all aspects surrounding our predicament. Marty and I are both hungry and thirsty and she wastes no time letting the culinarian know.

During the walk-through of our new "digs," she gives me a smile, "Can you believe this place? It's a fortress-like house." Trust me, she isn't kidding. On the first floor, historically authentic Medieval weapons are displayed throughout. Everything from battle axes to war hammers, crossbows, spears and swords line the walls. The basement has one bedroom, very high ceilings and zero windows, two bathrooms and what looks to be a hidden entrance/ exit door. The weapons on display down here are of the very lethal, extremely powerful and highly deadly modern variety — all beautifully displayed in locked, glass cases.

When we reach the bedroom on the second floor of this beautiful three-story home, we are introduced to our bodyguards — Special Agents Jacqueline Tiburzi and Wyman Bacharach. They will be taking care of us while we are inside the safe-house. Should we venture outside, there will be agents we can't see watching over us as they defend the perimeter. This is nice to know, of course, and we thank them for letting us know that our safety is in good hands. Marty smiles and excuses herself as she heads into the bathroom and closes the door. I notice this bedroom is a master suite with a reinforced sub-grade tornado/panic room. We're not just inside a fortress...we actually have another one right here in our bedroom. I pick my side of the bed and set up my CPAP on the nightstand. I give Marty the side of the bed closest to the bathroom. That's the side of the bed I usually sleep on, but I know better than to take it. I head into the living room and find Agents Goggin and Cope already lounging on the couch.

As we catch up on the latest updates pertaining to our plight, Marty interrupts our conversation bringing me a sandwich and a drink. "I don't want to bust up your meeting, but Sidney needs to eat," she says as she hands me a plate and a glass of water.

Taking my plate I think...*Where's my Captain and Coke*... but instead I remark, "Thank you sweetie." She gives us a puzzling look.

"Anything I need to know about?" Marty inquires.

"Not a thing babe...we're just catching up."

"OK then, I'll leave you three to catch up while I go and watch some HGTV."

When Marty exits, I tell the two Special Agents, "I think I should go sit with Marty while we eat...it will give her some reassurance. It's been a long stressful day for us both. We will talk more in the morning."

As I'm getting up to leave, they both stand and Agent Goggin says, "That's a wise decision Sidney. We'll talk over coffee at first light." We all shake hands and I head off to our bedroom to enjoy my sandwich and water with Marty.

I may have joined Marty, but she's fully engaged with the large screen TV. I usually know when to keep my mouth shut and this is one of those times. After all, if this HGTV show helps distract her from her hectic day, I'm all for it...besides they're showing island homes and I know she loves that. I slowly and quietly devour my sandwich while sipping my water as I watch her favorite show, Stacy Cellars Island Homes. As soon as I'm finished eating I whisper, "Are you ready for bed babe?" I get no response, so I stand and walk over in front of her waving my hands close to her face...still nothing... Marty's fast asleep while sitting straight up on the couch. I pause for a minute to see which island these folks from North Carolina are thinking about moving to. It's the Bahamian Island of Inagua and it all looks beautiful. I'm thinking… *Damn, I'd sure love to be there right now, sitting on that dock drinking a margarita with Marty and Stacy while watching the sunset and contemplating which magnificent, beautiful beach home to choose from. But NO, I'm in a well-guarded safe-house on the outskirts of Anchorage, Alaska, with mercenaries on a mission to cut my life short.* While watching this program, I softly say to myself, "I'll trade you even, your predicament for mine," Then I watch this couple as they purchase what I believe to be the wrong home. For two hundred thousand more dollars they could be living right on their own private beach. Instead they are two blocks inland and will probably have to spend two hundred thousand to fix it up. Right now I have my own problems...so I bend down while softly and quietly giving Marty a kiss on the forehead, before laying her flat on the couch and covering her with a throw blanket. Then I head into the bedroom, brush my teeth, put on my CPAP mask and head into La-La Land.

That's when the dream/nightmare takes off in full-force.

*   *   *

Marty seems to be staring at me while sporting a very concerned look, "Sidney, what are you doing? Why are you googling Billionaire Vodka? What's going on inside that head of yours?"

"If you really want to know sweetie...I'll tell you. I'm not sure how much time I have or what kind of trouble we may soon be in but I need to figure this out as fast as I can."

"Sidney, look at me...LOOK AT ME!" Oh, shit, I'm in trouble! I stop everything immediately and look up at Marty.

14

"I'm sorry sweetie...you have my complete and undivided attention as well as every right to ask me questions. My apologies! Please sit down. What do you want to know?"

"This latest dream/nightmare of yours has you really freaked out...you're scaring me. What do you believe it means and what do you believe is going to happen?"

"Good questions my dear. It's my belief Vladislav Surkov (Gray Cardinal) along with Dmitry Utkin, the founder of Wagner Group, are on a vengeance rampage. It seems that even though Utkin is retired from active service in the Armed Forces of the Russian Federation, he had neither the title of Hero of the Soviet Union or Russia, nor was he a cavalier of the Order of St. George. He may be looking for a feather to put in his cap."

"However, they are coming for us...not just you and me, but Hulk, Big Al and Pistol Pete along with Ross Brown, Chucci and Milton's son Dolph Jet Coley. In my dream/nightmare, they mentioned killing Whoman in New Orleans and Milton Coley last winter in Nuiqsut, Alaska. They also mentioned the need to rid themselves of Ross Brown at the Alaskan Pipeline. As you know, he now works with POTUS (President of the United States) as a security czar. Chucci was mentioned and as you know, he was an Army sniper and is the head of security at the Port of New Orleans. Milton Coley's son, Dolph Jet Coley, was just with us not long-ago fishing in Key Largo. He was an apprentice sniper on Chucci's team in Afghanistan and went on to be a CIA sniper — a job he still enjoys. Another name mentioned was Billionaire Vodka. I'm googling that now because it was mentioned in the dream/ nightmare and I need to know who owns it and what part this person may be playing in this new predicament we find ourselves in. After that, I'll need to notify all parties just mentioned. They will all need to be alerted immediately...if not sooner."

"What are you finding out about Vodka Man?" Marty asks.

"He's definitely a Russian oligarch. The term 'oligarch' derives from the Ancient Greek word *oligarkhia,* meaning 'the rule of the few.' Russian oligarchs are business oligarchs of the former Soviet republics who rapidly accumulated wealth during the era of Russian privatization in the aftermath of the dissolution of the Soviet Union in the 1990s."

The failing Soviet State left the ownership of state assets contested which allowed for informal dealings with USSR officials (mostly in Russia and Ukraine) as a means to acquire state property.

"The first modern Russian oligarchs emerged as business-sector entrepreneurs under Mikhail Gorbachev from 1985 through 1991, during his period of market liberalization. These younger generation entrepreneurs were able to build their initial wealth because of Gorbachev's reforms which effected a period when co-existence of regulated and quasi-market prices created huge opportunities for arbitrage. That's the buying and selling of securities, currency or commodities in different markets — or in derivative forms in order to take advantage of differing prices for the same asset. Do you understand any of this?"

"You learned all of this just now?" Marty asks.

"I'm a quick study sweetie...anyway, these oligarchs are multimillionaires or billionaires who stay in bed with Russian politicians, especially their leaders — in this case, Gray Cardinal. I'm sure he gets a cut of everything these oligarchs pull in monetarily. I'm also sure they'll be financing any mission Vladislav Surkov has planned for us. It may be time for you to go into hiding Marty."

"Not on your life, Sidney! I'm totally in! It's you and me NO matter what comes our way!"

That brings a smile to my face, but fear to my gut. Marty has never been one to back down from a fight, but this is going to be more than just a fight...it's going to be a fight to the finish. Give no quarter...no mercy, no clemency, no compassion, no pity, no leniency...SHIT! I excuse myself, walk to the bathroom and close the door. I take a good look at myself in the mirror and quietly ask the question, If Whoman was still with us, he would certainly ask, "What have you gotten yourself into this time Sidney?"

*   *   *

Agent Cope asks, "Are you going to tell her, or are you going to piss her off? I've gotten to know Marty over these past few months and it's my impression that if you don't keep her informed, you're in deep doo-doo."

I smile and reply, "Now I know why the FBI made you a Special Agent. Your intuitiveness is outstanding. That being said, I'm not telling her shit. She simply cannot come along. It's much too dangerous and it will only worsen. Marty will have to take it out on me later." Both agents look at me shaking their heads in the affirmative. We all know this is going to get ugly quick!

Special Agents Goggin and Cope check in with the security team watching the fortress and Goggins says, "We're good to go...you got everything you'll need Mr. Krogh?" I have my go bag, my sleep apnea machine, my cup of coffee and a change of underwear, so I shake my head "yes" as the three of us head out the front door.

*   *   *

17

Chapter 2

Ever since the Russian/Chinese worldwide disaster last year that brought us all into the Covid world, (4) Madam President has somewhat secretly put sanctions on almost every banking institution in the Soviet Union and some individuals (mostly Russian oligarchs or Chinese politicians and banking institutions) plus their family members, whether they live in our country or in their own. This is her way of sending a very strong message to both – Don't fuck with the United States of America or other friendly (NATO) nations!

Now that the United States and Madam President know there's a scheme afoot by both these nations, once again our President is tightening the screws... and I mean constricting the very blood vessels that keep Russian and Chinese economies alive.

* * *

In the world of the rich and beautiful, diamonds are an expression of pure luxury and inconceivable wealth. The precious diamond crystals not only decorate cleavages, wrists and fingers of ladies, they also enhance numerous other luxury goods that millionaires and billionaires like to be surrounded by. Our luxury designer Leon Verres sets the highest standards globally with his "Le Billionaire Champagne." With a price tag of $2.75 million, the Salmanazars-bottle contains 9 liters of the most valuable champagne bottled on Earth. These bottles aren't just filled with the most exclusive champagne in the world, they're also covered with one hundred sparkling diamonds and crowned with a shapka, a Russian fur cap. Only five bottles have been launched on the global market.

---

(4) Book Series II - *Bedlamites.* Russia and China purposely tried to spread Covid around the world.

18

The renowned designer Leon Verres is also the founder of Eau de Parfum, a 1.5-liter bottle of men's cologne with a price tag of $2.25 million per bottle. His perfume must pass through millions of dollars' worth of diamonds before one is fit to be sprayed on one's masculine body. Our wealthy designer has moved on to the most expensive vodka in the world, with a bottle priced at a record-breaking $3.7 million. This opulent, celebratory "Billionaire Vodka" comes in a 5-liter bottle with a distilling process fit for a king. (If the king happens to be a billionaire.) The process involves running crystal clear water and the finest wheat over millions of dollars' worth of diamonds. The bottle, in fact, comes encrusted with 3,000 scintillating white diamonds.

Billionaires from around the world have already enamored themselves with Leon Verres' glamorous collectibles.

Leon Verres is known as the planet's most successful and charismatic luxury designer of his time with the diamond versions of perfume, vodka and champagne. Even before the first bottle went across the counter, its reputation preceded itself and created sheer excitement among the luxury-spoiled rich around the world.

Whether in Dubai, Moscow, Saint-Tropez, New York or Shanghai, everyone who prides themselves as being special wants to belong to the privileged few who are able to score one of the sought-after diamond encrusted bottles.

This Russian oligarch is among the privileged few who gets to mingle with kings, queens and presidents, as well as ruthless dictators and autocratic leaders who believe in complete power. A government of one, if you will.

*   *   *

Then we have Roustam Tariko, the founder of the Russian Standard Bank, a credit card operation and a term life insurer in Russia.

Born in the town of Menzelinsk in Tatarstan on March 17, 1962, at the age of seventeen Tariko moved to Moscow to study. The economic reforms of the 1980s created new business opportunities which Tariko recognized and took advantage of. Unlike many other Russian businessmen who created their empires through the privatization of state enterprises back in the early 1990s, Tariko built his company from scratch.

While studying economics, Tariko had a part-time job as a street cleaner. He'd get up early, even when the temperatures fell to - 20 degrees Celsius, to begin his shift clearing snow from local streets and driveways. Tariko had an eye for making money. One of his first business ventures was a small cleaning company he established with two close friends.

Tariko also worked part-time as an independent guide. It was during this job that Tariko made an arrangement with a large government hotel. Clients of the guide service had been complaining about the condition of the hotel rooms. Tariko devised a plan that in exchange for a portion of room rent, he would take a part of it to renovate some of the rooms. This service to clients and hotels became an expanding portion of his enterprise, eclipsing his cleaning business.

In the late 1980s, Tariko began importing Kinder Surprise and Ferrero Rocher chocolates to the Soviet Union and selling them for rubles. Previously, such goods were only available in hard currency stores which were closed to average Russians. Tariko parlayed his success from selling Italian chocolates into an exclusive contract to import the alcoholic drink Martini. Russians really needed a product that was not as strong as Vodka and not as feminine as cheap sparkling wine, so Martini was the solution. Record sales of Martini enabled him to grow his company, Roust Inc., into the leading importer of premium spirits into Russia. He added Johnny Walker, Baileys and Bacardi to his portfolio.

In 1999, he expanded his empire into the banking business by founding Russian Standard Bank. This bank is the market leader in consumer finance and the country's largest consumer lending bank.

Both these Russian oligarchs came by their rubles from two different directions but they both enjoyed their lavish lifestyles. The exoticism and glamour that such trappings and seductiveness led to their egos was also accompanied by repulsiveness from those who had nothing and had to live paycheck to paycheck.

*   *   *

While still looking at myself in the mirror, I hear my phone ringing. Marty answers it and says, "Hello...yes, this is Sidney Krogh's phone. Who's this? Oh, hello Dolph...yes, he is," as she hands the phone over to me.

I take the phone from Marty — getting an uneasy feeling in the pit of my stomach — as I ask, "Dolph, how have you been doing? To what do I owe this pleasure?"

"Hello Sidney...it's good to hear your voice. However, I have some rather bad news to pass on to you. The NSA/CSS and U.S. Cyber Command have contacted the CIA director to pass on some interesting intelligence intercepts. It seems that you and the rest of your PSYOP team members, along with Ross Brown, Chucci and myself are on a 'priority one' hit list. This hit list has been initiated from inside Russia's War Room, The National Defense Management Center, also known as the National Defense Control Center (NDCC)."

I have to butt in quickly...and I ask, "Dolph, I'm going to assume that Madam President is aware of this, as well as FBI Director Cole Michael. But, when exactly did everyone become so enlightened?"

"It just came in last night. Everyone you've mentioned has been brought into the loop. I was asked to bring you in. You are being asked to bring your old PSYOP team into the fold. Everyone's safety is in grave danger. Airports are being monitored. All flight manifests entering the United States or Canada from eastern Europe or Russia are being scrutinized. All ships, entering both countries' ports, are under careful examination and observation."

I look down at Marty still sitting in the chair. The look on her face is one of bewilderment with a tad of perplexity as she's shaking her head and says, "Tell him about your dream, Sidney." Then I hear, "Sidney, SIDNEY wake-up," as someone is shaking me. I look up and Marty is staring me right in the eyes with a frightened look on her face — as she continues, "It's happening again isn't it Sidney? Those dream/nightmares are becoming real!"

*　　*　　*

The massive super-yacht Dilbar stretches one-and-a-half football fields in length. It boasts two helipads, berths for more than 130 people and a 25-meter swimming pool that is long enough to accommodate another entire super-yacht. Dilbar cost $648 million when it was launched way back in 2016, but it had to be retrofitted a couple years later for another $200 million. To refuel the Dilbar costs 1.1 million dollars. Dilbar is normally run by a crew of 80 who help maintain the super-yacht and wait on guests. When necessary, the crew capacity can be increased to a maximum of 96 crew members. This plush 512-foot vessel is said to cost up to $60 million every year, just to operate.

Its owner is Russian oligarch Alisher Usmanov, who loves to anchor near sun-splashed playgrounds in the Mediterranean or the Caribbean. Every once in a while Mr. Usmanov drops anchor in small nations such as the Maldives and Montenegro.

Montenegro, or "Black Mountain," got its name from the mountain forests that were so dense and thick that they looked black to outside observers. It is a country in Southeastern Europe. It is located on the Adriatic Sea and is part of the Balkans (the 11 countries that have all or part of their territory on the Balkan Peninsula) sharing borders with Serbia to the northeast, Bosnia and Herzegovina to the north and west, Kosovo to the east, Albania to the southeast, the Adriatic Sea and Croatia to the southwest and a maritime boundary with Italy. Podgorica, the capital and largest city covering 10.4% of Montenegro's territory, is home to roughly 30% of its total population of 621,000 citizens.

After falling under Ottoman rule, Montenegro regained its independence in 1696, under the rule of the House of Petrovic-Njegos, first as a theocracy (a system of government in which priests' rule in the name of God) and later as a secular principality. Montenegro's independence was recognized by the 'Great Powers' at the Congress of Berlin in 1878. In 1910, the country became a kingdom.

After World War I, the kingdom became part of Yugoslavia. Following the breakup of Yugoslavia, the republics of Serbia and Montenegro together proclaimed a federation. Following an independence referendum held in May 2006, Montenegro declared its independence and the confederation peaceably dissolved.

Montenegro has an upper-middle-income economy and ranks 48th in the Human Development Index. It is a member of the United Nations, NATO, the World Trade Organization, the Organization for Security and Co-operation in Europe, the Council of Europe and the Central European Free Trade Agreement. Montenegro is also a founding member of the Union for the Mediterranean and is currently in the process of joining the European Union.

Porto Montenegro is becoming the ultimate super-yacht sanctuary along the Adriatic coast. The coastal town of Tivat lies at the very heart of the lovely Boka Kotorska Bay. What makes this place stand out is its impressive flora (plant life of a particular region) which gathers a large array of tropical and peculiar plant species. The large town park is an oasis of beauty and peace where you can admire Tivat's lush vegetation. Tivat is rumored to be named after the Illyrian Queen Teuta who ruled part of Montenegro. She was attacked by the Romans in 229 B.C. and had to retreat from Lake Skadar to Risan in Kotor Bay. She then built herself a summer residence in Tivat.

Montenegro is quickly emerging as the new Monaco with the largest super-yachts and billionaire visitors, making it the most sought-after resort for the world's wealthiest individuals. Located on the shores of the UNESCO protected Boka Bay, Porto Montenegro is more of a city in itself offering everything a pampered visitor could dream of. Featuring an elegant nautical village (their version of Rodeo Drive) the bustling community is filled with restaurants, bars, boutiques and even a new Veuve Clicquot champagne bar.

According to the Constitution of Montenegro which was adopted in 2007, Montenegro has only one official language specified as Montenegrin. However, that is not the language being spoken aboard the super-yacht Dilbar. You see, Dilbar's owner, Mr. Alisher Usmanov, isn't just a Russian oligarch, he's aligned with the Kremlin and the language spoken aboard the Dilbar is Russian.

There are very few people in the world who personally own an Airbus A340-300, mostly because they come at a cost of over $200 million. However, Alisher Usmanov's eye-catching custom paint job sets his A340-300 apart from any other. The luxury remodeling puts its worth between $350 and $500 million, taking into consideration the interior decoration and implemented technology. The aircraft is registered on the Isle of Man (also spelled Mann). This island nation is a self-governing British Crown Dependency in the Irish Sea located between Great Britain and Ireland. The first letter of the jet's name is given after the 'Man' – M-IABU. The rest of the letters can be translated as 'I'm Alisher Bourkhanovich Usmanov'.

The super-yacht of Russian oligarch, Alisher Usmanov, is waiting at its berth for passengers, all of whom are arriving at Tivat Airport. They have been traveling in luxury as they disembark from a privately owned Airbus A340-300.

* * *

Chapter 3

Two days later...

This same privately owned Airbus A340-300, with a range of 7,400 nautical miles, has just journeyed some 6,506 nautical miles from Tivat Airport in Montenegro. The pilot asked for and was granted a private location for her passengers to disembark.

It didn't take long for the proverbial shit to hit the fan as the Wagner Group PMC mercenaries exited the aircraft, each man carrying a 3-foot-long Pelican case. These cases are known to all gun enthusiasts as rugged, waterproof transport cases for weapons commonly used by military forces. According to TSA rules, all these firearms must be packed and unloaded in locked cases and only in checked baggage. The second the Wagner commander caught sight of the FBI team, he went for the handgun at his waist. All his comrades, upon seeing this, made the same error in judgment, as suppressed FBI sniper rifles quickly sent six men to their deaths. All were dressed as private citizens and all now lay still, along with their Pelican cases, on the tarmac in a remote section of Los Angeles Airport (LAX). None of the six had a wallet or any other form of identification, just a very distinct tattoo on the left side of their necks...except for one.

The "trauma cleanse" vehicles had already been put on standby and they swooped right in. Better known as "cleaners," these specialists do quick forensic cleanup and body removal. All six mercenaries had been tagged long before they entered the United States. The NSA had put the FBI on notice...a six-man hit team would be entering the U.S. on a private jet from Montenegro. The jet was seized immediately and the pilot and crew were all arrested. The pilot was taken from her seat still trying to send an SOS, but the radio jamming device went into effect the second the first shots were fired.

The Wagner Group PMC (Private Military Contractors) work directly for the President of the Russian Federation – known to the Wagner Group as Comrade Supreme Commander and known to U.S. intelligence as Gray Cardinal.

Once you join Wagner Group PMC, you are no longer allowed to use any social network services...period! You are not allowed to post photos, texts, audio or video recordings. You're never allowed to tell anyone your location, whether you're in Russia or any another country. Mobile phones, tablets and any other means of communication are not permitted. Passports and other documentation are surrendered and in turn, company employees receive a nameless dog tag with a personal number and a secret tattoo on the left side of their neck. The company only accepts new recruits if a 10-year confidentiality agreement is established. Anyone who breaks this agreement is left in the cold and all rights are terminated.

Most of Wagner Group PMC are from the elite Spetsnaz forces and all carry the Kalashnikov AKMB assault rifle fitted with the PBS-1 silencer which produces almost no muzzle flash or smoke. This cadre of special operations units are controlled by the main military intelligence service GRU (Spetsnaz GRU). Since Spetsnaz is a Russian term, it is typically associated with the special units of Russia but other post-Soviet states often refer to their special forces units by the term as well because these nations also inherited their special purpose units from the now-defunct Soviet agency. The 5th Spetsnaz Brigade of Belarus is an example of a non-Russian Spetsnaz force. The NSA believes that one of these six men removed from the tarmac at LAX (the one without the tattoo) is from Belarus. The question is why? Why would the Belarusian dictator, Alexander Lukashenko, allow someone from his 5th Spetsnaz Brigade to accompany Russian private military contractors into the United States of America?

The FBI sniper team moved in quickly and confiscated all the weapons and two Iridium satellite phones. The Russian pilot and crew were handcuffed and taken away by a crack FBI interrogation team. The Iridium satellite phones went with them.

*   *   *

The circumstances that took Marty and me from our home in Whittier, Alaska, to the fortress outside of Anchorage are also playing out. At the same moment in Bold Knob, AK, Boston, MA, and Seymour, CT, Big Al and Kitty, Pistol Pete and Linda and Hulk and Candy are all being transported to safe-houses to be put into protective custody. Ross Brown seems to live in sequestration while working inside the offices of Alyeska at TAPS (Trans-Alaskan Pipeline System), not to mention Ross's latest employment as cyber-czar for POTUS (President of the United States). Ross Brown's office is in a place he calls "The Bat Cave" and this is where he staves off daily cyberattacks on the Alaskan Pipeline. Ross has estimated that 86,400 of these cyberattacks happen every second of every day. However, after the gutsy performance by POTUS a few months ago that took out the top hackers in Russia and China, the cyberattacks on the pipeline have greatly diminished. (5) That being said, I'm fairly certain that my dear friend Ross Brown is safe which leaves Chucci (the head of security at the Port of New Orleans) to worry about. I'm sure Dolph Jet Coley (CIA sniper) is fine, since he's the person who notified me about the attempts on our lives.

However, my dream/nightmare had already given me the heads-up on that. Although I'm certain the U.S. government is taking the greatest care to protect us all, it doesn't stop my tribulation.

(5) Book Series II - *Bedlamites*. Because of the Covid outbreak brought on by Russia and China, Madam President moved her Queen to Checkmate and took out government hackers from both countries without any repercussions.

It still warrants the question, why can't I just return to the lagoon dulcified life I believe I had before last winter? Even if I didn't have it, no matter what life I had is better than the one which has me always looking over my shoulder. This "smoke and mirrors" lifestyle just isn't for me. That's what I'm thinking when my phone rings…

*   *   *

Renowned designer Leon Verres' super-yacht left Barcelona two weeks ago. Sailing under the Bermuda flag, she's due to arrive in Key Largo, Florida, within 48 hours. This 460-foot super-yacht named, Milliarder Vodka (Миллиардер Водка in Russian) or Billionaire Vodka in English, has twelve very important guests aboard. They are very highly trained assassins who are sunning themselves on the top deck while enjoying free glasses of Billionaire Vodka...compliments of Mr. Verres.

The super-yacht Milliarder Vodka has made a pit stop in her home port at the Royal Bermuda Yacht Club in Hamilton, Bermuda, on its way to the millionaire/billionaire playground called Ocean Reef Club. Attached to the ship's hull are two Navy SEALs wearing rebreathers (closed circuit breathing apparatus which has a CO2 scrubber to absorb the carbon dioxide). This will give the SEALs four hours, tops, to do their work.

The U.S. government knows this super-yacht is registered in and sailing under the Bermuda flag, so the SEALs must wait for it to journey out of Bermuda's territorial waters. Intelligence reports show the captain's favorite route to the Keys is to head west/ southwest and follow the U.S. coastline south.

Beneath the ocean, lying in wait, is the Los Angeles-class submarine USS Philadelphia. Attached to the USS Philadelphia is a Shallow Water Combat Submersible (SWCS) operated by the U.S. Navy and United States Special Operations Command.

The Shallow Water Combat Submersible (SWCS) is a manned submersible and a type of swimmer delivery vehicle that is used to deliver United States Navy SEALs and their equipment for special operations missions. The SWCS has advanced computer systems for navigation including sensor mast with electro-optical periscope, wireless and wired communication between crew members, sonar detectors and sonar-assisted automatic docking. The SWCs carries six SEALs: a pilot, a co-pilot/navigator and four passengers. The SWCS can be deployed from surface ships, land, and Dry Deck Shelters (DDS) and submarines. In this case, the submarine option is preferred for stealth reasons.

The U.S. Navy trains its personnel to operate across a spectrum of conflicts from anti-piracy operations to all-out war. In many situations, it is desirable to stop a vessel and detain the crew (and or passengers) without destroying the vessel or causing casualties.

One way to stop a vessel is to stop the propulsion system, specifically to foul the propellers. NSWC Panama City is a research and development, test and evaluation and in-service support in Mine Warfare, Naval Special Warfare, Diving and Life Support and Amphibious and Expeditionary Maneuver Warfare Systems as well as other missions in the littoral battle-space (the area from the open ocean to the shore that must be controlled to support operations ashore).

NSWC Panama City Division's origins began with mine countermeasures research conducted during World War II at the U.S. Naval Mine Warfare Test Station, Solomons, Maryland. In 1945, equipment, facilities and personnel were transferred from that location to Panama City, Florida, to occupy a 373-acre tract of land owned by the U.S. Navy and considered to be in a caretaker status. This base has evolved over the years. From 1986 to 1991 it was named the Naval Coastal Systems Center (NCSC) and reported to the Space and Naval Warfare Systems Command. In October 1991, it was realigned under the Naval Sea Systems Command (NAVSEA). One of the experiments conducted at NSWC was to develop a nonlethal way to stop ships by using a synthetic version of the slime secreted by hagfish.

Hagfish are primitive eel-shaped fish that have evolved to now have a novel means of defense. When attacked, a hagfish secretes a clear thick gel that looks like egg white but is substantial and cohesive. The slime quickly balloons up to 10,000 times its original volume. If the slime is deployed against a ship's propeller, instead of locking the propeller(s) in place, the slime will congeal around the individual propeller blades, preventing them from scooping water and propelling the boat.

This is exactly what the Navy SEAL Team is doing as the super-yacht, Milliarder Vodka's screws are spinning at 250 revolutions per minute, yet the super-yacht is slowing to a stop.

One of the more esoteric acronyms that exist within the world of Special Operations Forces (SOF) is VBSS. The U.S. military is renowned for its multitudinous array of acronyms. VBSS is just one more that is mostly unknown even to a majority of military personnel. VBSS stands for Visit, Board, Search and Seizure. It refers to the act of approaching and boarding a maritime vessel for the purpose of searching it and possibly seizing it. In this case, the targets are twelve individuals believed to be members of Wagner Group PMC.

While the super-yacht's captain is trying to figure out what could possibly have gone wrong with his propulsion system, the United States Coast Guard Cutter Tarpon (WPB 87310) from Command Center Jacksonville is one mile away on her starboard side and closing fast. The cutter is already using its electronic jammers to deny the super-yacht access to the spectrum. The yacht will no longer be able to communicate with anyone, except verbally, to representatives of the United States Coast Guard.

U.S. Coast Guard Command Center Jacksonville is parent command to five cutters: Maria Bray, Hammer, Moray, Heron and Tarpon. They must cover a diverse and challenging AOR (area of responsibility). Sector Jacksonville utilizes Multi-Mission Station Mayport, Station Ponce de Leon Inlet and Station Port Canaveral, FL. Located within Sector Jacksonville's AOR are five Department of Defense installations, including U.S. Eastern Space and Missile Center, the Naval Ordnance Test Unit and Kennedy Space Center.

While this is happening above sea level, a Shallow Water Combat Submersible (SWCS) is 300 yards aft of Milliarder Vodka's position. The two Navy SEALs, who just slimed the super-yacht's propulsion system, are kicking their way back to the submersible.

Onboard the Coast Guard Cutter Tarpon are members of a specialized unit, the Maritime Security Response Team, who are well trained in VBSS drills. These law enforcement boarding teams are armed with SIG P229 pistols, Remington M-870P shotguns and rifles of the M-16 family, Mk-18 and M-4 SOPMOD. Also onboard the Tarpon is the ARG/MEU's Maritime Raid Force (MRF) from the United States Marine Corps 24th Marine Expeditionary Unit.

While the super-yacht Milliarder Vodka is drifting in the Atlantic approximately 30 miles off the Florida coast, the submarine USS Philadelphia is jettisoning another Shallow Water Combat Submersible (SWCS). Both mini-subs rendezvous at the stern of the super-yacht. While all of Milliarder Vodka's passengers and crew are watching the United States Coast Guard Cutter approaching from the starboard side of the super-yacht, eight Navy SEALs exit the two SWCSs. They proceed to drop their tanks and fins before surfacing with their BR4 Cutlass Maritime Defense Rifles which are used in these situations because of their NP3 coating.

This is the most advanced weapon coating available, electroless nickel with embedded Teflon bonded to the particles of nickel at the molecular level, providing self-lubrication throughout the entire coating. That's why this weapon was made — for use in harsh saltwater environments. As they board the super-yacht from the aft port side, only the yacht's chef glimpses the SEALs. He leaves his galley and is on deck to enjoy a cigarette. The chef's eyes grow large, but before he has time to open his mouth, a silent 330 Blackout round enters his forehead.

The second Master Chief O'Malley pulled the trigger, he remembered the words from Captain Thornton, "We need these dirt bags alive. The President wants answers that only they can give. Do what you have to do, but try to bring me one back who's breathing."

O'Malley was born and raised in Oklahoma. His dad was the local sheriff and his mom taught high school English. Thomas was the youngest of three children. He was the only male out of three and his father had to coax his mom into having a third child. Master Chief Thomas O'Malley is really Thomas O'Malley, Jr., and had been called Junior most of his young life — that was until he became a Navy SEAL. Once he was a SEAL, he was pinned with the nickname Celtic Charm (or Charms for short). Like the four-leaf clover, his team believes he has magical powers, or at the very least, he's a good luck charm. Charms had brought his team back home from many difficult missions and the men all look up to him. A few days after every mission, Charms takes the entire team out to Young Veterans Brewing Company, a micro-brewery owned and operated by veterans on the outskirts of Virginia Beach, for a green beer which is brewed especially for Charms.

As the Coast Guard cutter Tarpon closes in on Milliarder Vodka, the cutter's skipper, Captain Eldridge, calls out from the bridge on 1 Main Circuit (1MC). This is the term for the shipboard public address circuits on U.S. Navy and Coast Guard vessels. It also provides a means of transmitting general information and orders to all internal ship spaces and topside areas. It is loud enough so that all embarked personnel are able to hear it over the loudspeakers that are located throughout the ship.

"This is the captain of the U.S. Coast Guard cutter Tarpon. Prepare to be boarded... If you'll slowly turn around, you'll notice a Navy SEAL team. No one is to move or make any gesture which may be perceived as provocative."

Practically everyone onboard the super-yacht has slowly turned, only to see that every possible exit is covered by heavily armed frogmen. No one says a word. However, one of the Wagner Group mercenaries makes eye contact with someone downstairs on a lower level of the yacht and gives a slight chin movement. This is noticed by Charms as he moves swiftly to the opening that leads to a lower deck and turns.

Everyone hears poof, poof as two rounds take out an armed Wagner Group mercenary. Charms moves quickly to the 'contract killer' who gave his colleague the chin gesture and uses the barrel of his weapon to signal this man to his knees before asking, "How many more?" The man says nothing, so Charms puts the barrel of his weapon to the man's forehead... "How many?"

"Ten more," the mercenary replies.

The SEAL Team's headsets all hear, "Ten Bogies...stay alert!"

One minute later, the zodiacs are tied off to the super-yacht's starboard side as U.S. Marines and the Coast Guard's Maritime Security Response Team board the yacht. Now heavily armed U.S. military personnel have complete control of the situation. Within 15 minutes, every Wagner Group mercenary has had their hands zip-tied behind their backs. The entire super-yacht has been searched and all weapons and explosives have been brought to the yacht's bridge.

Coast Guard Captain Eldridge has boarded the super-yacht. She quickly gives orders to the yacht's commander. "Captain you're being placed under arrest and your boat is being seized by the United States government!"

Captain Eldridge then turns to the United States Coast Guard police (CGPD) law enforcement officer and says, "Get this man out of my sight." Immediately, the officer places handcuffs on the yacht's skipper, takes him into custody and escorts him off the bridge.

Captain Eldridge looks at all the weapons and explosives while shaking her head and thinking to herself...*This mission came together so quickly, it had to have come from the very top... It's prodigious on its face. That's a massive amount of firepower. What were these guys up to?*

* * *

Chapter 4

With my phone buzzing, I take a quick look and see it's my good friend Chucci.

Chucci was born and raised in the Louisiana bayou. Like his grandfather and his father before him, Chucci gave time to the United States Military by joining the Army. His grandfather (Gramps) was a Navy man in World War II. Though he stayed stateside for the war, he was the head of the Naval Ammunition Depot Hastings (NAD Hastings) near Hastings, Nebraska. Gramps has a unique hobby of following almost every ship at sea, knowing their port of call as well as their maritime flag. Chucci's father (Pops) was with the 173rd Airborne Infantry Brigade in Vietnam and always made sure that Chucci knew the importance of serving one's country. Chucci enlisted to become a paratrooper, sniper and a U.S. Army Ranger. He graduated first in his class from each course. Chucci went on to become a sniper for U.S. forces in Afghanistan and this is where he met Dolph Jet Coley. Dolph was Chucci's spotter on several missions and went on to become quite a sniper himself. Chucci is now the head of security at the Port of New Orleans. He's also a graduate of Louisiana State University – home of the LSU Tigers. Dolph Jet Coley went on to become a top-notch sniper for the CIA. (6)

Though Chucci and I only met a few months ago, we quickly developed a tight bond — the same bond cultivated among military personnel in combat.

"Chucci, I was just thinking about you...how have you been?" I ask euphorically.

(6) Book Series II - *Bedlamites*. Chucci and Dolph Jet Coley's story

36

"Hey Sidney, I guess we are all in the same boat, so to speak...and at least it's afloat. I'm at the Port of New Orleans now and it's never been this safe. The number of government people patrolling our perimeter is extraordinary. Are you and Marty out of harm's way?"

"Yes, we are! Thanks for asking. Marty is safely stashed in a safe-house outside of Anchorage and I'm in a van with Special Agents Goggin and Cope on our way to FBI headquarters. From what they've told me, the remaining members of the old team are all in the same set of circumstances...being driven to some hideout until this situation passes over."

Chucci says, "I've spoken with Biggin. He and I are now buddies. His half-brother, Special Agent Jennings Sanders, filled him in on your latest dream...which has been verified by NSA intercepts. I don't know how you do it, but I thank my lucky charms." We both get a snicker out of that. Normally I'd laugh, but things have gotten very serious. Chucci continues, "Sidney, I want you to know that Gramps (Chucci's grandfather), being an old Navy man, always keeps his eyes on most every ship on the ocean as well as their port of call. He is now enjoying his new calling — tracking down super-yachts. Since you've asked him to check on these mega-yachts and to determine which ones are flying a flag of convenience (FOC), he's come up with some very peculiar and baffling information. FOC refers to registering a ship or yacht in a sovereign state different from that of the ship's owner. It seems most of the super-yachts Gramps is tracking are owned by shell companies that are flying a flag of convenience in order to throw everyone off their scent. However, they have NO clue Gramps is on their trail. He's gathered up some of his salty dog Navy buddies and they've captured the scent. Once Gramps has that odor in his nostrils, it's usually game over."

Gramps has old Navy buddies he refers to as salty dogs, but these gentlemen were known as Port Watchers during WWII. The original Australian Coast Watch Organization was started in 1919 when selected civilian personnel in coastal areas were organized, on a voluntary basis, to report in time of war any unusual or suspicious events along the Australian coastline. The concept quickly spread.

During World War II, Coast-watchers, also known as the Coast Watch Organization, Combined Field Intelligence Service or Section C and the Allied Intelligence Bureau were Allied military intelligence operatives stationed on remote Pacific Islands. They played a significant role in the Pacific Ocean theater and South West Pacific theater, particularly as an early warning network during the Guadalcanal campaign.

In 1943, Lt. (jg) John F. Kennedy of the United States Navy and 10 fellow crew members were shipwrecked after the sinking of the boat PT-109. An Australian coast-watcher, Sub-Lt. Arthur Reginald Evans, observed the explosion of PT-109 when it was rammed by a Japanese destroyer. Despite U.S. Navy crews giving up the downed sailors as a complete loss, Evans dispatched Solomon Islander scouts Biuku Gasa and Eroni Kumana in a dugout canoe to search for survivors. The two scouts found the men after searching for five days. Lacking paper, Kennedy scratched a message on a coconut describing their plight and the position of his crew. Gasa and Kumana then paddled 38 miles through Japanese-held waters to deliver the message to Evans who radioed the news to Kennedy's squadron commander. The future United States President and his crew were rescued shortly afterward and 20 years later he welcomed Evans to the White House.

Some of Gramps' salty dogs still live on islands around the world and some have passed the Coast-watchers' creed on to their children. As Chucci continues, "Gramps asked me to inform you that within the week, you'll know who's after us and from which direction they're coming."

"God bless Gramps and those salty dogs wherever they are! And thank you Chucci. How are you holding up?"

"I'm fine Sidney. Thanks! What's your next plan of attack?"

"As soon as we know everyone's safety is assured and I've heard back from POTUS, we should have a good idea of what to look out for as well as more about Gray Cardinal's master plan. Until then, we're keeping our heads down."

Chucci and I wish each other well and make plans to stay in touch every day until we can meet up.

* * *

Back at FBI headquarters at 101 E. 6th Avenue in Anchorage, AIC Goggin tells us, "The rest of your old team's families are safely housed. Your old team members are being picked up from three different secure airports and flown here as we speak. You will be housed here at FBI headquarters until further notice. The meeting with FBI Director Cole Michael and the CIA Director will be virtual. Special Agent Jennings Sanders will be present along with Dolph Jet Coley who will be on loan from the CIA. You should know there has already been activity. Wagner Group mercenaries have been killed at LAX. They flew in on a Russian oligarch's private Airbus A340. The oligarch in question is Alisher Usmanov. His life will change forever later tonight as he's being kidnapped from his super-yacht in Tivat, Montenegro. This is being handled by Task Force 88, also known as Task Force Black. The unit is made up of the best that SEAL Team 6, Delta Force and the British SAS has to offer. No one from the government of Montenegro or any Foreign Service Officers (FSOs) at our U.S. Embassy there will be informed of the abduction. Secrecy is the only currency being used."

I ask, "What information do you have on Belarus dictator Alexander Grigoryevich Lukashenko's connection to all this?"

AIC Goggin continues, "It seems some of his men are among those embedded with Wagner Group PMC. What they are doing there is still a mystery. Military intelligence is turning over every rock and working very hard to try to figure this out. There is a working theory in which Lukashenko is playing along to stay in Russia's good graces. Or, Gray Cardinal could be manipulating the Belarusian dictator. Others believe Lukashenko wants to be a player on the world stage in order to make a name for himself which would tighten his grip on his own people." As I'm listening to all these theories, I quickly come to one conclusion...call Ross Brown.

Before I can even get my phone out of my pocket, in walks Special Agent Jennings Sanders and CIA sniper Dolph Coley. It's like the "Three Amigos" being reunited as we greet each other with hugs and smiles. I ask, "How have you two been? We need to stop meeting like this..." They both laugh, but we all know the seriousness of the situation. Jennings seems to be visibly cheerful...almost euphoric — before whispering to Dolph and me, "I have something to tell you both, however it must wait until after we've finished our virtual conversation with both directors." I'm thinking what could Jennings possibly be up to? But I ask, "How's your half-brother doing? Is Biggin still running his tours of the Louisiana bayou, Marshland Expeditions? I'd sure love to see that BIG fella again." (7)

Dolph chimes in, "Me too...I love that guy!"

Special Agent Jennings Sanders has a questionable look on his face as he asks, "Do you guys already know?" His thought stops there...and for good reason.

(7) Book Series II - *Bedlamites*. Special Agent Sander's half-brother, Biggin, is introduced. He lives in the bayou south of New Orleans.

Just then, the doors of the FBI office swing open and in walks Hulk, Big Al and Pistol Pete. Once again, it's hugs all around before Pistol Pete says, "As I see all these familiar faces I must say, Sidney, it looks like you've gotten the band back together again. I can even feel Whoman's presence." That brings a tear to my eye and as I look around, I can see I'm not alone. That's when Agent-in-Charge Goggin says, "Gentlemen, this way please, the screen is on and we need to take our seats."

* * *

Chapter 5

On the other side of the world, Belarusian dictator Alexander Lukashenko is standing next to a map which is detailing the strategic spot where Special Forces of Belarus will be deploying their own kill team on to American soil.

Alexander Lukashenko was born Alyaksand Ryhoravich Lukashenka on August 30, 1954, and has been the first and only president of Belarus since the establishment of the office on July 20, 1994, making him the longest sitting European president. Before his political career, Lukashenko worked as director of the state farm (sovkhoz) and served in the Soviet Border Troops as well as in the Soviet Army.

Lukashenko continued state ownership of key industries in Belarus after the dissolution of the Soviet Union and retained important Soviet-era symbolism, which can be seen in the coat of arms and national flag of Belarus. The Russian language was given the same status as Belarusian and economic ties with Russia were strengthened. This led to the creation of the Union State with Russia...this allows Belarusians to freely travel to work and to study in Russia and vice versa.

President Alexander Lukashenko is the Commander-in-Chief of the Armed Forces of the Republic of Belarus.

Belarus is slightly smaller in size than Texas and is a landlocked country. Roughly 23 percent of Belarus' territory was contaminated by radioactivity when the reactor at Chernobyl exploded on April 26, 1986. The area affected was home to more than two million people. Besides the radioactive fallout, Belarus inherited its special forces (Spetsnaz) units from the remnants of the Soviet armed forces, GRU and KGB.

A six man team will be neatly sliced from the 5th Spetsnaz Brigade and their only mission is one of assassination. The commander for this politically motivated 'execution mission' is Major General Vadim Denisenko.

Officers for special operations forces are trained by the military intelligence department at the Military Academy of Belarus. Students are trained in the following specialties: management of units and telecommunication systems and field and practical exercises with the use of weapons and military equipment, which are held at a field training and material base. Future special forces officers are trained by military universities in the Russian Armed Forces, the Novosibirsk Higher Military Command School and the Ryazan Higher Airborne Command School. After five years of training, cadets receive the military rank of lieutenant. Their official motto is "Nobody but us". However, they have an alternative motto which is "Anywhere, anytime, any task". It seems those two mottoes will be in direct conflict with the FBI's motto "Fidelity, Bravery, Integrity" and the Navy SEALs' motto "The Only Easy Day Was Yesterday."

*   *   *

The highest ranking member of this hit squad is a senior NCO in the Belarusian Army who enjoys the rank of *Praparščyk,* which has two stars, and his name is Yuryi Alyakhnovich. One of his closest friends is also a senior NCO but with the rank of *Staršy* Sápmi *na* which is a thick single stripe with a small stripe embedded inside the thick stripe. His name is Artsyom Kavalyow. The rest of this team consists of junior NCOs. All are expert marksmen and divers and are airborne qualified.

The team will be making its way to Russia via helicopter. They will land at the Russian Air Force base in Kaluga Oblast. This is a large airfield with hangars and an extensive alert area for Russian fighter jets. The Russian Air Force is the air force of the

Russian Federation. It's believed that Russia enjoys the third largest air force in the world. It is currently under the command of Lieutenant General Viktor Bondarev.

Once they arrive at the Kaluga Oblast Air Force base, they will board a Ilyushin Il-112V Russian transport aircraft for their flight to Anadyr, Russia's Ugolny Airport. The airport is a mixed-use military and civil airfield in the Russian Far East, located 11 km east of Anadyr. It has a long, concrete reinforced, heavy load-bearing runway, complete with a modern terminal. It's roughly the midpoint of the northern trans-Pacific routes. Anadyr has also been a prominent base for Soviet Air Defense Forces due to its close proximity to Alaskan airspace and home to the 529th Fighter Aviation Regiment PVO.

* * *

Just outside of Murmansk Oblast, Russia, is the naval base of the Russian Navy's Northern Fleet. Geographically, Murmansk Oblast is located mainly on the Kola Peninsula almost completely north of the Arctic Circle and is a part of the larger Sápmi (Lapland) region which spans four countries.

The oblast borders with the Republic of Karelia in Russia to the south, Lapland Region in Finland to the west, Troms and Finnmark County in Norway to the northwest and is bounded by the Barents Sea in the north and the White Sea to the south and east.

The climate is harsh and unstable due to the proximity of the Gulf Stream on one side and the Arctic cold fronts on the other. Sharp temperature changes accompanied by high winds and abundant precipitation are common throughout the year. However, the waters of the Murman Coast in the south remain warm enough to remain ice-free even in the winter.

The Sámi people (also spelled Saami) are a Finno-Ugric-speaking people inhabiting the region of Sápmi (formerly known as Lapland). Today Lapland encompasses large northern parts of Norway, Sweden, Finland and Murmansk Oblast, Russia, occupying most of the Kola Peninsula. The Sámi have historically been known in English as Lapps or Laplanders. These terms are regarded as offensive by the Sámi people who prefer the area's name in their own languages, e.g., Northern Sámi Sápmi. Their traditional languages are the Sámi languages which are classified as a branch of the Uralic language family.

Customarily, the Sámi have pursued a variety of livelihoods including coastal fishing, fur trapping and sheep herding. Their best-known means of livelihood is semi-nomadic reindeer herding. Currently about 10% of the Sámi are connected to reindeer herding which provides them with meat, fur and transportation.

No one is exactly sure how many Sámi people there are, but estimates range from between 50,000 – 200,000! On February 6 every year, they celebrate Sámi People's Day. They wear traditional clothing, eat traditional food and fly the Sámi flag.

The Sámi are semi-nomadic, meaning they don't stay in the same place all year. Sámi herders migrate with their reindeer during the seasons, heading to the mountains for winter and coming back together with the community in the summer. On the journey, Sámi herders will camp in a traditional tent called a"lavvo." A lavvo is a circular frame of poles leaning inwards toward a pointy top, similar in style to the teepees and wigwams used by the indigenous people of America. Archaeological finds revealed that the Sámi livelihood was part of the Viking culture.

The Sámi do have a parliament and a chairman of the board. The current president is Per Olof Nutti.

One thing to remember about the Sámi semi-nomadic reindeer herders is that they speak their own language, pay no taxes to any of the four countries they roam (Sweden, Norway, Finland and Russia) and they always stay above the Arctic Circle. The only other thing to remember is that Per Olof Nutti always keeps a close eye on the comings and goings of the Russian Naval ships, most especially the submarine fleets. Mr. Nutti is in possession of the Iridium Extreme 9575 Satellite phone. This phone is seldom used, but when it is, it enjoys global coverage and comes with a PvR Bluetooth voice encryptor. The Iridium Extreme 9575 has a direct line into a massive five-sided concrete and steel building in Langley, Virginia. Mr. Nutti's code name is Reindeer.

The Reindeer's latest sat-transmission stated...approximately 85 days ago a BS-64 Delta-IV-class nuclear-powered ballistic missile submarine departed navy base Gadzhievo outside of Murmansk, sailed upriver and headed east into the Barents Sea.

*　*　*

It's almost midnight when Russian oligarch Alisher Usmanov finally shows his face on the forward deck of his super-yacht Dibar. Successful men are known to flaunt their confidence as well as their cigars. Who can forget the pictures of the indomitable Winston Churchill plugging away at his beloved Cheroots as he plotted the downfall of the Nazi empire? Many men smoke cigars while enjoying a good time with their friends in order to portray an image of sophistication or to simply celebrate a happy occasion. The best cigars are crafted by specialist hands and made from top quality leaves. For these reasons, leading cigar brands command a hefty price tag. Mr. Usmanov loves this time alone to light up his Gurkha Royal Courtesan cigar infused with Rémy Martin Black Pearl Louis XIII - and why not at a cost of $1 million? This cognac is aged in the c100-29 century-old tiercon. All Louis XIII de Rémy Martin are a blend of 1,200 eaux de vie between 40 and 100 years old, aged in oak barrels that are several hundred years old and cost about $2,400 a bottle.

Before Alisher Usmanov even lights his Gurkha Royal Courtesan cigar, he closes his eyes as he puts it up to his nose and slowly smells its entire length. Just before he's able to light up, even before his eyes have reopened, he is out cold and being handed over the starboard side of his yacht. His cigar along with his $79,000 Ligne-2 Champagne lighter fall from his hands into the waiting palm of one of the "Snatch and Grab" team members before it even has time to hit the deck of the multimillion-dollar yacht. SEAL Team 6 Master Chief Thomas O'Malley (Charms) looks at the lighter and notices it's made of solid 18-carat white gold and embellished with 468 brilliant cut diamonds. Even though the Master Chief doesn't count each diamond, he just shakes his head as he follows his team members back into the dark, pristine waters of the Bay of Kotor.

*   *   *

The Situation Room, officially known as the John F. Kennedy Conference Room, is a 5,525-square foot auditorium and intelligence management center in the basement of the West Wing. Along with the President and her staff is her National Security Advisor, the Homeland Security Advisor and the White House Chief of Staff. This room is used to monitor and deal with crises at home and abroad and to conduct secure communications with outside (often overseas) persons. The Situation Room is equipped with secure advanced communications equipment for the President to maintain command and control of U.S. forces around the world. Today they are also joined by the Joint Chiefs of Staff.

The Joint Chiefs of Staff is defined by statute (written law) and consists of a chairman (CJCS), a vice Chairman (VJCS), the service chiefs of the Army, Marine Corps, Navy, Air Force, Space Force and the Chief of the National Guard Bureau. Their role is to provide professional military advice to the President and Secretary of Defense.

The morning briefing begins with the Pledge of Allegiance. The President then tells everyone, "Please sit...this morning we've invited the Joint Chiefs to join us. It seems this combined live-fire exercise with Russian and Belarusian forces has escalated beyond its normal range." The President looks at the Joint Chiefs and says, "General, the floor is yours!"

General Adams' is the 20th Chairman of the Joint Chiefs of Staff, the nation's highest-ranking military officer. Prior to becoming Chairman, General Adams served as the 39th Chief of Staff of the U.S. Army. He received his commission from Army ROTC at the prestigious Princeton University in 1980.

General Adams 42 year career has taken him from commanding the 1st Battalion, 506th Infantry, 2nd Infantry Division; the 2nd Brigade, 10th Mountain Division; Deputy Commanding General, 101st Airborne Division (Air Assault); Commanding General, 10th Mountain Division; Commanding General, III Corps; and U.S. Army Forces Command to where he is today, as Chairman of the Joint Chiefs of Staff.

General Adams' operational deployments include the Multinational Force and Observers, Sinai, Egypt; Operation Just Cause, Panama; Operation Uphold Democracy, Haiti; Operation Joint Endeavor, Bosnia-Herzegovina; Operation Iraqi Freedom, Iraq, and three tours during Operation Enduring Freedom in Afghanistan.

In addition to the General's bachelor's degree in political science, he also has a master's degree in international relations from Columbia University as well as one from the U.S. Naval War College in national security and strategic studies.

The General stands and acknowledges the President. "Madam President, Joint Chiefs and distinguished U.S. intelligence officers...Russia and Belarus currently have a total of 115,000 troops near the border of Ukraine. The Russian Defense Minister, Sergei Shoigu, and Belarusian Minister of Defense, Viktur Khrenin, along with other high-ranking military officials from both sides are jointly observing this military exercise. It seems Moscow helped Belarusian leader Alexander Lukashenko weather the huge anti-government protests after his country's last election saw his 26-year rule was coming to an abrupt end. After the election, mass protests broke out against electoral fraud when the official exit poll gave Lukashenko 80% of the vote. The opposition candidate, Svetlana Tikhanovskaya, although very much in the lead, ended up a distant second. Thousands took to the streets and Belarusian security forces imprisoned almost 7,000 protesters. As detainees were released, there were many reports of vicious beatings and torture which only added fuel to new demonstrations. Lukashenko's Soviet neighbors came to his rescue and it's our belief that he felt very obligated to join forces. Now both countries are saying these military exercises are defensive, but from what our analysts are seeing and hearing, this is not the case. We expect Russian troops to cross the border into Ukraine within one week's time. Ukrainian President Volodymyr Zelenskyy has been put on alert, along with NATO Secretary-General Jens Stoltenberg, Madam President." General Adams finishes and yields the floor back to the President.

Madam President stands and in a very authoritative voice begins to speak, "Thank you General. As General Adams has just stated, I've spoken with President Zelenskyy and NATO's Secretary-General. We are in communications with all NATO countries and I'll be speaking with Russian President Vladislav Surkov (Gray Cardinal) later today. (8) I will spell it out to him in no uncertain terms — this invasion into a sovereign nation will not be tolerated.

(8) Book Series I - *Hypersomnolence*. Vladimir Putin was assassinated. He
     was replaced by second-in-line, Vladislav Surkov (Gray Cardinal).

We will have NO such communication with the authoritarian dictator of Belarus. The United States of America will make it a point of never giving him credibility or status in the free world in which we live."

"We have a lot of work to do people and I want everyone on this. All department heads...get your people up to speed instantly. I want complete updates tomorrow morning. My thanks to the Joint Chiefs and my staff. Let's get to work!"

*   *   *

In Los Angeles, the FBI interrogation team has been joined by the High-Value Detainee Interrogation Group (HIG). This is a three-agency entity — FBI, Central Intelligence Agency (CIA) and the Department of Defense (DOD) — established in 2009 to bring together intelligence professionals to conduct interrogations that will strengthen national security and be consistent with the rule of law.

The director of the HIG is an FBI representative. He has two deputies — one from the DOD and the other from the CIA. The HIG is staffed by trained professionals from across the U.S. Intelligence Community.

The HIG deploys expert Mobile Interrogation Teams to collect intelligence that will protect our national security. These teams deploy both within the United States and abroad. Team members have extensive interviewing and interrogation experience. They are also trained based on the latest scientific research.

Special Agent Favitta has led this HIG team for three years now. As a graduate of Arizona State University, which is considered one of the best schools if you're wanting a life with the FBI, his duties have taken him around the world and put him into quite a varying range of situations. His superiors noticed one special quality that would always stand out – Special Agent Favitta was a natural born interrogator.

The crew aboard the billionaire Russian oligarch Alisher Usmanov's Airbus A340-300 consisted of two private pilots with five attendants in the cabin. All seven employees of Mr. Usmanov were armed when they were taken into custody. One of the Iridium satellite phones, which was confiscated at the time of their arrests, has been ringing off the hook.

The Airbus' pilot in command is Russia's first female military pilot, Colonel Valentina Stepanovna Grizodubova. She has been awarded the title, "Hero of the Soviet Union" and the only female also awarded the title "Hero of Socialist Labour." She asks her interrogator, Special Agent Favitta, "I'd like my phone back...as you can hear someone is trying to contact me." The Special Agent has left one of the phones in the room with the detained colonel on purpose, just to watch her reactions. "You have NO right to detain me or my crew!"

The Special Agent gives a very slight snicker before saying, "Colonel Grizodubova, you've brought firearms into a foreign country, namely the United States of America, without prior authorization or permission. This means you and your crew are in criminal possession of firearms which has resulted in the arrest of you and your entire crew. Furthermore, you were transporting a group of assassins into our country, all of whom were also in possession of illegal firearms. So, NO... I won't be handing over any phone to you, much less a satellite phone that directly links you to your handler(s)."

Colonel Grizodubova tries to hide her look of bewilderment asking, "How do you know my name while I do not know yours?"

*   *   *

51

The President already had a team of Operational Technology Division (OTD) agents from Quantico, Virginia, deployed to Los Angeles.These FBI operatives develop and deploy technology-based solutions. These multi-disciplined agents are highly skilled engineers, electronic technicians, forensic examiners and analysts who support our most significant investigations and national security operations with advanced electronic surveillance, digital forensics, technical surveillance, tactical operations and communications capabilities.

This particular group of FBIs (OTD) agents has been hard at work on the encryption and over-the-air rekeying of one of the two Iridium satellite phones which was confiscated from the Airbus A340-300.

While that's going on in one part of this massive building, interrogations are underway in another section. The composition of an interrogation team varies based on the unique circumstances surrounding each interrogation. Ideally, the team consists of a team leader (in this case Special Agent Favitta) along with an interrogator and trained observers. One or two interrogators interact with the detainee while other members of the team observe and provide feedback. Every second is filmed and analyzed. Specifically, observers are focused on the words used, facial expressions and attitude.

Before the interrogation begins, everyone on the team systematically organizes all available facts (i.e. what is definitively known) and intelligence (i.e., what is believed or known about the detainee) based on available information and the potential motivation of the detainee. Then the team designs its questioning plan to achieve its objectives.

The Russian Colonel, Valentina Stepanovna Grizodubova, knows the three stages of interrogation. She's thinking to herself...*this FBI man will first interview me but I will say nothing.*

Then he will politely question me, but I will still say nothing. NO, I will stay strong and wait for this interrogation. She has been schooled in Moscow to master the effects of isolation, anxiety, fatigue, lack of sleep, uncomfortable temperatures and chronic hunger. She understands that most living organisms cannot entirely withstand such assaults, yet she stands ready to see how her training will be put to the test as she says to herself, "I will give them nothing."

*   *   *

Chapter 6

The Kola River flows out of Lake Kolozero from the north into the Kola Bay of the Barents Sea. Along this river are the towns of Murmansk and the Severomorsk and is the main administrative base of the Russian Northern Fleet.

After about an hour's drive along the river, you find the berths of Olenya Guba, the special purpose sub Losharik, intelligence ship Yantar and several of the most secretive spy vessels of the Russian Navy.

From this base, located about 30 km north of Murmansk City, nuclear-powered submarines and surface vessels regularly sail out on special missions. The small town on the Barents Sea coast houses the 29th Special Submarine Squadron.

The Northern Fleet's Head Commander Aleksandr Moiseev is rarely seen in the town of Murmansk. However, thirty days ago he was with the Regional Governor, Andrey Chibis, enjoying lunch at Restaurant Tsarskaya Okhota on Kolskiy Avenue 86 in downtown Murmansk.

The fact that Russians start their day with vodka and have vodka at all business meetings is more than a cliché and true to their stereotype. The Commander and the Regional governor were both getting tipsy. After all, they were old friends and the Commander loved to brag as he just let this tidbit slip..."Two months ago, I was given strict orders to have a submarine prepped and ready for departure...and these orders came directly from the President of Russia, Vladislav Surkov (Gray Cardinal). Not just any sub was prepped...this Top-Secret mission needed a BS-64 Delta-IV-class nuclear powered sub." Regional Governor Chibis appreciated the fact that Commander Moiseev enjoyed his vodka and that the more he drank, the more he loved to talk...Mr. Chibis's CIA code name is "Governor."

54

* * *

Back at the George H. W. Bush Center for Intelligence (better known as the headquarters of the Central Intelligence Agency) in the unincorporated community of Langley, Virginia, Major General Johnathon Stanley is receiving his morning briefing. "Sir, we received word from both 'Reindeer' and 'Governor' that stated approximately 79 days ago a Russian sub was being readied for departure. The mission was ordered from the top by Russian President, Bladislav Surkov...code name "Gray Cardinal." The only submarine giving our satellite a bright signature was the BS-64, a stretched DELTA-IV-class. It's one of two massive Russian submarine motherships, each one capable of carrying one or two deep diving submersibles. This BS-64 has both submersibles attached. She has a full crew who have been onboard making preparations for over 24 hours before her departure. As I've mentioned, we have confirmation from our two sources on the ground."

Major General Stanley says, "Ms. Bikowsky, I want to thank you for volunteering to be the liaison between the CIA and the United States Armed Forces. Your resume speaks for itself."

"Thank you General!"

In the movie "Zero Dark Thirty," the CIA operative hunting Osama bin Laden was a headstrong agent code-named Maya. In real life, Alfreda Frances Bikowsky joined the agency before the Sept. 11, 2001, attacks on the United States of America. She served as a targeter — a position that involves finding targets to recruit as spies or for lethal drone strikes. She was one of many women who sifted through communication intercepts, interrogation reports, snippets from human spies and satellite images, trying to make their analysis operational during Desert Storm. Then the agency put her to work at the Bin Laden Issue Station, also known as Alec Station, with one mission: find Osama bin Laden! While working for

55

months trying to track the terrorist leader, one thing kept coming back to her as she examined and reexamined several potential trails — the al-Qaeda use of couriers to hand-deliver messages. To whom? To where? Finally, she got her break...to a compound in Islamabad, Pakistan. For her work, Alfreda Frances Bikowsky was given the CIA's highest honor, the Distinguished Intelligence Medal. Navy SEALS may have killed Osama bin Laden, but a woman led them to their prey.

"Ms. Bikowsky, we need to know where she's (the Russian DELTA-IV-class Sub) going. As you know, the Russians have implemented some mysterious "Top-Secret" plan. The underlying intentions or motives of the particular plans are yet to be determined. We do know that the contrivance on their part has us watching an old Army PSYOP team. I'm sure these gentlemen want their lives back just as much as we want to know what the hell is going on. Your team has the lead in the field. We do have a few of their operatives in custody who are being interrogated. Anything we get from them will be passed on to you immediately."

"Thank you General! We are in contact with our agents on the ground in Russia and along the coast of Alaska. Sound buoys picked up her scent from the Barents Sea, past Novayka Zemlya Island to Wrangel Island, into the Arctic Ocean. All intercepts suggest she'll be traveling in a straight line from Murmansk toward the Alaskan coast and she's currently at flank speed. Each sound buoy has her at 24 knots. She should pass between the Alaskan and Russian coasts within the next 24 hours. As stealth as the Russians think this sub may be, she won't get past us. If she stops, we'll know...if she deploys one of her underwater submersibles, we'll know and it too will be followed."

*   *   *

The time is 6 AM before the crew of the super-yacht Dibar realizes the yacht's billionaire owner, Russian oligarch Alisher

Usmanov, was no longer on his own vessel. Both helicopter tie-downs were inspected and secured... the two pilots had been interviewed by the captain. They knew nothing! The skipper is scratching his head as he makes his way to the pilot house. He's contemplating his next move when he receives radio calls from members of his crew... "The Worx C-Researcher 3 submersible is still in her cradle Captain."

"10-4...thanks."

"Captain, the 388 Skater race boat and all nine jet skis are accounted for, as are the Hobie Cat and the two laser dinghies."

"10-4," he says with a bewildered look on his face.

The head of the super-yacht's housekeeping has already informed the captain that Mr. Usmanov did not sleep in his bed last night and the yacht's security personnel has informed him that the billionaire owner never left the ship...so his mind is spinning...where the fuck is he? Just then, the head of the super-yacht's security team addresses the skipper by radio, "Captain, Mr. Usmanov's satellite phone is ringing."

*   *   *

Back at the FBI office in Anchorage, Alaska, the screen has just gone blank as our VoIP internet call with FBI Director Cole Michael and the CIA Director has finished. They fill us in on their version of our dire situation. I take Hulk, Pistol Pete and Big Al over to a corner of the office and remark, "Do you believe that bullshit? No one, and I mean NO one, is spending that much time and effort just to get to us. We are in a stratagem...an artful ploy keeping the attention on us. I have a call in to Ross Brown but he has yet to call back. I'm sure he's busy being head of Cybersecurity for the President, but there's lots more to this story and we're being kept in the dark. I feel as though we're the dangling carrot."

Pistol Pete says, "You're absolutely correct...none of this makes sense." Hulk and Big Al both feel the same way, so we call Special Agent Jennings Sanders over for a consultation. Dolph Coley sees this and moves to a different corner of the room to join Special Agents Goggin and Cope. We fill the agent in on our misgivings and ask that he come clean should he know anything we don't (which, at this point, is everything).

Special Agent Sanders slowly looks around the room...I can see his facial expressions changing by the second...he's pondering what to do next and he knows blowing smoke up our six is off the table. Then he bends down and whispers, "The powers that be know the Russians are playing some very long secretive game. You're part of their ruse and they will lose as many of their own people as it takes to keep their scheme alive. Whatever it is, you're part of it. They will definitely try to kill all of you. They don't give a shit about human life. To them, you are only cannon fodder and so are any and all of their own people. They'll do anything they must for this secret ongoing Russian op. To them, you're a means to their end. No one from the NSA, CIA, FBI, DOD or any other intelligence agency from our NATO alliance has a clue what this end is. We have to let it play out until we can figure it out."

Hulk has a look of disgust on his face. He uses both hands to pull Agent Sanders close. When their noses are almost touching, Hulk whispers back, "All you had to do was ask, asshole. Who are you, and what have you done with our friend Special Agent Jennings Sanders? After all we've done for your country, you deceive us! Who the fuck do you think you are?"

"I'm sorry Hulk," Agent Sanders says, as he looks around at all of us before continuing, "I'm under orders not to say a word. If anyone knew I spilled the beans they'd have my head on a stick...my life as an Agent would be over. I'm sorry...I love you guys and so does POTUS (President of the United States). She has three layers of guards keeping you safe...shooters and snipers 24/7. She even keeps a shooter in Ross Brown's office with him. It's driving him nuts." No one says a word for what seems to be an hour but was probably 15 or 20 seconds...so I break in, "Your secret is good with us. Mum's the word! We'll play this game of yours, but make NO mistake about it...we want to be armed and we want a heads up before any action takes place anywhere near us. Don't try to play us again! Do you understand?" Sanders is biting his lip and contorting his fucking face again before saying, "OK, OK, that's fair...I'll get you Glocks and extra mags. I'll tell them you all insisted on being armed. I can pull that off."

Big Al chimes in, "You fucking better!"

Before our little powwow breaks up – I had to ask, "So, Special Agent Sanders, according to the FBI and CIA directors, they've taken out assassins at LAX arriving on some Russian oligarch's jet and they've captured and killed some more at sea off the coast of Bermuda on their way to the Ocean Reef Club in Key Largo, FL. My question is — what does any of that have to do with us?"

He could only squint his eye in wonderment...before saying, "Good question!"

At least now I know why I haven't heard from Ross Brown.

*   *   *

After the commando raid on the super-yacht Dibar, Master Chief Thomas O'Malley (Charms) and his "Snatch and Grab" team have safely transported the unconscious Russian billionaire Alisher Usmanov to a waiting Shallow Water Combat Submersible (SWCS). He was then transported past Sveti Nikola Island and out into the open waters of the Adriatic Sea where an MH-60R Seahawk helicopter assigned to the Raptors of Helicopter Maritime Strike Squadron (HSM) 71 from the Nimitz-Class nuclear-powered super-carrier, the USS John C. Stennis (CVN-74), hoisted him aboard. Mr. Usmanov was then transported south with the chopper flying low and under the radar. The Raptor's pilot was making sure to stay west of Greece over the Ionian Sea on his way out into the Mediterranean Sea, before landing onboard the United States aircraft carrier and dropping off the package into the waiting arms of a CIA doctor and the interrogation team. This is when the physician gives Mr. Usmanov a shot of Physostigmine to counteract the Propofol injected by the "Snatch and Grab" team. As the oligarch blinks his eyes and tries to focus — he asks, "Who are you...and where the hell am I?

*   *   *

Chapter 7

The FBI operates 56 field offices and 350 resident agencies across the country. Within the U.S. Department of Justice, the FBI acts as a national security organization and the country's primary investigative agency. The FBI carries out intelligence and law enforcement responsibilities to protect the country against security threats. The local FBI office in Los Angeles investigates crimes within its district as well as supporting Los Angeles County and California law enforcement agencies.

There are four FBI offices in Los Angeles County and one of those field offices is located inside the Federal Building at 11000 Wilshire Blvd. This morning, the receptionist is enjoying her coffee when a gentleman enters, walks through the metal detector and right up to her desk. He asks, "Excuse me Madam, may I speak with the FBI officer in charge?"

She looks at the screen on her desk, then back up at the gentleman and replies "Sir, would you kindly take a seat?" as she gestures to a vacant seating area before continuing, "There will be someone with you shortly."

Marat Gabidullin has spent 10 years as an officer in the Soviet army with their airborne forces. Until recently, he was a member of the "proxy force" – Wagner Group. Marat has entered the United States illegally.

Within minutes, Special Agent Todd Rhea appears in the reception area and walks up toward the gentleman who's getting up out of his chair and extending his hand. The Agent says, "Hello, I'm Special Agent Todd Rhea...how may I help you?"

As they shake hands, Mr. Gabidullin Marat remarks, "Agent Rhea, my name is Marat Gabidullin." Agent Rhea already knew who he was speaking with. The office receptionist had his picture on her computer screen and gave Agent Rhea the heads-up before he left his office. Maintaining his poker face he continues…"Mr. Gabidullin, I believe your name has come up in our daily briefings over the past week and a memo and photo of you was received this morning from FBI Headquarters in Washington. What brings you into my office this cock-crow?"

Marat Gabidullin appears perplexed and it shows on his face as he says, "Well Agent Rhea, then you must know that I've left Wagner Group. This is something one does not do. They don't just kill you for desertion, they videotape you being sledgehammered to death, then they show the video to others to make sure they don't make the same mistake. I have entered your country illegally and I would like asylum. I have some highly classified information I'd love to share with your government. In my opinion, this information needs your immediate attention."

Special Agent Rhea knows this is way above his pay grade as he turns and says to the receptionist, "Please put a call through immediately to Director Michael in Washington."

She nods her head in the affirmative and is already on it as Agent Rhea looks back at Marat and says, "Please have a seat"…as the agent uses a hand gesture toward the chair he'd already been sitting in…before continuing to speak. "May I get you something to drink?" Marat shakes his head yes as Agent Rhea disappears from the reception area and closes the solid door behind him.

The architectural style, Brutalist, intentionally attempts to look raw, haphazard or unadorned. That's the style of the J. Edgar Hoover Building 935 Pennsylvania Avenue NW in Washington, D.C. It is the headquarters of the Federal Bureau of Investigation (FBI). The 2,800,876 square feet of internal space has numerous amenities as well as special, secure system of elevators and corridors to keep public tours separate from the rest of the building. There are three floors below ground as well as an underground parking garage. The structure is eight stories high on the Pennsylvania Avenue NW side and eleven stories high on the E-Street NW side. Two wings connect the two main buildings forming an open-air, trapezoidal courtyard.

Somewhere on the tenth floor, FBI Director Cole Michael is being connected to a secure phone as he says, "This is the Director."

"Sir, this is Special Agent Rhea at the Los Angeles field office. Mr. Marat Gabidullin has come in this morning, of his own free will, and has asked for asylum. He's stated that he's in possession of highly classified information that needs our immediate attention. I have an agent with him in the lobby. How would you like me to handle this?"

The Director knows exactly what he wants done. "I want you to immediately put him under arrest for entering the United States illegally. Tell him this is just a formality — no handcuffs needed. Does he have a firearm?"

"No Sir...not with him…"

The Director continues, "I will have a Gulfstream V on the tarmac at LAX in one hour. I want you both on it. I believe Special Agent Monica Wynnie has wrapped up the crime scene and the forensics from the LAX shootings. I want her on the jet with the two of you."

"Thank you Director, I'll make it happen."

The second the FBI Director hangs up he is quickly back on the phone with HIG team leader and top interrogator Special Agent Favitta. "So, tell me Agent Favitta, how is your interrogation of

Russian Colonel Valentina Stepanovna Grizodubova going?"

Agent Favitta explains, "Director, she has definitely been trained and is skilled at evading our questions. We are in phase three and her sleep deprivation is in full swing."

The FBI Director smiles as he says, "I have information which might help you along with your questioning. We may know why the Russian/Belarus 'assassination team' landed in Los Angeles."

As soon as the director hung up, he was immediately back on the phone to the FBI's Miami field office located at 2030 SW 145th Avenue in Miramar, Florida. Located on a 20-acre site, the 330,000 square foot facility has 1,000 employees. One of those is a trusted confidant of Director Michael. Her name is Bennye Wolfe. When she's given a mission, she not only sees it through to its conclusion, it's done capably, skillfully and competently. This is what he needs, and he needs it done quickly.

The Director calls Special Agent Wolfe on her cell. She looks at the number and quickly answers. "Director, to what do I owe the pleasure?"

"Special Agent Wolfe, how have you been?"

"Just fine Sir...how may I be of assistance?"

The Director continues, "I need someone with your skill set tout-de-suite. As I'm sure you know, every intelligence agency in the free world has been on high alert the past few weeks. Something's amiss! We've taken down a group of assassins at LAX and we've captured a Russian oligarch's super-yacht on its way to Key Largo with an assassination team onboard. I'm beginning to believe we have ourselves a concatenation. I need you to pack your things and be at Ft. Lauderdale Executive Airport by 5 PM this evening. A Gulfstream V will take you to Jacksonville. There you will interview those onboard this yacht. We want to know who was or is the target or targets in Key Largo. Also, dispatch a two-person team of agents to the Ocean Reef Club in Key Largo. Not sure what they'll be looking for. Lots of yachts and millionaires hanging out there. It also has its own private airport. They are to be discrete and yet turn over every rock. That's your mission! I want answers! This is to be as surreptitious as possible...understood? We need to discern what we're dealing with...ASAP!"

"Understood! You'll have your answers Director!" Both phones go dead.

Bennye Wolfe spent 15 years in Army Intelligence. Her specialty is advanced interrogation techniques. In military terminology, a black site is still a location with clandestine jails where prisoners generally are not charged with a crime, yet have zero recourse and NO bail. One of these locations was positioned at 34 degrees 34'36.48" N - 69 degrees 17'25.80" E outside of Bagram Air Base in Afghanistan. It's code-named The Salt Pit and Cobalt. This is where Special Agent Wolfe honed her skills.

*   *   *

At the FBI office in Anchorage, Alaska, I am brushing my teeth when my cell phone begins vibrating in my pocket. I wash my mouth out quickly and while reaching into my pocket, I see I've hung up on my caller. Big Al walks into the bathroom and notices me looking at the screen on my phone as he asks, "Who's calling?"

I squint to see and look up with a smile. "It's Marty...I'm in trouble!"

Big Al starts laughing as he's opening his Dopp Kit and grabbing his toothbrush — before sarcastically blurting out, "Sidney's in *deep doodoo!*" I smile while shaking my head in the affirmative as I exit the restroom.

65

While standing in the hall, I hit redial immediately and even before it rings once I hear, "Sidney, how could you?" *Oh, shit...here it comes,* I think to myself. "You promised!" Now, right here I could tell her I had my fingers crossed behind my back when I made that promise, however, I figured out quickly that I'd be digging this hole deeper, so I just let her vent and I took it like a man. "We were supposed to do this together...as a team! Yet you just take off in the middle of the night...not even saying goodbye!"

I break in right here, "In my defense, Marty, I kissed you on your forehead and told you I loved you before I left. I knew you'd be pissed, but this *is not* something you can be involved in. The other wives and Candy will be joining you today." Then all I hear is a click and my phone goes dead. Oh shit! As I'm standing there thinking about what to do next, my phone rings again...It's her! She actually waited two minutes for effect. It worked! Damn she's good!

"Hello sweet lady..."

"Hello yourself...asshole." She can even call me an asshole in a very sexy way. I hadn't noticed that before.

"Listen, I'm sorry sweetie. I knew it would take a while for it to sink in, but you must have known that this is for the best. I don't know where this is going to take me, but I'd be worrying about you and not staying focused on what needs to get done. Do you understand that?"

"Oh, sure...you think by stating the obvious I'll totally understand." I'm thinking that I'm becoming a bit more adroit in the way I deal with situations. Give thanks and praises! I do believe I've got her...so I say, "Thank you dear lady. You know I love you and I know you love me. This will all be over soon and I'll come home to my gal."

66

Marty finishes by saying, "Love you too Sidney. You best stay in touch."

As she hangs up, Big Al is exiting the bathroom and says, "Well played asshole. I love the way Marty calls you an asshole...very sexy!" I smile at Big Al, but I'm thinking...*my goodness, he heard it in her voice too!*

*   *   *

Chapter 8

U.S. intelligence has recently noticed the resumption of the cross border freight train operations between North Korea and China. There had been a five-month suspension due to the Covid-19 outbreak and China's zero tolerance campaign.

The P'yŏngŭi Line is an electrified main trunk line for the Korean State Railway of North Korea. The train with more than 10 cars was seen leaving the Beijing railway station last evening and was spotted again crossing a bridge on the northern border city of Sinuiju. We've known for years that China is North Korea's closest and most influential ally in economic terms. This suspension was lifted by Beijing because they were given assurances from Kim Jong-un that victory over the Coronavirus and Omicron variant was over and his people were virus free.

This evening's train from Beijing to Pyongyang will have no tourists. There will be no long waits for customs and immigration clearance at the Sinuiju Station which is the border stop from China to North Korea. On today's train, there will only be the People's Liberation Army Rocket Force commander, General Li Yuchoa, who's also a member of the 19th Central Committee of the Chinese Communist Party and General Xu Zhongbo who is currently serving as political commissar of the People's Liberation Army Rocket Force. Other Chinese military leaders from the Intelligence Bureau of the Joint Staff Department (PLA) - Li Xuanliang and Li Yen, along with their staff officers, fill out the list of passengers on today's manifest.

The People's Liberation Army Rocket Force (PLARF), formerly the Second Artillery Corps, is the strategic and tactical missile force of the People's Republic of China. The PLARF is the 4th branch of the People's Liberation Army (PLA) and controls China's arsenal of land-based ballistic missiles — both nuclear and conventional.

The Intelligence Bureau of the Joint Staff Department of the Central Military commission is one of the People's Republic of China's primary intelligence organizations and the principal military intelligence organization of the People's Liberation Army (PLA).

*   *   *

On this morning inside the White House Situation Room, the day begins with a fully loaded Morning Book. Present at today's meeting is the President, Vice-President and all senior White House staff. Also, in attendance is the President's National Security Advisor, the Joint Chiefs of Staff, Secretary of Defense and the Director of the National Security Agency (NSA) U.S. Army General Shuji Miyasaki. He also heads U.S. Cyber Command (Shuji means principal, important or chief in Japanese).

General Miyasaki is the 3rd Commander of United States Cyber Command and the 18th Director of the National Security Agency. Born in White Bear Lake, Minnesota, he is the son of Edwin Miyasaki, a second-generation Japanese American and a retired United States Army colonel who served in the Military Intelligence Service during World War II. Throughout the Korean War Colonel Miyasaki served with the Nisei (2nd generation American) linguist soldiers. This unit served in a specific and unique way, through the Japanese language — serving as interrogators, translators, message interceptors or interpreters. These soldiers were trained interrogators and assigned at every level from the front lines with the U.S. and South Korean Divisions to the Corps, Army and even POW levels. Many of these Japanese-American linguists were often ordered to operate behind enemy lines in order to collect intelligence — and many never returned. Retired Colonel Edwin Miyasaki's wife and General Shuji Miyasaki's mother is Fusae Miyasaki (Fusae means house of blessing or kindness in Japanese).

The General grew up in White Bear Lake, Minnesota, and attended White Bear High School. He is married to Hiroko Miyasaki (Hiroko means tolerant, generous or abundant in Japanese).

General Miyasaki attended St. John's University where he received a commission as military intelligence officer in 1986 through the Army Reserve Officers Training Corps program. He also attended the University of Southern California, the National Defense Intelligence College and the United States Army War College, earning a Master's degree from each institution. He's also a graduate of the United States Army Command and General Staff College.

The morning briefing begins with the Pledge of Allegiance. The President then tells everyone, "Please sit...this morning we've invited the Joint Chiefs to join us. Also in attendance is our National Security Advisor and Head of Cyber Security, General Miyasaki. OK General Miyasaki...I'd like for you to lead us off and then we'll hear from General Adams."

General Miyasaki stands, looks at the President and speaks to those in attendance. "Thank you Madam President, Joint Chiefs and all other presidential staff and advisors, a good morning! Last evening a North Korean train left Beijing for an overnight ride to Pyongyang, North Korea. Onboard were most of President Xi Jinping's top generals including the head of Rocket Force, General Li Yuchao and his second in command, General Xu Zhongbo. Also onboard this train is the leader of the Joint Logistics Support Force and the Western Theater Command plus their staff. General Li Yuchao was born in Sui County, Henan, in November of 1962 and joined the People's Liberation Army in December of 1980. He graduated from the PLA National Defense University. He served in the Second Artillery Corps and commanded the 53rd Base, the 55th Base and the 63rd Base before being assigned chief of staff of the People's Liberation Army Rocket Force where he rose to become

70

commander earlier this year. He was then promoted to the rank of major general. General Xu Zhongbo was born in Rushan, Weihai, Shandong province in October of 1960. He enlisted in the People's Liberation Army in March of 1978. He served in the 20th Group Army from 1978 – December 2003 and was eventually promoted to political commissar in 2013, taking over the 83rd Group Army. He went on to become political commissar of the Western Theater Command Group Force and the Joint Logistics Support Force of the Central Military commission. He was just promoted to major general and has become the political commissar of the People's Liberation Army Rocket Force. The Rocket Force created a streamlined command in charge of all three legs of China's nuclear triad. Rather than just controlling land-launched nuclear missiles, they are now in control of their nuclear-missile-armed submarines and strategic aircraft with nuclear bombs and missiles. Our intelligence reports that this force has already held its first drills practicing mobile combat operations and missile launches. We know President Xi Jinping calls PLA Rocket Force 'The core force of the strategic deterrence, a strategic buttress to the country's position as a major power and an important building block in upholding national security.' Our problem, Madam President, is why these particular generals and staff are onboard this train heading to North Korea? Where is the train going to stop and who's going to be there to meet it? We have America's sharpest and smartest minds working on this problem, running every scenario imaginable to figure it out. We're very limited as far as assets on the ground. We do have satellite coverage in Pyongyang and we're watching the Nyongbyon Nuclear Scientific Research Center in North Korea's major nuclear facility located in Nyongbyon County in North Pyongan Province, about 100 km north of Pyongyang. Other than that, we're blind."

*   *   *

71

The Pyongui railroad line is not known for its punctuality, but this morning it pulled in on time to Pyongyang Railway Station. Before the fifteen members of the Chinese military and their staff exited the train, Major General Li Yuchao noticed that they had rolled out the red carpet — military band and dignitaries present, including the Supreme Leader, Kim Jong-Un.

Kim Jong-un is the son of Kim Jong-il. The latter was North Korea's second supreme leader from 1994 to 2011. He is also the grandson of Kim Il-sung, who was the founder and first supreme leader of North Korea from its establishment in 1948 until his death in 1994. Kim Jong-un is the first leader of North Korea to have been born in the country after its founding in 1948. Kim rules North Korea as a totalitarian dictatorship. His leadership has followed the same cult of personality as his father and grandfather before him.

Japanese rule over Korea ended on August 15, 1945, with the surrender of Japan in World War II. The armed forces of the United States and the Soviet Union subsequently occupied this region and failed to agree on a way to unify the country. As a result, in 1948, they established two separate governments. These post-war administrative areas were succeeded respectively by the modern independent states of North and South Korea. Japan officially relinquished its claims to Korea in the signing of the Treaty of San Francisco on April 28, 1952.

The Korean War began on June 25, 1950, when some 75,000 soldiers from the North Korean People's Army poured across the 38th parallel, the boundary between the Soviet-backed Democratic People's Republic of Korea to the north and the pro-Western Republic of Korea to the south. This invasion was the first military action of the Cold War. By July, American troops had entered the war on South Korea's behalf. After some early back-and-forth across the 38th parallel, the fighting stalled and casualties mounted with nothing to show for them. Meanwhile, American

72

officials worked anxiously to fashion some sort of armistice with the North Koreans. The alternative, they feared, would be a wider war with Russia and China...or even, as some had warned, World War III. Finally, in July of 1953, the Korean War came to an end. In all, 5 million soldiers and civilians lost their lives in what many in the U.S. refer to as "The Forgotten War."

In the Situation Room, General Miyasaki continues to speak..."Madam President, Joint Chiefs and distinguished intelligence officers, please give your attention to this live feed from our satellite over Pyongyang Railway Station. Analysts are sending us facial recognition and putting names to them as I speak. Kim Jong-un is there along with North Korea's new defense chief, No Kwang Chol, and their army's chief of general staff, Ri Yong Gil. Those wearing white robes are suspected to be the scientists we've nicknamed 'nuclear duo' and the 'missile quartet.' It's believed the two standing next to Kim are Jang Chang-ha, 53 years old and president of the Academy of National Defense Science and Jon Il-ho, age 61, and commonly described as an official in the field of scientific research. Pyongyang Railway Station is across the street from Yonggwang Station. This is part of the Chollima line of the Pyongyang Metro, one of the deepest metros in the world, with its track approximately 360 feet underground. This metro area also serves as one of North Korea's many bomb shelters. The station presently has three floors above ground level as well as a basement. The ground level houses a ticket desk exclusively for government employees. On the first floor there is a waiting room, toilets, a ticket desk for the civilian population and access to the trains. On the second floor there are offices for the staff and on the third floor is the office of the station master. If Kim Jung-un is taking these Chinese Generals and their staff somewhere by Metro, they are probably going to Platform #5. It's the deepest underground line and only used by the military and top government officials. Where they will exit is anyone's guess, but we are putting our money on the Nyongbyon Nuclear Scientific Research Center. At this point, Madam President and distinguished intelligence officers, I'd like to add – A South Korean researcher who runs NK Tech, a database of North Korean scientific publications, has given us a lot of information over the past few months. I have compiled a list…" General Miyasaki momentarily looks down at his notes before continuing. "First of all…they've never heard of Kim killing scientists. Second, he's elevated science in the regime's propaganda and put his fondness for scientists and engineers on prominent display across North Korea. Third…he's opened a sprawling complex shaped like an atom that showcases the nation's achievements in nuclear science. Fourth…Kim has opened a six-lane avenue in Pyongyang known as Future Scientists Street, with gleaming apartment towers for scientists, engineers and their families. Fifth…Kim's propaganda posters around Pyongyang show North Korean rockets soaring into space and crashing into the United States Capitol. And last, but not least…after a successful test, scientists and engineers are honored with huge outdoor rallies passing thousands as they are cheered along the parade route. Even with United Nations sanctions prohibiting the teaching of scientific material with military applications to North Korean students, these students still enter countries such as China, India and even Germany to study. The internet has also been a gold mine for the North. While the state blocks public access, it allows elite scientists to scour the web for open-source data under the watch of security agents. The smartest science students are funneled into military projects, knowing they may someday enjoy one of those gleaming apartments on Future Scientists Street in Pyongyang. We will stay on top of this — collect all the data possible, and keep you informed immediately of any updates. I yield the floor Madam President…"

"Thank you General Miyasaki," the President remarks as she looks around the room. "As you can see, we have multiple serious security issues in play at one time. We will break for snacks and a bio break and then we'll hear from our Chairman of the Joint Chiefs, General Adams."

* * *

Chapter 9

At the present time 6,000 satellites circle our planet — 60% of these are defunct satellites. Of the other 40% (2,666 operational satellites) 446 are used for observing the Earth, 97 are used for navigation/GPS purposes and 1,007 are for communication. The rest are military/spying, etc. Two of those are FORTE (Fast On-Orbit Recording of Transient Events) P94-1 U.S. spy satellites. This spacecraft was designed and built by the Los Alamos National Laboratory (LANL) along with Sandia National Laboratories (SNL).

The project was sponsored by the United States Department of Energy as a testbed for technologies applicable for the detection of nuclear detonation and used to monitor compliance with arms control treaties. It has a resolution that allows it to read a six-inch object from its 155-mile high orbit, even on a cloudy day, and find nuclear weapons buried more than 15 feet underground.

One of these birds has been put on-site over southeastern Russia, while the other has recently changed its orbit and is on-site over North Korea.

The bird (spy satellite) that's presently hovering over Russia is showing an NSA analyst that a BS-64, (stretched Delta-IV-class Russian nuclear submarine) is surfacing off the coast of Anadyr, Russia. The second this information was relayed to Ms. Bikowsky, she called Major General Johnathan Stanley and asked him to please join her inside the sensitive compartmented information facility (SCIF) at the Pentagon. Within fifteen minutes, they were both enclosed. Ms. Bikowsky is the first to speak. "General Stanley, since our phone call we've intercepted radio transmissions from a Soviet Ilyushin Il-112 Military Transport that they will are on final approach into Anadyr. That information, along with the Delta-IV-class-sub surfacing just east of Anadyr, Russia is cause for concern.

Anadyr has an 8,200 foot hard-surface runway that is very capable of receiving the Russian transport plane. This airstrip was used by Russia's long-range aviation bombers. Sir, the sub is now located in the Gulf of Anadyr and moving toward the Anadyrsky Liman, an estuary on the Gulf. The estuary is divided into three parts...we believe they'll use the inner bay called Onemen Bay to transfer personnel from the plane to the sub. It has been confirmed by two sources, including the FORTE satellite. The FORTE zoomed in and both submersibles are still attached."

"Good work, Ms. Bikowsky! Do we have an ETA on this flight?"

"We do sir...it should land within fifteen minutes."

* * *

With the restroom and snack break finished, everyone returned to their seats in the Situation Room, The President turns her gaze to the Chairman of the Joint Chiefs and says, "General, the floor is yours..." but Madam President quickly realizes the General is engaged in serious conversation.

General Adams has a very concerned look on his face as he returns to the podium. "Madam President and distinguished members of America's intelligence agencies...earlier today we began tracking a Chinese surveillance balloon in our airspace. This is a clear violation of our sovereignty as well as international law. That is unacceptable! Officials of the U.S. Department of Defense confirmed that the military was tracking the balloon as it flew into United States airspace at an altitude of about 60,000 feet. It entered our skies from Canada, floating over Malmstrom Air Force Base in Montana. The base houses the 341st Missile Wing which operates nuclear intercontinental ballistic missiles. The Chinese Foreign Ministry is telling us the balloon was a civilian weather airship intended for scientific research that was blown off course. However, we have already confirmed the spy balloon has propellers to help

76

steer it which means an operator is clearly in control of its path. China's foreign minister has again described the incident as a result of a force majeure for which it was not responsible. We have categorically dismissed this claim and made it clear to the Chinese that this object is undeniably a surveillance balloon and it's flying over sensitive sites collecting intelligence. We have a Lockheed U-2, high altitude reconnaissance aircraft nicknamed 'Dragon Lady' sending back pictures of the gasbag in real-time. Just to help put this in some context, the United States Air Force had a unit from 1958 to 1986 that was tasked with catching 'falling stars.' This unit was the 6493rd Test Squadron/6594th Test Group. They would fly out of Hawaii and catch film canisters falling from America's first spy satellites. These satellites were part of the Corona program, orbiting the Earth and taking photos of Soviet Russia. The satellites would then drop their film canisters over the Pacific Ocean where these Airmen would try to snatch the canisters out of the air. The recovery process was surprisingly low-tech. A plane with a large hook beneath its tail would try to catch the canister's parachute as it fell. When the planes failed to make the grab or the weather was too bad to attempt it, Coast Guard rescue swimmers in the unit would fish the film out of the water. The unit boasted a perfect record with more than 40,000 recoveries in 27 years. When these airmen weren't snatching film from the air, the unit supported rescue missions near Hawaii and is credited with 60 saves. My point being, this Chinese system is so antiquated it seems like a joke. It's easily jammed and can be downed anytime we like. However, we've been using it to our advantage. This spy balloon is literally a gas-filled balloon that does fly high enough to disrupt our commercial air traffic. It has sophisticated cameras and imaging technology on it, all of which are pointing down at the ground while collecting information through photography and other imaging. The game is: what imaging are they seeing and collecting? This part of the game is where our best PSYOPs personnel come into play. With that being said I hand the podium over to Madam President."

As the President stands, she makes her way over to where General Adams is seated. Leaning, she speaks candidly, "Thank you General Adams." Then, adjusting the microphone, she looks out at all of those individuals who've spent countless hours protecting our country before saying, "All of our military toys along this balloon's path have been put away and a E-3 modified Boeing 707/320 Sentry (AWACS) or airborne warning and control system will shadow this intruder along its entire path. We temporally jammed the intruder's capability to send any signals back to China. The PSYOP unit out of Fort Bragg, NC, is in the process of putting together a plan that we will inform you of within the hour. Take another break and any calls made will be on secure phones only.

*　　*　　*

Inside the Russian Ilyushin Il-112V military transport, the Belarusian Major General Vadim Denisenko is going back over the plans with his two top NCOs Yuryi Alyakhnovich and Artsyom Kavalyow, as they are wheels down in two minutes into Anadyr, Russia, and Ugolny Airport.

After the Il-112V taxied to the gate, the six-man special unit, sliced from the 5th Spetsnaz Brigade, grabbed their gear and piled it all into a Trekol – Russian made large all-terrain amphibious vehicle for the short ride to the Anadyr Helicopter Base just minutes away. With zero fanfare, General Denisenko and this six-man team of shooters board a medium-sized, twin-engine Mi-8AMT Russian helicopter for the short hop to the Gulf of Anadyr. This helicopter was chosen because it's fitted with the LPG-150M winch and SLG-300 hoist system that will lower the team of assassins to their transportation...a Russian Delta-IV-class nuclear submarine.

*　　*　　*

With break time over, the Joint Chiefs, Cyber Command and all other intelligence agencies and their staff present, the President walks to the podium and begins speaking. "The plan we've put together is one I'm very proud of. It took all departments represented here to help finalize a very fascinating and captivating plan which I'll lay out for you now. With the help of the PSYOP unit out of Ft. Bragg, our plan will be one of deception...an old 'Ghost Army' tactic used in World War II. So, with all of your help and input, PSYOPS has quickly organized some great new visual toys for the Chinese cameras to discover on their way east. These visuals will not be discussed here. Some are being labeled as Top-Secret. Just know that the game is in play. We will not shoot down this surveillance gasbag while it's over the continental U.S. The debris field could cause loss of life and/or destruction of private property. For this reason we will wait until it floats off the Carolina coast and then shoot it down. A trio of Navy warships will be on-station...the guided missile destroyer USS Oscar Austin (DDG-79), guided-missile cruiser USS Philippine Sea (CG-58) and amphibious warship USS Carter Hall (LSD-50). Navy divers are currently embarked aboard the warships off the coast and will assist in the debris recovery. The FAA will issue a ground stop in parts of North and South Carolina as soon as the Chinese gasbag exits our coastline. At that time, a United States Air Force F-22 Raptor from the 149th Fighter Squadron, based at Langley Air Force Base, Virginia, will use a single AIM-9X Sidewinder to shoot this intruder out of our skies. The two fighters will have the call signs Frank-1 and Frank-2, which will be in reference to World War 1 ACE Army Air Corps 1st Lt. Frank Luke, whose nickname was the Arizona Balloon Buster. Frank Luke is credited with 19 aerial victories, ranking him second among United States Army Air Service pilots after Captain Eddie Rickenbacker during World War I. On 1st Lieutenant Frank Luke's final flight, witnesses on the ground later recounted a five-minute aerial dogfight, one lone American in a French-made SPAD against ten German Fokkers (often known simply as the Fokker Triplane which was a World War 1 fighter aircraft built by Fokker-Flugzeugwerke). As 1st Lieutenant Luke

79

was shooting down two Fokkers, his own aircraft was being riddled with bullets from enemy machine gun fire. Trailing smoke his SPAD aircraft began a slow spiral toward the ground. Luke struggled with the controls, leveling off at 150 feet he took aim at the enemy's Drachen observation balloons and opened fire with both of his Vickers 11-mm weapons. (Vickers machine gun was built by Vickers Limited in the United Kingdom. It's one of the first machine guns used in wartime.) As he did, he felt his own airplane shudder under a hail of bullets. He rocked back in his seat as something slammed against his chest. Again he banked, turning toward Murvaux where one more black Drachen was being feverishly hauled back to earth by its frantic ground crew. Holding down the triggers of his own guns, 1st Lieutenant Luke swooped low on the third balloon and yet again, gasses exploded and the night sky lit up with the telltale signature of the American Ace of Aces...three balloons in less than 15 minutes. Luke was flying dangerously low after nailing the third balloon and the odds finally caught up with him. His wound was leaking warm blood into the lining of his flight jacket but he was still breathing and his SPAD was still flying. In his last act of defiance, he saw a troop of German soldiers along the city's main street. Tipping his nose ever so slightly, Luke opened up as he passed over them, smiling as he saw half-a-dozen enemy soldiers fall. He then noticed a small field on the outskirts of the village and put his crippled airplane on the ground. An enemy patrol called out to him to surrender, but instead Luke pulled out his pistol and began shooting. Within seconds, his body was quickly riddled with enemy bullets." The President continues to speak…"Luke Air Force Base, Arizona is named in his honor. Lt. Luke died fighting for his country at the age of 21 and is buried in Meuse-Argonne American Cemetery and Memorial in France. His military awards included the Medal of Honor, the Distinguished Service Cross with Bronze Oak Leaf Cluster, of which he has two, the Purple Heard and the War Merit Cross awarded to the Lieutenant by Italy. When the recovery is complete, we should have another piece of this Chinese, North Korea, Russian 'Trojan Horse.' We will get to the bottom of this and when it's over, there will be but one victor! I thank all of you for the time and efforts you've put forth to protect our democracy and our homeland...the United States of America!" With that, the President turns to leave as the entire U.S. intelligence community and Joint Chiefs stand and applaud her perceptiveness, cleverness and leadership.

*   *   *

Chapter 10

Back at the FBI office in Anchorage, Alaska, my cell phone alerts me to an incoming text. Looking down at the screen puts a smile on my face as I read...*Sidney, give me a call at your earliest opportunity...Gramps has information for you!* I go straight to my favorites and hit the name Chucci. After a couple of rings, I hear his voice. "Hello Sidney! How are you my friend?"

"Hey Chucci...always good to hear your voice."

"Sidney, we have a lot going on here so let me cut right to the chase. You know Gramps and his old Navy buddies 'the salty dogs' have been on the hunt for these mega-yachts and working hard to find some kind of pattern...which they have! Are you ready?"

With an even larger smile on my face I reply, "I have a pencil in my hand and a clean sheet of paper. I'm ready."

Chucci continues..."There seems to be a massive seizure of super-yachts world-wide. Every one of these is owned by Russian oligarchs and all have ties to the Kremlin. For instance, Italy impounded four super-yachts including Sailing Yacht A owned by Andrey Melnichenko, billionaire Russian oligarch who lives in St. Moritz, Switzerland. They also seized Lady M, Lena and Scheherazade. Spanish authorities have detained the megayachts Tango, Amore Vero, Lurssen, Crescent and Valerie. Croatia has impounded Royal Romance while Gibraltar has seized the Axioma. Even the island of Fiji, at the behest of the United States, has seized the 348-foot super-yacht Amadea. In total, this is about 4 billion dollars' worth of recreational vessels. I say at the behest because this seems to be a concerted effort by the U.S. government and NATO nations to send a very loud and clear message to the Russian oligarchs. This can only come from the very top...from Madam President." Chucci pauses for a second then resumes..."There are three mega-yachts which it seems the U.S. has purposely let through this net. Gramps and the salty dogs say these three are showing anomalous behavior. The Galactica Super Nova is owned by the CEO of a Russian oil firm called Lukoil; then we have the yacht Graceful it's been reported that this yacht belonged to Vladimir Putin. (9) Lastly, we have Nirvana Potanin (a second mega-yacht owned by our old pal Putin). Two of these yachts are docked at the Ocean Reef Club in Key Largo and one is due to arrive there later today. The funny thing about the two Putin yachts is who's on them. The Russian billionaire, Mikhail Fridman, is on one and his billionaire buddy, Oleg Deripaska, is on the other. Both have cut ties with the Kremlin and have taken their money and, shall we say, 'floated quickly away.' The Oil tycoon who owns the Galactica Super Nova is Vagit Alekperov. He also owned the Heesen Shipyard which he just sold for millions in gold before hightailing it across the sea and out of Russia's grip."

I can't believe what I'm hearing! I know I must get this info posthaste to Special Agent Sanders who will in turn make the call to FBI Director Cole Michael.

"Chucci, I'm not exactly sure what Gramps and 'the salty dogs' have uncovered, but I do know it's part of this puzzle. I've known about and spent lots of fun times at the Ocean Reef Club growing up in Key Largo. I can't believe the Ocean Reef Club (ORC) has been brought up so many times during this fiasco. It is definitely a major playground for the rich and famous. I'm going to pass this on quickly and I'll let you know what comes of it. Please give Gramps and the salty dogs' my best and many thanks to you brother!"

"You're welcome Sidney. My best to you, Big Al, Pistol Pete and Hulk... Good luck!" We both hang up and I'm already on the run to find Agent Sanders.

---

(9) Book Series I - *Hypersomnolence*. Putin was assassinated by a Saudi Arabian hit squad. If I could kill hime again, I would!

The second Agent Sanders hears the latest from Chucci, he's instantly on the phone with FBI Headquarters in Washington, DC. From there, the FBI Director is on the phone with Bennye Wolfe. Not only will this help her with her interviews regarding the crew and the Wagner Group mercenaries (who've been detained aboard the super-yacht, Milliarder Vodka), but it will also give the agents from the Miami office a heads-up on who they're looking for at ORC.

While that's going on, I'm in a spare office at FBI Headquarters in Anchorage on a secure FBI computer trying to find out everything I can on Mikhail Fridman and Oleg Deripaska. Fridman was born in Western Ukraine and his parents lived there until their death from Covid-19 over a year ago. In every picture of Mr. Fridman, he kind of looks like Miss Piggy if she were a man. His face, especially his eyebrows, looks as though he never likes what he's hearing. Mikhail was chairman of Alfa group, a private conglomerate operating primarily in Russia and the former Soviet states that spans banking, insurance, retail and mineral water production. The Alfa Bank is Russia's fourth largest financial services group and its largest private bank. His net worth is $11.4 billion and it looks as though he's on the run from Mother Russia and has taken all his money with him.

Oleg Deripaska sports a smile everyone should be very leery of and he never shows his teeth. I wonder what that's all about? He seems to be in a lot of trouble with U.S. authorities. The United States Attorney for the Southern District of New York and the Assistant Director-in-Charge of the New York Office of the Federal Bureau of Investigation have an indictment charging Oleg Vladimirovich Deripaska with bank fraud. He also has links to Russian organized crime. He owns En+ Group, a Russian energy company and he's head of the United Company Rusal, the second largest aluminum company in the world. However, it seems he's no longer in charge of either and a large hotel complex in Sochi, owned by Deripaska, was seized by the Russian authorities.

These three Russian A-holes are on the run with all the money they could possibly stuff down their pants and they're either already there or headed to the Ocean Reef Club in beautiful Key Largo, Florida. *Holy shit...this is getting good!*

* * *

An FBI Gulfstream V has just touched down at Elmendorf AFB just a few miles from the safe-house near Anchorage. Elmendorf Air Force Base is a United States Air Force (USAF) facility in Anchorage, Alaska, originally known as Elmendorf Field, it became Elmendorf Air Force Base after World War II.

It is the Headquarters for Alaskan Air Command. In 2010, it was amalgamated with nearby Fort Richardson to form Joint Base Elmendorf-Richardson.

Fort Richardson was named for the military pioneer explorer Brigadier General Wilds P. Richardson who served three tours of duty in the rugged Alaskan territory between 1897 and 1917. Richardson, a native Texan and an 1884 West Point graduate, commanded troops along the Yukon River and supervised construction of Fort Egbert and Fort William H. Seward (Chilkoot Barracks). As head of the War Department's Alaska Road Commission from 1905 to 1917, he was responsible for much of the surveying and building of early railroads, roads and bridges that helped the state's settlement and growth. The Valdez-Fairbanks Trail, surveyed under his direction in 1904, was named the Richardson Highway in his honor. The joint base's mission is to support and defend U.S. interests in the Asia-Pacific region and around the world. It provides units who are ready for worldwide air power projection that increase the points your planes contribute to air superiority, while being capable of meeting United States Pacific Command's theater staging requirements. In other words, planning today for military options needed tomorrow.

As they exit the FBI Gulfstream V, the ladies are giving hugs to the two FBI pilots, Drake and Cash who seem to be their very own private aircrew. (10) One of the Fly Team is already on the tarmac with his weapon locked and loaded, scanning the surrounding area. A 2023 white Ford Transit cargo style van, INKAS Armored Vehicle with an all-wheel drive 10-speed automatic 3.5 liter V-6 engine, pulls up to their secure location for passenger pick-up. With everyone safely seated, the Special Agent from the FBI office in Anchorage pulls out onto Fairchild Ave. as he chauffeurs this group to the "fortress" a few miles outside of Elmendorf AFB.

The second the armored van pulls into the "fortress" (safe-house) driveway, Marty is already out the door and on the run to meet the girls. Even though the four of them know the circumstances of their gathering, they are all still screaming and hugging each other. With the hand off complete, the Fly Team gets back in the armored van and leaves these screaming women in the capable hands of their two FBI bodyguards. Before these four females have calmed down enough to notice, the safe-house chef is walking their way carrying a tray which is balancing a pitcher of margaritas with four glasses. The chef smiles knowing he's in for a wild evening.

*　　*　　*

With the Belarusian hit team safely aboard the Russian BS-64 - Delta-IV-class nuclear sub and all their gear neatly stowed, the sub's captain, Admiral Feliks Gromov, is on the bridge. He is enjoying the beautiful sunset as his helmsman is reversing course and exiting the estuary (named Onemen Bay) and heading back into the main body of the Gulf of Anadyr.

(10) Book Series I - *Hypersomnolence* / Book Series II - *Bedlamites*
Drake and Cash are FBI pilots in both books.

The helmsman has set a heading of east by southeast. It should take them until dark to enter the Bering Sea. Admiral Gromov is taking in the evening's breeze while watching the day get put away. The skies on the western horizon are crystal clear and he's hoping to witness a green flash or anything that might possibly give his mission some good luck. But when the sun finally touches the sea, the rarest of all green flashes occurs. Known as a green ray, it shoots a beam of green light straight up a few degrees above the green flash. Truly a beautiful sight! As a broad smile is now expanding on the captain's face he thinks, "This is a great sign...a submariner's dream...a sight seldom witnessed at sea. Our mission is protected."

When the sub reached the Chukchi Sea Shelf, the eastern most part of the Continental Shelf off Russia, Captain Gromov picks up the comms and orders, "Osnastka diya pogruzheniya. Ochistit' most! (Rig for dive! Clear the bridge!)" After everyone clears the bridge and the hatch is sealed, the captain gives his next orders from the Control Room, "Dive, dive, dive!" At the same time the diving alarm is sounded, the order is repeated by the diving officer and BS-64 begins her downward trim and disappears beneath the calm seas. The second the sub is completely submerged, the captain orders, "Ustanovka diya besshumnogo bega! (Rig for silent running!)"

*   *   *

Chapter 11

The Gulfstream V from Los Angeles arrived at Andrews Air Force Base (Andrews AFB, AAFB) delivering Special Agent Monica Wynnie (she's also a crime scene investigator and forensic scientist) and Special Agent Todd Rhea along with his prisoner, asylum seeker Marat Gabidullin, who's AWOL from Russia's Wagner Group. Within minutes of landing, a Bell 407 helicopter from the HRT Tactical Aviation Unit is airborne and headed for the rooftop of FBI Headquarters located at 935 Pennsylvania Avenue, NW, in Washington, D.C.

As soon as the chopper touches down, Marat Gabidullin is immediately escorted off the rooftop and into the belly of the beast by two FBI agents. Special Agents Rhea and Wynnie are collecting their files and personal belongings while tapping the pilots on their shoulders and thanking them for the lift.

Both agents take the elevator to the dungeon, the bottom floor basement area, where members of the domestic and international terrorism, foreign counterintelligence agents and cybercrime are all seated and waiting for the Director to join them. As Agents Rhea and Wynnie enter the room, everyone stands and greetings are exchanged. Before anyone has time to sit back down, Director Cole Michael enters the room. The room goes quiet as the Director speaks. "Please be seated. As you know, all agencies are in crisis mode as we try to determine just what's going on with Russia, China and now North Korea. There is a lot of disturbing chatter between the different intelligence divisions...however, if I may use a metaphor, we may have scored a touchdown. A Russian operator with Wagner Group, Marat Gabidullin, entered our FBI office in Los Angeles asking for asylum. It's now our thinking that the Wagner Group assassins, taken out by our FBI team at LAX, were on a sanctioned mission to eliminate Mr. Gabidullin because he knows too much. Interrogations are continuing in LA with the pilot and crew of the aircraft that brought them to our soil. It is also our belief that the crew and Wagner Group assassins onboard the mega-yachts Billionaire Vodka, captured by the United States Coast Guard along with a SEAL team, was on its way to Ocean Reef Club in search of three Russian oligarchs. These people may also be holding pieces of the puzzle. We need every piece we can get. Mr. Gabidullin is going to be interviewed by a special FBI interrogation team upstairs. All of you will be witnessing this live from this very room. Make yourselves comfortable and let's get some answers people!" The FBI Director turns and walks out the door.

* * *

While the Alaskan girls are drinking and laughing it up in the living room, Marty gets up to use the ladies' room. As she's walking past the kitchen, she hears the chef whispering in a language that she's heard before. She proceeds to peek around the open door. The chef has his back turned to her and is wildly waving his hand while softly, yet emphatically, speaking into a satellite phone. Marty quickly backs away from the door frame, however her hand hits the wall with a quiet but startling thump. She then turns and commences to walk back toward the ladies when she hears the chef saying, "Hello...Miss Marty, may I help you?"

Marty turns around and sees the chef standing outside the door with his left hand hidden behind the door frame. Smiling she says, "No thank you Chef, I'm a little lost and tipsy, but I now remember where the ladies' room is located. Thank you!"

Chef smiles back before asking, "Is there anything else I can do for you ladies this evening?"

Marty stops, and as she is turning back toward the chef, she notices a slight change in his demeanor. She continues to keep her cool and broadens her smile before saying, "No Chef...you are the best and I can't thank you enough for your kindness and the care you're taking of my girlfriends and me. As you know, things have been getting a bit stressful for us. If we need anything else from the kitchen this evening, we can fetch it ourselves. Have a good night."

"Well, thank you Miss Marty. I'll see you ladies in the morning."

Marty is hoping he bought it, but not being totally sure, she walks straight upstairs to the bedroom, walks in and closes the door. Marty quickly goes to her Go Bag and removes her Walther PPK and the three magazine clips. Since these magazines are stored for long periods of time, she knows there are only 3 rounds in each which helps to preserve the power of the coil spring. She quickly and methodically inserts the ammo until each is packed. Marty chambers a round ejects the magazine and replaces the round that she just chambered. She now knows she must count her shots and she has 11 rounds to start off with, should she need them. All the while she's thinking to herself, *Something's not right in this so-called safe-house.* She flips on the weapon's safety and heads into the bathroom where she quickly opens the vanity and places the handgun and the two extra magazines on top of the rolls of toilet paper and covers them with a hand towel. Just for good measure, she decides to flush the toilet before exiting the room.

Marty is leaving the bedroom and heading for the staircase, that will take her back downstairs when she notices the chef is heading up the staircase to the third floor. As he looks down at her, he waves before saying, "Good night."

Marty smiles, returning the wave before saying, "Good night Chef."

*   *   *

A couple of things you should know about Marty...besides being my lover and best friend, she's as cool as a cucumber when she's under pressure. Some of the most seasoned warriors don't know how to maintain such calmness when certain the walls may

90

be closing in. She's very competitive at the gun-range...no hesitation or fear when it comes to pulling a trigger. She's my kind of gal!

*   *   *

That's when my cell phone startles me but frees my mind from some unpleasant thoughts. When I see its Marty, I shake those irksome images immediately out of my head as I answer, "Hey sweetie...how you doing?"

"Hi Sidney...I'm fine...I think." I quickly ask, "What's wrong babe?"

"It may be nothing, but the chef is strange. Is there any way you can check him out?"

"Why, what's he doing?"

Marty continues, "It's a feeling. Nothing concrete, but he's sneaky and he makes my skin crawl. You know that sixth sense you feel when something's not right? Well, something's not right Sidney!"

I'm thinking, *Wow, this is all we need...a fox in the henhouse.* However, in order to calm Marty, I remark, "I'll get right on it sweetie. I'll get back to you ASAP with an answer."

"Sidney, we've been here for over three days now. Card and board games are fun, but get us out of here."

I reply, "I'll get right on it babe. In the meantime, why don' t you mention this to Agent Tiburzi and give her a heads-up?"

Marty sighs before saying, "Maybe I'll have a quick chat with her in the morning."

91

"Sounds good…I love you babe, I respond."

"Love you too Sidney." As we're hanging up, I'm quickly heading over to Special Agent Sanders' bedroom.

*   *   *

Admiral Feliks Gromov takes the comms of the Russian BS-64 – Delta-IV-class nuclear sub and states, "All stop! This is what we train for gentlemen. Prepare the underwater submersibles. General Denisenko, please ready your men to exit the sub. All hands stand-by." With those orders, the nuclear sub begins to quietly settle into position for the six-man commando team to exit one craft and enter another. All are dressed in their dive gear and all weapons are stored in waterproof/airtight containers. There will be three Belarusian assassins in each submersible, each mini-sub containing all the gear needed to complete their mission.

The journey from the sub to the shore of the western coast of Alaska is approximately twenty miles, straight into Ugashik Bay where one can spot the small lighthouse near the town of Pilot Point.

*   *   *

The chef has taken his preplanned night off and is at the Elmendorf AFB boarding his personal Aerospace twin turboprop eFlyer 800. This all-electric eight-seater is preparing to lift off for Pilot Point Airport.

*   *   *

Chapter 12

Major General Stanley and Ms. Bikowsky have been spending countless hours over the last two days in contact with every U.S. intelligence agency trying to find the Russian BS-64 nuclear sub. It's been all-hands-on-deck! The last sighting was when the Delta-IV was leaving the Chukchi Sea Shelf off the eastern most part of the Continental Shelf of Russia, and the last thing they heard the captain say was, "Rig for silent running." Since then, this sub has been a ghost. That was until two mini-subs broke free from their mothership and were picked up by a sound-buoy located along the Alaskan coastline inside the Cape Newenham National Wildlife Refuge, giving them new hope.

Ms. Bikowsky is ecstatic as she picks up the phone for her call to General Stanley. "Sir, I believe we have them. They didn't travel far, so it's believed they weren't just silent running but also moving quite slowly. It's believed they're on some mission timetable. The noise the sound-buoy picked up is believed to be the mini-subs detaching themselves from the hull."

General Stanley, though quite pleased they found the sub, still needs more answers, "Great work Ms. Bikowsky! What's their location and what, if any, intelligence do we have on the mini-subs' possible mission?"

Ms. Bikowsky continues, "Sir, the location is about twenty miles off Alaska, directly west of the small town of Pilot Point. They do have a small runway there, as do most of the small towns in Alaska. As for their mission, we have everyone in on it. They're working up different scenarios now."

"Thank you, Ms. Bikowsky, I'm heading your way shortly."

While General Stanley is finishing his coffee, he's thinking, *This is going to be one hell of a long day!* He starts his car and is on his way to CIA Headquarters in Langley, Virginia.

Simultaneously, Chef is landing at Pilot Point Airport as the Belarusian Special Forces assassination squad is abandoning their mini-subs and coming ashore.

* * *

I finally find Special Agent Jennings Sanders closing down a bar a few doors down from the FBI Headquarters in Anchorage. As I'm helping Sanders out the door and down the sidewalk, Hulk and Pistol Pete have exchanged their pajamas for proper attire and are running to help me. Big Al has already started a pot of coffee out at the front desk and is bringing out the mugs as we enter the front door.

The FBI agent who's performing night duties has already booted up a computer for us to use. Our mission is to find out everything we can about the chef at the safe-house. It's mind-bogglingly to me that no one here seems to know his real name. Agent Fossil (a nickname we've given the overnight agent because he looks too old to still be an agent) is going through the file cabinets trying to find the chef's personal information. While Pistol Pete is pouring coffee down Sanders' throat, the rest of us join Agent Fossil at the file cabinets. That's when I have an epiphany and ask Agent Fossil for Agent Tiburzi's or Bacharach's cell number.

* * *

As the Aerospace twin turbo-prop eFlyer 800 lands back at Elmendorf AFB, chef does his aircraft picketing or tie-down of his non-hangared airplane. He salutes his comrades before saying, "Give me a twenty-minute head start. I have some unfinished business, then let's get this done!" With all their dive gear sitting on the coast of Alaska ready for their exfil (exfiltration), or as we'd say in Vietnam, "Di di mau," they are now dressed in their BDU black camo with matching balaclavas checking their weapons. (11)

As chef is pulling into the safe-house, he's confronted by Agent Tiburzi who asks, "How was your night off chef?"

Chef smiles and says, "It's been great...I was able to meet up with some old friends for dinner."

"Very good! Well, you know the drill...pop your trunk!" Chef pops the trunk open. As Tiburzi is walking back to look in the trunk, she uses her flashlight to check out the back seat of the car. Happy with what she sees, she waves the chef in.

Upstairs and looking out of her window, Marty is wide-awake as she watches the chef returning to the safe-house. She's been pacing the floor all night while the other ladies slept. She has a bad feeling about the chef and can't understand why no one else has picked up on it. She watches as he parks his car and is met at the side door by Agent Bacharach who unlocks the door and lets the chef pass through before relocking it. The chef turns to Agent Bacharach and remarks, "I'm going to the kitchen for a minute and then up to bed. Have a nice night Agent Bacharach!"

"Thank you...same to you Chef."

Chef goes into the kitchen and heads straight to the pantry where he's left his .22 pistol with suppressor and subsonic ammo which will make it even quieter! Knowing he doesn't have much time before the assassination team arrives, he heads upstairs. For some reason, he wants to kill the women himself and he wants to start with Marty. He slowly approaches the bedroom door and listens. Not hearing anything, he slowly opens the door. As he walks in, he notices a light coming from under the bathroom door.

(11) France occupied Vietnam before the US, thus the Vietnamese added
      French terms to their language and dialect. "Di di mau" means in French,
      "Move quickly!" but to us in combat it meant, "Get the fuck away!"

95

He brings his weapon up as he carefully approaches the door. He hears a flushing sound just as his hand is moving to the doorknob. Then he hears, "Is that you Chef? I've been hoping you'd come pay a visit." As Marty is opening the door, Chef is putting the weapon behind his back with his right hand. Marty opens the door with only a towel on and her right hand hidden from view behind the doorframe. With the flick from her left hand, the towel falls to the floor and the chef's eyes pop wide-open, giving Marty the split second needed to get the upper hand. Marty pulls the trigger three times in quick succession. With no suppressor on her Walther PPK, the three 9-mm rounds enter from the Chef's neck to his left eye. He falls in a heap to the floor along with the metallic sound of his weapon.

It seemed like only seconds when all the girls came running into the room. Candy goes over and places two fingers on the Chef's neck to feel for a pulse, but no joy. She looks up at Marty and asks, "Are you OK?"

Marty is shaking her head in the affirmative while saying, "Yes! I'm OK." They all hear the banging at the side door and head down the stairs. This is where they find the body of FBI Agent Bacharach lying against the door. Linda and Kitty each grab an arm and pull the dead agent's body away so that Special Agent Tiburzi can finally get through the so-called safe-house door. Tiburzi's phone is ringing as she sets foot inside...that's the exact same time a bullet enters her left shoulder and knocks her to the floor. Candy slams the door shut and locks it as Linda and Kitty help the agent back to her feet. Marty starts yelling from the basement door, "Quick...this way!"

*   *   *

With no one answering their phones at the safe-house, I'm yelling to Agent Fossil, "Get all the law enforcement people you can to your safe-house!" Then looking at my old PSYOP teammates I continue, "Grab your weapons and lets get moving!"

96

Dolph Coley comes walking into the FBI lobby wiping his eyes after just waking up. "What the hell's going on?"

Without explaining I say, "Something's not right at the so-called safe-house. We need you!" With that, Dolph immediately turns around running and returns in two minutes fully dressed and armed to the teeth. As the FBI battle-wagon pulls up to the front door, we all jump in and we are off...full speed ahead!

I make one more call to wake up the Anchorage Chief of Police Wayne. "Why you calling me so damn early?"

"Sorry Chief Wayne...I didn't want to bother you, but I do believe we need a SWAT team to roll out immediately. I'll send you the address. Marty may be in trouble."

Chief Wayne sits straight up in bed and says, "Anything you need Sidney!"

The chief's wife, Nita, is awakened. "What's going on Wayne? Is everything alright?"

I am busy typing the so-called safe-house address into my phone before I tell Chief Wayne, "The address is on its way, Wayne...I thank you ahead of time. I'll be in touch. All the best to Nita," I reply as I'm hitting end.

*   *   *

Back at Langley, Ms. Bikowsky asks, "General Stanley, what is the exact location of the PSYOP team?"

His answer is not what she wanted to hear... "Their exact location...I don't know, but...they're somewhere around Anchorage, Alaska. You don't think...?" Those were the last words out of the general's mouth before he was on the phone. Ms. Bikowsky was also in quick communication with every U.S. Intelligence Agency.

97

Every branch was immediately put on high alert while any and all resources in and around Anchorage were informed of all possibilities...including the assassination team on the ground, in or around the same location as the old PSYOP team.

When word reaches Madam President, she calla Deputy Jon Finer, the National Security Advisor.

"Yes, Madam President..."

"Deputy Finer..."

*   *   *

Chapter 13

Special Agent in charge Bennye Wolfe didn't need to spend much time at U.S. Coast Guard Sector Jacksonville. She figured out quickly that these Wagner Group killers were on their way to Ocean Reef Club to exterminate some fellow Russian citizens who had turned themselves into a group of thorns in the side of the Russian leader Gray Cardinal. She knows that once you cross a certain line, you either walk out of a five-story window to the street below or somehow give yourself ten blows to the head with a sledgehammer...All considered suicides in Russia.

That being the case, Agent Wolfe meets up with the two agents from the Miami FBI office at the ORC Pubic Safety Department. The two agents, Agent Allen Willis and Nigal Androtti, had already met with the ORC Commodore as well the dock-master earlier in the day. They instantly figured out who the persons were that needed to be interviewed.

Ocean Reef Club is a private club with amenities which include 36 holes of golf, a 175-slip marina, tennis, private airport, medical center, a wide variety of dining options, plus a fire department and public safety department. The public safety department also manages the front gate and welcome center. Officers assigned to the front gate and welcome center are responsible for ensuring that all members, guests and employees gaining access to ORC have proper clearance. The dock-master is responsible for verifying the identity of all boat traffic coming into the Marina and performing on-site inspections for all registered vessels. The ORC Association maintains a highly trained fire department ready to respond to any and all emergency situations.

As Agent Wolfe enters the ORC Pubic Safety Department she is met by Bobby Harris, the Security Commander. Commander Harris escorts the agent into a private room where she smiles before greeting the men. "Great job Special Agent Willis and Androtti!" Then she looks at the three gentlemen seated with their hands handcuffed behind their backs before continuing, "We need to get these three out of here...pronto!"

Agent Willis says, "Yes Ma'am..." as he and Agent Androtti turn and begin helping the three Russians to their feet. Agent Bennye Wolfe is quite pleased with this quick outcome and certain that FBI Director Cole Michael will be very satisfied with these results as well. She thanks Commander Harris and his department for all of their assistance and offers a promise that the Public Safety Department will be receiving a commendation from the FBI Director.

Agent in charge Bennye Wolfe is driving as they pull up in their golf cart to the Ocean Reef Club's private airport... with Agents Willis and Andrade and the three Russian oligarchs in handcuffs. The Gulfstream V is already fired up and waiting when co-pilot Drake comes running up to Agent Wolfe yelling above the jet blast, "Excuse me Agent Wolfe, we've just received a phone call from Special Agent Sanders that the FBI safe-house outside of Anchorage, Alaska, has been hit and we have agents down. Sanders is on site and has asked us to head out immediately to New Orleans to pick up three passengers at Louis Armstrong International for transport to Anchorage."

Agent in charge Wolfe asks, "Why not go to the New Orleans Lakefront Airport, it's right next to FBI Headquarters?"

Drake is shaking his head and biting his lip as he's saying, "It's Sanders...who knows what he's up to, but we've been hit and he's on the scene. You know he always plays it close to the edge."

Bennye Wolfe knows Agent Sanders' reputation all too well and says, "Give me a minute," as she quickly walks over to the airport lounge where a young man wearing an Ocean Reef Club shirt is standing and asks, "Young man…are you in charge of the airport?"

"No Ma'am…" he replies. "That would be Mr. Towers and he took off in a golf cart a bit ago. He didn't say where he was going."

"So, who's in charge while he's gone?"

"Well, I guess I am, Ma'am."

Agent Wolfe looks at a beautiful jet setting idle on the tarmac and asks, "Whose jet is that?"

"Ma'am that's the jet that brought Jimmy Buffett and his Coral Reefer band here for a private birthday party. They have a departure time in about 30 minutes."

The agent asks, "Where's the pilot?"

"He's onboard Ma'am."

Agent in charge Wolfe walks over to the golf cart embodying Agents Willis and Androtti and while pointing at Mr. Buffett's jet says to them, "That's our jet…put the Russians onboard and I'll be there in a minute." As the Agents drive the golf cart to the beautiful Embraer Legacy 600 and walk up the steps into the jet, Agent Wolfe is getting on her satellite phone (an anti-wiretapping encoded GSMK CryptoPhone with voice encryption algorithms). After changing the frequency, she pushes the squawk button twice before hearing, "This is the MAJOR."

Inside a soundproof glass room, a man sits with his Bilsom 303 earplugs in, he's surrounded by large screen televisions showing live action from around the world. Very few operatives in the intelligence community even know who the MAJOR is and

101

much less about where he's located...all they know is when you call him, he takes care of business. "This is Cobra Venom," says Agent Wolfe. She has only spoken with the MAJOR on a few occasions, but it's her belief that he never smiles. He's no nonsense and never gives a hint of what he may be thinking as the MAJOR dictums, "You've been verified...state your business."

As Agent Wolfe is speaking with the MAJOR, five golf carts come rolling up to Ocean Reef Club's (ORC) airport lounge. As the passengers are exiting the golf carts, Agent Wolfe is folding down the satellite phone's antenna and walking up to the young man in charge of the airport who happens to be speaking with a gentleman with a receding hairline. Special Agent Bennye Wolfe is smiling as she sticks out her hand and says, "Hello, you look like you might be Jimmy Buffett."

"Yes, ma'am," he replies. "I am...and I hear you've put some people on my airplane."

"Yes, I have...it is now temporarily the property of the United States government. At least for the next eight or so hours," as Agent Wolfe puts a finger up while saying, "Please give me a minute." She walks over to co-pilot Drake and says, "You've been cleared to Louis Armstrong International Airport and then all the way to Anchorage. You both stay safe and give them whatever help they need. I want you wheels-up in five minutes." Drake is already running back to the Gulfstream V to join the pilot, Special Agent Cash.

As Bennye turns back around, Mr. Buffett asks, "Are you allowed to do that? I need to be in Savannah, Georgia, tomorrow night for a string of concerts at the Enmarket Arena."

Agent Wolfe replies, "You'll be on time...we are taking your bird to Andrews Air Force Base and then your pilot is free to go, with a full tank of gas and 'THANKS' from your Uncle Sam. I'll

102

make sure that you and your band are taken care of and uncle Sam will gladly cover all expenses. I'll keep you notified of any changes and give you a heads-up when your jet is 30 minutes out and ready to pick you up."

Before Mr. Buffett can open his mouth, an explosion goes off behind him. Agent Wolfe is looking straight into a large flume of smoke as Buffett turns around to see it for himself. As the Gulfstream-V is getting ready to speed down the runway, Special Agent in charge Bennye Wolfe is going up the stairs of the Embraer Legacy 600 saying to the pilot, "You get this bird in the sky… NOW!" Then she turns to her agents. "Agent Willis, you're in charge. You and Agent Androtti get these three Russians to Washington." Then looking back at the Legacy 600s pilot she says, "You've been cleared all the way to Andrews and back. There'll be someone to meet you and get you gassed up. Now, get moving!"

Agent Wolfe is down the stairs quickly and back on the phone. On the other end of the connection she hears, "This is FBI headquarters Washington, how may I help you?"

"This is Special Agent Wolfe for the Director. Secure line only."

"Please hold for the Director."

While Bennye Wolfe is holding for the Director, she is walking back toward Jimmy Buffett and the Coral Reefers. As she's sliding up behind Mr. Buffett, who's still looking at the billowing smoke she says, "When today is over, I may be needing a new home. Any openings in one of your Margaritavilles?"

With a serious look on his face Jimmy asks, "So, it's been that kind of day? Well, from the looks of things it's far from over!"

Bennye hands Mr. Buffett her card and says, "If you need anything please give me a call."

103

Then she hears, "This is Director Michael...I'm on a secure line." Agent Wolfe turns and takes a few quick steps away from the Reefers and Mr. Buffett while putting a finger into her right ear before saying, "Sorry Director, it's hard to hear right now as we have a jet taking off. There's been an explosion at Ocean Reef Club. It looks like it took place at the marina. I've put Willis in charge and he and Agent Androtti are on a plane heading to Andrews. That roar in the background is them going wheels up." Knowing that's not the truth, she continues..."I'm going to need reinforcement here...local, state, send them all! I'm on my way to ground zero now."

"Stay on top of this Agent Wolfe. I'll get the cavalry to you ASAP. Secure that crime scene."

With sirens blasting Bennye says, "The ORC fire department is already en route. If this is one of the megayachts, I'll need the other two secured and swept for explosives quickly!"

The Director continues, "We already have the Monroe County Sheriff's Department Hazardous Device Squad en route and we're on the phone to Miami FBI headquarters now. They'll be choppering in to ORC Airport with everything you'll need."

"Thank you sir, I'll send you constant updates."

As they both hang up, the Director is thinking, *I chose well by putting her in charge.* At that moment, he is handed a note... After a quick read, he learns that Special Agent in charge Bennye Wolfe has gone over his head to another agency before contacting him. But this agency is unknown to the Director and has him wondering, "Who are they...and why did she contact them?"

*   *   *

Chapter 14

Chief Master Sergeant Jessica L. McWain from the 673rd Security Forces Squadron at Joint Base Elmendorf-Richardson was the first on the scene at the FBI safe-house. When the call came in from the National Security Advisor, Deputy Jon Finer, she knew immediately there was a serious breach in security and lives were at risk. With a five-man team, she opened the armory and within minutes her squad was on Fairchild Avenue heading for the safe-house.

Chief Master Sergeant McWain has never run from a fight. She was the Security Forces Manager for the 386th Expeditionary Security Forces Squadron, Ali Al Salem Air Base, Kuwait. In this capacity, she led a 219 Total Force Security team and 14 contractors in the security of the installation, base security zone, plus 4,200 base personnel. She's also deployed in support of peacekeeping, contingency, and combat operations in the Balkans, Haiti and Southwest Asia. Her awards include the Air Force Meritorious Service Medal with two oak leaf clusters, Air Force Commendation Medal , Army Commendation Medal, Air Force Achievement Medal with two oak leaf clusters, Air Force Combat Action Medal, Afghanistan Campaign Medal with one star, Iraq Campaign Medal with one star, NATO Medal and the Nuclear Deterrence Operations Service Medal.

By the time we arrived, the action was over and bloody bodies were lying very still on the safe-house grounds. Anchorage SWAT pulled in 30 seconds after our FBI battlewagon. As they exited their vehicle, I could tell they were as dumbfounded as we were. Chief Master Sergeant McWain walks over to us and explains, "We were first on the scene. Nothing's been moved. The women are all safe and in the house with a wounded FBI agent. The women and the wounded agent broke into the weapons locker in the basement and somehow got the upper hand." As she is telling us, she turns and points to the bodies before continuing…"The ladies shot and killed these five men that are wearing black. There are two FBI snipers who were killed outside the house. Inside the home there is another dead FBI agent and someone the women refer to as Chef. One terrorist was wounded and limped off in that direction (as she points towards the west, in the direction of the Knik Arm... the waterway into the northwestern part of the Gulf of Alaska). Three of my men are in pursuit."

I quickly ask, "Are the ladies all OK?"

The Chief Master Sergeant responds, "They seem a bit shaken, but other than that...look around. They took care of business!"

Special Agent Sanders is kneeling next to one of the dead FBI snipers who is lying on the lawn. As I start to walk over to him, he stands and looks at me shaking his head no. His face is despondent as he moves on to the second agent whose body is lying about thirty yards away.

Knowing the ladies are OK, I decide to go through the pockets of each of the five terrorists when the Chief Master Sergeant remarks, "The coroner officer is on his way. Please let him finish his job before we handle any of the bodies."

"With all due respect Ma'am," I reply..."I need any information I can get as fast as I can get it. Every second counts! This is only a small part of a very large puzzle, of which you've not been read in. However, you'll be brought up to speed soon." The whole time I'm talking to her, I'm padding down every inch of each terrorist.

Hulk, Big Al, and Pistol Pete have gone inside the house with the ladies and the wounded agent. I'll join them as soon as I finish foraging for information from these five scumbags. I notice

106

that none have the tattoo of the Wagner Group. That surprises me! Then, I find a piece of paper in one of their socks. I don't know what it says, and I don't believe it's in Russian.

I look at the SWAT commander and ask, "Is it alright to enter the safe-house? I know it's a crime scene."

He replies, "Your friends certainly didn't care about that when they entered. Chief Wayne told me you had carte blanche. So, you do whatever you deem necessary and we'll work around you." I thanked the commander and headed for the safe-house door. That's when the ambulance and the coroner's vehicles came screaming in.

*   *   *

Back in Langley, Ms. Bikowsky and General Johnathon Stanley are receiving the sad news that three FBI agents have perished while one was wounded and in stable condition. At the same time, they also get word that five of the assassins are also deceased after a horrific gun battle in which one was wounded and scampered off.

General Stanley is quickly on the phone with National Security Advisor Finer. After he elucidates the entire situation, the general goes on to tell Deputy Jon Finer how he and Ms. Bikowsky are interlocking every morsel of information they can find and will soon have something concrete. The General ends the conversation with, "You have my word on it!

With that, the General asks Ms. Bikowsky, "Find that sub? A Russian BS-64 Delta-IV nuclear sub can't just disappear. The sub must be sitting there waiting for this team of assassins to return. We know *that's* not going to happen, but they may not know that. Where would the mini-subs have landed, and how did they get to Anchorage so quickly? We need a U.S. Navy Boeing P-8A Poseidon anti-submarine aircraft in the air immediately."

Ms. Bikowsky responds, "I'm on it, Sir!"

Ms. Bikowsky promptly finds out that only last year there was a reorientation leading to more emphasis on Arctic operations, including the region around Alaska. Some Navy Boeing P-8As are actually located at Naval Air Station Adak on Adak Island and call the Aleutian Islands home.

Within the hour, a Navy Boeing P-8A is airborne and dropping sound-buoys off the coast of Alaska. Sound-buoy's emit acoustic waves underwater and when these waves hit the hull of a submarine, they bounce back so the operators on the plane can detect direction, distance and depth. The crew can encircle the exact location and follow the submarine's route.

The Boeing P-8A Poseidon Maritime Surveillance and Patrol aircraft excels at anti-submarine warfare, anti-surface warfare, intelligence, surveillance and reconnaissance and search and rescue. It can fly higher (up to 41,000 feet) and get to the fight faster (490 knots), or 304 mph.

* * *

Aboard the Russian BS-64 – Delta-IV-class nuclear sub, Admiral Feliks Gromov is receiving a radio message from his radar officer, "Captain Gromov, we are being pinged. Many sound-buoy's are in the water all around us. They are honing in on our echo. It will only be a matter of time, Sir."

The captain looks at his XO and Belarusian General Vadim Denisenko and says, "We must wait for the team to return. We're in international waters and as far as they're concerned, we're minding our own business." As he speaks, he's thinking to himself…*This Belarusian Special Forces team may have been eradicated. If so, I should get out of these waters as fast as I can. However, before we submerged I watched the sun touch the sea and I witnessed the green flash expand into the green ray shooting a beam of viridescent light straight into the sky. This is the proof that our mission is protected.* For that reason, the sub's captain calms down and feels reassured that he can sit tight.

* * *

Chapter 15

As an FBI Gulfstream V is approaching the Louis Armstrong International Airport in New Orleans, Chucci and his tugboat captain Hal, are waiting at the general aviation ramp of the private jet terminal (FBO) with Biggin (Biggin is Special Agent Jennings Sanders' half-brother).

As the Gulfstream's pilot FBI Special Agent Cash and his co-pilot Special Agent Drake are taxiing to the private jet terminal, the aviation fuel truck is already on standby. With the engines still running, the fuel truck goes straight for the single point fueling system located under the wing and quickly starts the refueling process. The airport may be owned and operated by Charleston County Aviation Authority (CCAA), but the director of aviation is Kevin Dolliole. He was given orders over an hour earlier that our second Gulfstream V lands, it was to be refueled immediately...no questions asked!

While Agent Drake is opening the passenger door, Agent Cash is on the radio. "Special Agent Sanders, we are picking up our package in New Orleans and taking on fuel, heading your way in fifteen minutes. How are things there?"

"Long story...have a safe flight." Agent Cash is shaking his head as Biggin, Chucci and Captain Hal enter the airplane. Biggin gives Cash a high five before saying, "You're a sight for sore eyes. It's great seeing you again...it seems every time we meet it's always under dire circumstances."

Cash smiles and says, "Great seeing you again also. The circumstances do seem to be grievous, but maybe one day we can go fishing...for fish...not people!" They both chuckle as Biggin takes a right to enter the fuselage to take his seat.

With everyone seated and the aircraft fuel handlers backing away from the aircraft, pilot Cash takes the comms. "This is your captain speaking. Please stay seated with your seatbelts fastened. There will be no smoking and we only have Adam's ale to drink. I've been ordered to tell you to get all the sleep you can because the second we touch down you'll be on the move immediately. Where to...only God knows..."

The air traffic control tower (ATCT) at Louis Armstrong International Airport remarks to Pilot Cash, "All incoming and outgoing traffic is on pause until you're airborne. Please taxi to runway 2/20 for takeoff." Pilot Cash is thinking to himself...*I radioed ahead for fuel and they already had a truck ready for me while other aircraft were here first and waiting and now an entire International Airport is on pause until I'm airborne. Who the hell is pulling these strings?*

*   *   *

It doesn't take long for investigators to discover that Chef was the owner of the all-electric eight-seater Aerospace twin turbo-prop eFlyer 800 that's tied down at the Elmendorf-Richardson airbase. It took a few extra hours of digging to discover that Chef was the last living relative of a family of Russian sleeper agents. This blew my mind and brought me back to the TV show, "The Americans."

After some more digging, we learned the real name of his parents were Andrei Bezrukov and Elena Vavilova. They were both born in the Soviet Union. They had undergone training in the KGB and been dispatched to Alaska as part of Soviet deep-cover secret agents. As active agents for the SVR, the foreign spy agency of the modern Russia, they had two children — one was named Alex. We all knew him as Chef. He possessed an American passport, driver's license, pilot's license, a degree as a "Top Chef" from Holland College Culinary Institute of Vancouver, Canada, and last but not least, background checks showing him to be reliable, trustworthy and suited for the job.

111

Mr. Chef, or should I say Alex, never sent up any "red" flags and was always dutiful, compassionate and thoughtful...that was until Mother Russia gave him his operational orders. His parents have passed away and his sister, Sylvia, is believed to have also passed on, but there is no record of where or when she passed away.

In spy lingo, Alex was a "sleeper" and now he's a dead "mole." Another thing spies usually do is expatiate every situation to its end. So, where is Sylvia?

I had already taken a picture of the piece of paper I'd taken off of the one dead scumbag assassin and sent it to Ross Brown (in the hopes he might call me) and to FBI Director Cole Michael. I'm hoping to hear back from someone soon as my phone starts vibrating. "Hello, this is Sidney Krogh."

"Yes, Mr. Krogh, my name is Alfreda Bikowsky, I'm working on the Joint Task Force and I'm calling from the Pentagon. I'm on a secure phone and I know that you are not. However, I know you're on the scene at the safe-house and FBI Director Michael forwarded the photo you took of a note which was in one of the terrorist's sock. I have a few questions if you don't mind?"

"No Ma'am, go ahead."

"Do any of these men have a tattoo on their neck?"

"Ma'am, none of these men are Wagner Group. That surprised me! Now, I have a question for you. In what language is the note written?"

"I'm sorry Sidney, I can't divulge that information."

She continues to speak, but I loudly voice over her, "Then this conversation is over," and I hung up.

Twenty-seconds later, my phone begins vibrating again. "YES!" is all I say, before I hear, "Mr. Krogh, please find a secure satellite phone and call me back on the number I'm texting you."

"Yes, Ma'am!" I found an FBI Special Agent who quickly handed over his sat-phone. I headed over to a quiet spot and typed in Ms. Bikowsky's number. As soon as she answered I heard, "It's Belarusian...more to the point East Slavic language. Now, may I ask you a few more questions, Mr. Krogh?"

I responded with, "Only if you'll do a one-for-one. Do you understand?"

"Yes, Mr. Krogh...I understand." "Good! Then you may go first."

I figured out during our conversation that she's been charged with putting this massive puzzle together. Ms. Bikowsky is collecting all the pieces and then trying to make sense of them. I believe I've added a bit to her collection, while at the same time, she was adding to mine — kind of an arrière-pensée between two consenting adults.

*   *   *

As I am entering the front door of the safe-house, I can't help but see the blood stains on the floor. I hear Hulk talking with Candy and it sounds like they might be in the kitchen, so I head in that direction. That's when I hear, "Sidney…Sidney…" Looking up I see Marty coming down the stairs. While she's now taking two stairs at a time, I'm sprinting her way. We embrace at the bottom of the stairs and I can feel the fear being released from her body. "Thank God you're here! I think I've just gone through another UBM."(12)

(12) Book Series I - *Hypersomnolence*. UBM means Uncle Bob Missions. The story of Sidney's Uncle Bob and how he died in WWII. Anytime my old PSYOP team returned from a tough mission, we called it a UBM.

"I'm so sorry I wasn't here for you sweetie. Air Force Chief Master Sergeant McWain filled me in on most of it but I want to hear it all from you. Firstly, are all the ladies OK?"

"Yes, everyone is fine! Candy jumped right into action when Special Agent Tiburzi was wounded. She sure knows her stuff. We got her downstairs into the basement quickly and locked that door. I knew something was wrong with Chef. You've always told me to listen to my sixth sense, so I had already loaded my PPK and put it in the bathroom vanity of our bedroom. Then I went downstairs into the basement and broke into the weapons locker. I'm not sure which rifles I took, but the ammo fit and I loaded three of them...just in case."

Marty is a real piece of work. She went out the hidden door in the basement with Kitty and Linda while Candy took care of Agent Tiburzi. Marty gave Candy her PPK for protection. The three ladies watched as one of the FBI snipers fell to the ground after being shot. Instead of being scared, Marty got pissed off and started giving hand signals to the ladies. To her amazement, the ladies understood her hand signals and then to her bewilderment, she could see that these professional assassins had broken two "golden rules." One of concealment — instead of hiding in the shadows, they were silhouetted by a far-off streetlight. After shooting/killing the three agents outside, and making sure that Chef had finished off the agent inside the house and hopefully our ladies, they broke rule number two...that of assumption — never let your guard down by assuming anything. They either aren't trained very well or they're stupid and arrogant.

Marty put up three fingers and started the countdown as she began bringing them back into her hand one at a time until the last finger was gone and all three women opened fire. She said it was over in seconds and that one of them was screaming and probably cussing...but in a language she didn't understand. The ladies ran back into the basement. After a few minutes, they went back outside

114

with Candy to check on the FBI snipers. They were both deceased, along with Agent Bacharach!

They took the five scumbags' weapons and were heading back to the basement door when they saw the flashing lights in the distance. Within a minute they had a new girlfriend, Chief Master Sergeant Jessica L. McWain.

It was then that she started crying on my shoulder before asking, "Sidney, is it always going to be like this? Are people going to keep trying to kill us?"

"NO, Sweetie! I promise you! When this is over, we'll make some changes to our lives and all of this will be a distant memory." I know that may have sounded good, but how the hell am I possibly qualified to make such a statement. SHIT! Now I really have something to work on.

*　　*　　*

Chapter 16

Back at Ocean Reef Club, the main gate is closed to anyone except first responders. All hotel room guests have been evacuated to other accommodations in Key Largo and Card Sound Road has been shut off at U.S. Highway-1 at Florida City. All ORC employees are allowed to leave the island, but only after first being interrogated and their cars searched. Only the homeowners are being allowed to stay and only if they don't leave their homes until they get the all clear.

The airport has been also been closed to any outgoing or incoming traffic unless it's been cleared by the FBI. There are three federal helicopters and one jet parked on the tarmac.

Jimmy Buffett and the Coral Reefer band were put on two air-conditioned buses and will be meeting their jet, on it's return flight from Washington D.C., at the Fort Lauderdale Executive Airport. Special Agent Bennye Wolfe made sure everyone onboard the buses had a box lunch and a LandShark Lager for the one hour and forty minutes, police escorted drive.

The bomb squad from the Monroe County Sheriff's Department, as well as FBI bomb technicians have been on the scene for a few hours clearing every yacht docked at the Ocean Reef Clubs marina. The ORC marina is a 175-slips, world-class mega-yacht private harbor, with berths costing somewhere in the three-million-dollar range.

FBI officials are with the ORC Public Safety Department Commander Bobby Harris in the office of the Dock-master, going over the entry logs from the last three weeks. Both yachts that were previously owned by Valadimir Putin, Graceful and Nirvana Potanin, are still docked and bomb free. While the Galactica Super Nova, which is owned by Vagit Alekperov, the ex-CEO of Lukoil in Russia, is a burned-out ex-super-yacht hull.

Special Agent Bennye Wolfe has made the rounds and is quite pleased with the security and complete lock-down of the club. Even police and Coast Guard boats are securing the property from the sea. Local TV and radio stations are broadcasting the necessity for everyone to stay clear of this area. Agent Wolfe knows it's time to call her boss, Director Cole Michael, and update him on the progress of the ORC investigation. She also would like to know if Agents Willis and Androtti have safely dropped off the three packages. While she's still thinking of making that call, her sat-phone rings, "Hello, this is Special Agent Wolfe."

"Yes, Agent Wolfe, this is Ms. Alfreda Bikowsky and I'm working with General Stanley at the Pentagon. I'm the Dissectologist in this quagmire of world events and your reputation as a puzzle enthusiast, proceeds you."

Special Agent Wolfe smiles before saying, "If this is the Ms. Bikowsky who tracked down Osama bin Laden, then it is I who should be saying, your reputation proceeds you. How may I be of assistance Ms. Bikowsky?"

*   *   *

FBI Pilot Cash brings his Gulfstream V in for a perfect landing at Joint Base Elmendorf-Richardson, outside of Anchorage, Alaska. The FBI battlewagon is there to pick up Biggin, Chucci and Capt. Hal and transport them to the so-called safe-house. Other FBI agents are en route to Anchorage from California and Washington State to help bolster their depleted force. FBI Special Agent, Crime Scene Investigator and Forensic Scientist, Monica Wynnie, is also airborne and en route to our location.

*   *   *

With the information I've received from the massive puzzle solver, Ms. Bikowsky, we now know the Belarusian dictator,

117

Alexander Lukashenko, sent this team to our shores — a present for Wagner Group founder, Dmitry Utkin. Pistol Pete and Chucci have been on the computer checking into the dictator's life and we've come up with a plan. We may all die trying to pull it off, but we aren't thinking about that at the present time.

The dictator has a power circle, all recruited from his own private security service. This asshole had to do this because so many of his own countrymen and women wanted his head on a stick. Our mission is to try to help them with the impaling...and move that concept along as rapidly as possible.

At first, I had no idea why Chucci brought Captain Hal along, but soon learned he's not only a boat captain, he's also a highly thought of pilot with training and competence in a variety of flying machines. We have in our possession an Aerospace twin turbo-prop eFlyer 800 whose old owner will no longer be in need of its service. We also have plenty of weapons thanks to the FBI safe-house weapons locker that Marty had broken into. Special Agent Sanders tried to tell us we couldn't use any of these weapons, but as he's talking, Pistol Pete began laughing and walked right past Sanders carrying three high powered M240B gas-operated, air-cooled, belt-fed weapons. They fire the 7.62-mm rounds with a maximum range of 1,100 meters. When Agent Sanders put his hands into the air and turned to walk away, we knew he'd given up and the locker was ours. Big Al noticed the M4A1s sitting around doing nothing, so he grabbed two. Hulk always loves to make a lot of noise...and this is his favorite toy...a compact 5.56 Colt Rifle with M203 Grenade Launcher. You should see the smile on his face.

To carry the ammo we'd need, we procured four TT-3 Day Assault Packs and filled them to the brim...including C-4, the old basic plastique dynamite substitute, just in case the need for pyrotechnics arose.

The safe-house may just start to live up to its name as over twenty-first responders (many with weapons) are on the grounds, with more agents arriving later today. Knowing this makes it easier to say our goodbyes to the ladies.

*   *   *

Captain Hal has calculated our flight plan and says we have a need to add a whole extra set of quad-redundant batteries to make our flight. Lucky for us, Mr. Chef was one very prepared commie bastard. The captain gives us the rundown on our new airplane, "The safety features are to die for...we have two wing-mounted electric motors, each with dual redundant motor windings, quad-redundant battery packs and a full airplane parachute. Additional features include: emergency auto-landing system, intelligent algorithm ensuring envelope protection, terrain avoidance and routing for emergency auto land. This babies got everything! The only problem I see is the battery packs will only get us 500 nautical miles and we need to traverse 903. With the additional pack we should be covered. Any turbulence or other unforeseen obstacles could cause us a problem."

With that being said, we anticipate a two-hour flight heading west with the sun. The saying, "The weather is here, wish you were beautiful," has us taking off into a gorgeous sunset...one we'll be able to watch for the next few hours.

Onboard we have our two snipers, Dolph Coley and Chucci. Biggin wanted to come along but we needed the extra battery packs. They're both about the same size but Biggin probably weighs more. Hulk will be carrying his (blooper), a Colt Rifle with M203 Grenade Launcher. Big Al will be handling the M4A1 while Pistol Pete will be armed with the M240B. Pete and I will also be in charge of any pyrotechnics and other forms of explosions. All of us have Glock 34s with suppressors. Needless to say, but I will

119

anyway, we have a secure satellite phone and we possess an Enence instant two-way language translator. Though it can instantly translate 36 languages, we believe we'll only need Russian and Ukrainian.

As for our sat-phone, we need all the security we can get so the feds sent us off with a GSMK Cryptophone 13 satellite adapter. This puts us on the Thuraya satellite network, meaning no tangos can listen in and we have perfect communication with the feds and other U.S. government officials. We are looking at each other as the eFlyer 800 takes to the sky. That's when we all start exchanging stories about Whoman.(13) We miss you brother, but you're with us in spirit!

*　*　*

We all try our best to get quick catnaps before we hear Captain Hal on the comms. "We are over the Gulf of Anadyr 15 minutes until touchdown." Our plan is simple...land at the Ugolny Airport, kill anyone who gets in our way and steal the Russian Ilyushin Il-112 V military transport aircraft. This is the same airplane that brought the Belarusian scumbags to our shores. It's our belief that their mission was to kill our women which would instantly bring us back to the safe-house. With the kind of explosives they carried with them, we further believe it was their plan to set in place enough high explosives to bring the house down, killing us all. Nice plan, except for the fact that three women with very little or NO training at all killed five highly trained Special Forces from the 5th Spetsnaz Brigade!

Captain Hal figures he'll be able to decipher the Russian aircraft's instrumentation panel and get us airborne. We're hoping the Russian military transport has been gassed up and is ready for its return flight, but we're ready and willing to do whatever has to be done.

(13) Book Series II - *Bedlamites*. Whoman died in the book and also died in real life while I was writing this book. Rest in peace brother.

Just as we're on approach Captain Hal says, "All batteries are dead...the last 15% of our battery power dropped in a matter of seconds...we'll never make the runway." *Holy shit*...is all that is running through my mind, but then I remembered something our captain had said. "Captain...I recall hearing you say something about a full airplane parachute. Do you know how that works?"

"I've never used one before, nor have I ever been in an airplane that was equipped with one. That being said, we're about to find out! One thing I do know is that this system is only intended to save our lives...the aircraft will most likely be destroyed." *Oh, GREAT*...is what I'm thinking, just as Captain Hal activates the handle in the cockpit and an igniter fires a rocket motor to extract the parachute from the rear of the aircraft. We can only hope no one sees a white parachute with an airplane dangling from it floating to Earth. It would also be nice if we were out of earshot as we smash into the ground. What a way to start a mission! Murphy's Law on day one...not good!

When the parachute fully deploys, our aircraft swings downward so fast you get a blood-rush that almost makes you faint. It takes a few minutes to comprehend what has just happened. At that very second, the nose of our airplane smashes into the ground and we're being dragged backward. That's when the airframe hits the ground as the floor beneath our feet cracks open. Within seconds, we come to a complete and very abrupt stop. The only sound we hear is Pistol Pete laughing. I had to ask, "Just what the fuck is so funny?" This only makes Pete laugh harder!

When he finally gets himself under control he says, "You know what Whoman would say right now?"

In unison the old team says, "Another fine mess you've gotten us into, Sidney."

121

We figured our crash landing puts us about a mile from the Ugolny Airport. The captain was right...the aircraft is destroyed but the passengers, crew and weapons are all intact. Hulk and Big Al quickly roll up our white lifesaving parachute and stuff it back inside our busted fuselage.

We all check each other out — no bruises or broken bones, just an airplane that's seen better days. All of our weapons and gear are fine. The initial plan was to taxi right up to the Russian transport aircraft, but with that option no longer available, we begin our hike to Ugolny Airport on foot. I figure we should arrive in about 15 to 20 minutes. We don't want to do a real power walk because we're going to need every bit of energy to "slash and burn" once we get there.

Pistol Pete, Captain Hal and I will check out the Russian Ilyushin Il-112 V, military transport aircraft while Hulk and Big Al set the perimeter. This will allow Chucci and Dolph to go straight to the airport hangar and take care of anyone there. We're all hoping this phase of our operation will be a little stealthier than our landing.

As we approach the Ugolny Airport, we notice two men smoking beside our (soon-to-be) transport aircraft. One of them stops and begins field stripping his cigarette. This the act of rolling his cigarette back-and-forth between his fingers until the lit end falls to the ground. They seem to quickly finish their conversation as one begins walking back toward the hangar, while the other one is entering the airplane. I turn and start to give Chucci and Dolph a hand signal but they're already shaking their heads in the affirmative. You don't need to tell either of them anything. They already know what to do.

When the one still smoking enters the hangar, Pete, Hal and I sprint the last 50 yards to the aircraft. Pistol Pete does the honors

122

of putting him in a choke hold but as soon as I see his Belarusian uniform, I instinctively know he's an officer and possibly a pilot, so I tell Pete, "Don't kill this guy...he may just be our dream come true." Pete zip ties him quickly and does a body search. He finds a handgun, radio, pack of cigs, lighter and wallet (with pictures of his family — wife and kids). This is a goldmine! He has a family he'll want very much to get home to...alive.

I ask Captain Hal, "Can you drive this thing?"

He replies quickly, "Piece of cake. Tanks are full and so is the extra fuel bladder. I'll crank her up when you give me the word."

With the airplane secure and full of aviation fuel and most everyone at the base probably sleeping, Pete and I are letting Chucci and Dolph take care of the explosions on this phase of our operation. We need to blow their communication tower. The intel report we received before we began this mission told us that this communication tower also serves the town of Anadyr. This way both the town and the airport will lose all Wi-Fi and radio contact with the outside world. We also need to blow up all of their radio gear which is usually housed in an office inside the hangar. Then it's the aviation fuel and one MiG-31 interceptor (that wasn't supposed to be here, and won't be in a few minutes). I figured we'd use over a quarter of our C-4 explosive here at the airport, but with the MiG included, it's now around half. Big Al and Hulk have moved closer to the hangar and Hulk has disappeared inside. As soon as Chucci and Dolph pass Big Al, he signals Hulk and everyone is now heading toward the aircraft. As Hulk gets closer, I see he's wearing a Belarusian military uniform and carrying a number of packages. He throws them into the aircraft and says, "Look at these...ironed and folded very nicely. When we arrive, we will be Belarusian officers, and I want us all looking like stack soldiers." Hulks uniform had blood on it, but I decided I didn't need to know how that happened.

Chucci says, "Sidney, we have a five-minute window before everything goes BOOM!"

I tell our pilot, "Captain Hal, crank this baby up!" With that, both Klimov TV7-117S modular turboprop engines come to life. The advanced digital avionics light up inside the glass cockpit, which features navigation equipment, communications, flight displays and monitoring systems. Our two six-bladed propellers slowly begin moving us forward as we are making our first turn toward the runway. No one has gotten out of bed to stop us, as we hear our first explosion igniting the aviation fuel dump. Within two-seconds the communication tower is on its way to the ground. As for the MiG... well this one won't be following us and the hangar no longer exists.

With a Belarusian officer unconscious and zip-tied at our feet, we take to the air on a very beautiful evening for flying. We make one quick pass over the Ugolny Airport to see firsthand the destruction we are leaving in our wake. Captain Hal sets his heading west/southwest...full speed ahead for Belarus.

* * *

Back at FBI headquarters at 935 Pennsylvania Avenue, NW, Washington, D.C., the members of the domestic and international terrorism, foreign counterintelligence agents and the cybercrime unit are all seated in the dungeon, the bottom floor basement area. Earlier, Special Agent Todd Rhea escorted Marat Gabidullin from the Los Angeles FBI field office, to be interviewed about his status in the United States and his need for asylum, even though everyone knows this ex-Wagner Group commander is AWOL from his unit, has a price on his head and is a treasure trove of information.

As the very large TV screen comes to life, the dungeon crowd goes quiet. All eyes are on the monitor as this interrogation begins.

Special Agent Rhea notices both FBI interrogators are polite and cunning at the same time. This is a craft he's always wanted to engage in with the bureau. To watch these two skilled professionals at work gives him a sense of pride. It also seems that Marat Gabidullin is the gold mine of information they've all heard about. He seems to be coming completely clean. After an hour of questioning, just before taking their first break, he said something that alarmed everyone in the dungeon... "above-ground nuclear explosion."

* * *

A few blocks down the street from FBI headquarters are the beautiful grounds of the Executive Mansion. America's White House is one of the most iconic buildings in the city and yet most do not know the origin of the name. When the White House was first created, it didn't have a specific name. Typically it was referred to as the "President's House," the "Presidents Mansion" or the "Executive Mansion." However, there was also the nickname: "The White House." Despite the nickname, the term was not official until 1901. That's when President Theodore Roosevelt decided it was time for a change. Since every state had an "executive mansion" for their governor, Roosevelt decided there should be some distinction for the presidential house. That decision made the nickname official.

The White House has 132 rooms, 35 bathrooms, 147 windows, 28 fireplaces and a whopping 412 doors. Behind one of those doors, Madam President is not believing what she's hearing... "A WHAT?"

"Yes, Ma'am...that's exactly what he said. An above ground nuclear explosion. He has no knowledge of where, when or the weight in megatons...just that it's happening soon."

With this knowledge, Madam President calls her Chief of Staff. "I want the Joint Chiefs, the heads of the FBI, CIA, DOD and

125

NSA in the situation room in one hour." As she's putting the phone down she's thinking...*Have these people gone completely mad? What could they possibly be thinking? Mutual destruction can't be in their equation...so what is...what could they possibly do that they believe they could get away with?*

*   *   *

Three hours into our flight Captain Hal has our stolen Russian aircraft on autopilot we are cruising at 30,000 feet with an airspeed of 345 mph. Our range is 5,400 miles on a tank of gas. We're expecting to land at the Machulishchy air base in nine hours. The Air Force and the Air Defense Forces of the Republic of Belarus are located in Machulishchy, Minsk Region, Belarus. From Ugolny Airport to Machulishchy air base is 4,086 miles, give or take a mile or two. With the aviation bladder full, this should give us plenty of petro to get there and still have enough for our exfiltration.

Everyone seems to be asleep except for our Belarusian prisoner and me. I'm without my sleep apnea CPAP machine and I know I'd snore everyone awake if I even tried to sleep, so I take out my Enence instant two-way language translator and ask, "Do you understand English or Russian?" I hear my translator say, "ty govorish' po-angliyski ili po-russki?" Our prisoner gives me a strange look before saying, "Russki."

*   *   *

Chapter 17

Back at the Pentagon, Ms. Bikowsky and General Johnathon Stanley are on a secure speaker phone hookup with the President, the Joint Chiefs and all the other government intelligence acronyms. The President asks, "General Stanley, do you or Ms. Bikowsky have any information from any other source which would collaborate with Marat Gabidullin's statement?"

General Stanley glances at Ms. Bikowsky before answering, "Madam President, the big picture does have the Chinese generals and scientists still with their counterparts and Kim Jong-un, about 100 km north of Pyongyang at the Nyongbyon Nuclear Scientific Research Center. The satellite is being monitored 24/7 and no one has exited the complex." "General Stanley, this is General Adams, Joint Chief of Staff. How are you today, sir?"

"I'm fine General Adams. It's a pleasure, sir."

"As you are probably well aware, we have every intelligence apparatus around the world working on this...it seems all fingers point to Nyongbyon. I'm sure you're cognizant of the fact that we try to keep the United States Armed Forces at DEFCON 5 (exercise term – Fade Out, meaning least severe) however, we are going to go to DEFCON 4 (exercise term – Double Take). We don't want to alert any of our advisories at this point, but we do want our commanders around the world to understand that defense readiness conditions are heightened. Should we have to go to DEFCON 3 (exercise term – Round House), this will put all of our Air Force units around the world at the ready for complete mobilization within 15 minutes which would immediately throw up a 'RED' flag to Russia, China and North Korea. It seems there will only be one reason to go to DEFCON 3 and that is this above-ground nuclear explosion information that has just surfaced. We'll need to know the instant anything changes at Nyongbyon. Keep your eyes wide open and your ears to the ground."

127

"Yes, sir! You can depend on us General Adams." With that, both secure speaker phones go dead.

* * *

Inside the Nyongbyon Nuclear Scientific Research Center, Chinese Major General Li Yuchao is speaking to North Korea's defense chief, No Kwang Chol, and their army's chief of general staff, Ri Youn Gil as he tells them, "Guojia Zhuxi Xi Jinping (English translation) "State Chairman Xi Jinping would like us to move up the timeline. It seems both of your nuclear scientists, Jang Chang-ha and Jon Il-ho, have put together something that the world believes only the Americans can properly produce. Our scientists believe your staged thermonuclear weapon is ready and Major General Li Yuchao and General Xu Zhongbo of our Rocket Force think you can launch this destructive device aboard your newest intercontinental ballistic missile within a week's time."

Both of the North Korean scientists are all smiles and shaking their heads affirmatively as North Korean Defense Chief, No Kwang Chol says, "Our Supreme Leader, Kim Jong-un, is looking very much forward to this detonation into the atmosphere over our biggest enemy. We will have it ready for launch within the week."

North Korea's Supreme Leader is standing thirty feet away with a wide grin on his face. He's thinking, *Finally, I get my payback.* Then he starts snickering to himself.

* * *

Back in the Pentagon, General Johnathon Stanley is on a secure phone as he calls the President's chief of staff, "This is General Stanley for the President."

"Yes, General... she will be with you momentarily."

Momentarily turned into five minutes before the General heard, "Hello General...this is the President."

"Madam President, Kim Jong-un and the Chinese Generals are back above ground. No scientists are with them. It's believed they are still subterranean. Only military personnel and their staff have boarded the Pyongyang Metro from the Yonggwang Station and it's believed they are heading back to the North Korean capital. There is a train ready for them at the Pyongyang Railway Station for their trip back to Beijing."

"Thank you, General. I'd like for you to join us in one hour in the Situation Room."

"Yes, Ma'am!"

The President then calls her Chief of Staff.

"Yes, Madam President…"

"Get everyone back in here...one hour,"she says firmly as she places the phone back in its cradle.

*　　*　　*

As our Russian Ilyushin Il-112 V military transport aircraft enters Belarusian airspace, everyone is up and doing their weapon checks. Our prisoner and I had an enjoyable conversation during the flight. He definitely would love to live through this ordeal and return to his family. Though I can't guarantee his safety, I too would love for him to help us land safely at the Machulishchy air base and taxi our aircraft to a safe place — like an out-of-way hangar. We've all changed into our Belarusian military uniforms. Hulk, of course, enjoys the rank of Генэрал-палкоўнік, or three-star Air Force

General. I can only imagine how he must have killed the general and taken his uniform. It does beg the question, what was a three-star Belarusian Air Force General doing at the Ugolny Airport in the first place? As I'm thinking about that, my sat-phone rings... "Hello, this is Sidney Krogh."

"Hello, Mr. Krogh. This is Navy Master Chief O'Malley. I need for you to listen carefully...when your aircraft lands at Machulishchy air base, I want you on runway 1/19...is that clear?"

"Yes, Master Chief..."

"You will taxi to the end of the runway, then turn to port and go straight to the first hangar. Do you copy?"

"Loud and clear Master Chief."

"Good! See you in a few minutes."

We all look at each other completely dumbfounded. Who the hell is Master Chief O'Malley...and how could he possibly know who or where we are?

That's when I notice that our prisoner is also looking dumbfounded. Does he understand English? Were my instincts right about him or are they taking a quick turn? He is sitting in the co-pilot's seat and everything he says to the air traffic controller is being fed back to us over my new favorite toy...the Enence instant two-way language translator. We have his family photos from his wallet...are they real? If so, does he have a mistress, namely the Belarusian military? We find out quickly as our prisoner tries to divert our landing onto runway 15/33 instead of 1/19. This son-of-a-bitch understands English. I immediately put my Glock to the side of his head and say into the Enence, "You fuck with me and you're dead!" And our prisoner hears in Russian, "Ty trakhayesh'sya so mnoy, I ty mertv." I know...I know...he probably understands English perfectly, but I simply can't take that chance at this moment in time. Our prisoner works for one of the most ruthless (in truth he's a second-rate scumbag) dictators on the face of the Earth, so I have to ask myself, *Why would he put his life in immediate danger unless he's fully aware of what this dictator prick would do to his family should they ever figure out he helped us?* I guess my Glock aided in his ultimate decision of putting us on the proper heading for runway 1/19 because the tower has just given us clearance to land on the correct runway. I take our prisoner's headset off and re-zip-tie his hands behind his back as Captain Hal regains control of our aircraft.

Being a twelve-hour flight from Ugolny Airport to Machulishchy air base, we arrive around 9 AM. We touch down and taxi to the end of the runway and as we turn to port, we see a gentleman wearing a reflective safety vest and a helmet with acoustic earmuffs, holding marshaling wands with handheld beacons. He's directing us toward a dilapidated old airbase maintenance facility. As soon as this ground handler crosses his hand-held beacons into an X, Captain Hal hits the brakes and we come to a complete stop. However, that's when our wand handler directs Captain Hal into a hard-left turn. With his foot on the port wheel brake our captain winds up the starboard engine causing our aircraft to do a 180 degree turn. Only then are we given the signal to cut the engines. As we exit our stolen aircraft, we find ourselves helping to push it back into the dilapidated maintenance building.

As I'm trying to figure out who Master Chief O'Malley is, I hear some radio chatter going on, "Master Chief, we have two bogies in a jeep heading your way."

The gentleman walking toward me is answering, "Roger that!" Then he looks at me and says, "You have a Belarusian prisoner with you, is that correct?"

131

"Yes, we do," as I point to our prisoner.

The Master Chief walks over to the Belarusian officer and remarks while he's cutting our prisoner's zip-tied hands-free, "When this jeep gets here, you will tell them that this is a preplanned stopping point for this aircraft and that they should just move along. Keep it short and get rid of them! Do you understand?" Our prisoner nods his head in an agreeing manner as the Master Chief looks at Hulk and says, "General, I want you standing close by, but you let him do all the talking. If anything goes south, you end it immediately. You understand what I'm saying?" Hulk nods his head in the affirmative as the Master Chief continues, "One of my snipers will be watching the events through his scope. We can't fuck this up...it's not an option!" Then he hears on his comms, "Ten seconds, Master Chief," as the rest of us are quickly herded deeper into the abandoned building. Captain Hal, still in the cockpit seat, promptly ducks down and out of sight.

As the Russian-built Tigr 4x4 multipurpose all-terrain infantry mobility vehicle (armored jeep) comes around the corner from the far end of a long row of abandoned buildings, it's inbound to our location. As the Tigr draws near, our prisoner is signaling for them to stop.

Both windows of the vehicle are down as the driver comes to a complete stop and says, "Good morning General." He looks past the prisoner as he's saluting Hulk. Hulk nods his head and looks away. The driver turns his attention to our prisoner and he continues, "What are you doing in this abandoned section of the airport?"

Since the entire conversation is in Russian, Hulk only takes casual glances toward the two men in the Tigr jeep. When Hulk believes the conversation has gone on long enough, he turns toward the two Russians. That's when he hears very distinct poofs coming from over his shoulder. It seems the expression on the face of the

132

passenger in the Tigr jeep had changed and he was picking up his radio. However, before he could broadcast anything to anyone, the side of his head received a shot that caused a gaping hole...in a millisecond second, so did the drivers.

Hulk quickly grabbed our prisoner taking him by the back of the neck and planting him face first into the tarmac. Two of the SEALs ran out to help. One pushed the dead driver over and on top of his dead buddy. The other one helped Hulk get the prisoner to his feet and inside our (no longer) abandoned building. They were followed closely by the Jeep. The two dead Russians were taken out of the Tigr and dragged into the farthermost corner of this dump.

I'm thinking...*This can't be good. We may be up shit's creek without a...*I had to hold that thought as Hulk handed me the "paddle."

"I've recorded their entire conversation on my phone. Do you still have your Enence translator?" Hulk remarks.

Master Chief O'Malley is finally able to introduce himself along with two of his team members, Rags and Skids. I'm always into nicknames and can't wait to hear how these two got theirs. With the formalities over, we begin feeding the Enence translator the recording from Hulk's phone. Besides hearing something unintelligible at the beginning of the recording, we did receive some good news. Both Russians had just gotten to work and hadn't even checked in with their superiors when they watched our aircraft land and taxi over to these abandoned buildings. They both knew that no one had used this section of the airfield in years and their curiosity definitely got the best of them. The bad news, at some point someone is going to be out looking for these two. Again, on the plus side, we do have their radio and are now in possession of a very fine Russian-made 4x4 multipurpose all-terrain infantry mobility armored jeep.

The other bit of intel we finally recognized is that our prisoner/pilot is not friendly. Therefore, he will be used until he's no longer needed. We won't necessarily dump him off with his two dead Russian friends, but he's no longer to be trusted any farther than you can throw three dead Russians. He's been re-zip-tied — hands and feet, with one of the SEALs sitting next to him in the back of this dump.

Master Chief O'Malley is truly calm under the circumstances and seems to be fully in control as he asks, "Mr. Krogh…"

I stop him right there and ask, "Excuse me Master Chief but I have to ask, how the hell did you know we were heading here...and how we were getting here...or when we'd arrive?"

All he said was, "That's a story for another day. Right now we want you to know that your plan is solid." As he looks at Dolph and Chucci he continues, "Glad to see that they've brought the two of you along. I've done a quick study of you both and we're always glad to have extra shooters...especially ones as highly trained as you two are." He then looks at (Генэрал) General Hulk, (Лейтэнант) Lieutenant Pistol Pete, (Генэрал-маёр) General-Major Big Al and myself, (Капітан) Captain Krogh and says, "Everyone appreciates what you've done for our country, from Vietnam to Prudhoe Bay, Alaska, and New Orleans. But you guys are in your early 70s now."

Once again I butt-in, "Excuse me, Master Chief, you do know that the Belarusian dictator, Alexander Lukashenko, tried to kill our wives and his girlfriend (as I point to General Hulk) a day or two ago? (I think it was a day or two ago...lack of sleep does that to me.) What would you have done? Age doesn't matter when some asshole is trying to kill our loved ones."

"Mr. Krogh, I'd be right where you are. I believe all of us would. So, let's cut to the chase. My team and I will be doing the snatch-and-grab. We will take Dolph with us and Chucci will be

134

taking a sniper position on that high perch over there," he says as he points to a crumbling concrete wall that's barely left standing next to our dilapidated airbase maintenance facility. "We have a few hours before dark, we need to eat and hydrate ourselves and get some rest, then we will go over the plan with you."

I take O'Malley aside and inform him, "Master Chief, I have a few items I've taken off of our prisoner." I hand him the officer's handgun, radio, pack of cigs, lighter and wallet (with pictures of his family — wife and kids).

All he said was, "Good work." He takes all the items and heads over to our prisoner. I watch as O'Malley, once again, cuts the zip-ties from our prisoner's hands, takes a cigarette out of the pack and hands a smoke to the Belarusian officer. He takes the cancer stick and leans forward as the Master Chief gives him a light. They sat together and chatted for a good thirty minutes.

While we're resting, Lieutenant Pistol Pete brings up the fact that he's the lowest-ranking man wearing one of our stolen Belarusian uniforms. General Hulk reminds him that we all are wearing the uniforms that fit us and that rank had nothing to do with who got what. However, a snickering General-Major Big Al loves the fact that he outranks Pistol Pete and I notice him laughing under his breath.

About a half hour before nightfall, we hear over the radio, "Master Chief, I've received the signal."

"10-4, green light them in." Hearing this conversation leaves me wondering, just who the hell else has been invited to this party?

The Master Chief looks at me before saying, "Mr. Krogh, what do you know about BYPOL, the Belarusian resistance?"

Chapter 18

The Chinese generals and their entourage have boarded train number K27 as it departs from Pyongyang Train Station for its 24-hour return trip to Beijing. The U.S. has a geosynchronous orbit (GSO) satellite following the train. This particular GSO has a fixed orbit of 40.3399 degrees N, 127.5010 degrees E, directly above North Korea. A satellite in a geostationary Earth orbit appears stationary to ground observers because it's always at the same point in the sky. The GSO satellites constantly stay above a patch of Earth at a distance of 22,223 miles, thus providing constant 24-hour surveillance of a geographic area. By contrast, low Earth orbit (LEO) satellites such as the U.S. KH-11 spy satellites are closer to Earth, so the Earth's rotation exceeds their speed (meaning that they cannot maintain continuous surveillance over specific locations).

With this GSO satellite busy keeping some folks at the Pentagon up past their bedtime, the supreme leader of North Korea is off to his presidential getaway in Wonsan. Kim has a few choices of transportation to his lavish mansion estate — sometimes he flies there on one of his helicopters or private jets. When he has a mistress accompanying him, he may take his underground train. If he feels like slumming it, he always has his very own private and well-protected highway.

Wonsan is the Rocketman's preferred massive seaside estate and he and his family are the only ones who live there. All the beaches are kept combed and there are yachts and dinner boats constantly at the ready. This private hideaway has swimming pools, tennis courts, soccer fields, waterslides and a sports stadium complete with basketball courts (just in case Dennis Rodman comes to visit) all fronting east to North Korea's beautiful Sea of Japan's beaches. The Korean people may be suffering but Kim's organized crime family is way too busy masquerading as a nation-state to give them any notice.

Today the Rocketman is quite giddy as he looks out over the countryside from his Sikorsky S-76 helicopter. The Sikorsky S-76 is an intermediate-class twin-engine commercial helicopter powered by two turboshaft engines both driving the main and tail rotors. They are designed and produced by the American helicopter manufacturer Sikorsky Aircraft. The U.S. is still trying to find out how the hell Rocketman got one and where he gets his spare parts. The supreme leader knows that the prospects of the "master plan" he's put together with his closest ally, China, will finally put his name in neon lights around the world while at the same time destroying his sworn enemy...namely the United States of America.

But the true "master plan" is quite different because across the border to the North, the leader of the People's Republic of China, Xi Jinping, doesn't call Kim by any name except the "little fat man." Xi can't stand Kim Jong-un and only puts up with him when it helps Xi with the long-term goals he's set forth for his own country.

To Xi, this means he can kill two birds with one stone. Or as they say in Chinese: Yī fèn gōngzuò wánchéng liǎng xiàng rènwù. Transliteration: Complete two tasks with one job.

Xi knows when he wants to get rid of "little fat man" it will be easy. Manipulating such a fool as Kim is simply child's play. However, he is still simmering inside after the Covid-19 fiasco and the way an old adversary played him. He can't seem to get over the fact that this United States female President became his puppeteer and was able to manipulate his moves over the past year. Xi can't stand the thought of performing as a puppet for others. He's the one who's supposed to be pulling all of the strings. He won't make the same mistake this time around.

However, he may be forgetting another famous Chinese proverb: "He who seeks revenge digs two graves."

*   *   *

Back inside the Situation Room, Madam President is asking, "Just how far along are the North Koreans with their nuclear program?"

The director of the DOD says, "Madam President, it's now believed that they may have developed a staged thermonuclear weapon. Essentially, they are arranged in two or more stages, mostly two. The first stage is normally a boosted fission weapon. Its detonation causes it to shine intensely with x-radiation which illuminates and implodes the second stage that's filled with a large quantity of fusion fuel. This will set into motion a sequence of events that will result in a thermonuclear, or fusion, burn. A fireball occurs with temperatures similar to those at the center of the sun."

The president has a bewildered look on her face as she asks, "And we're just finding out about this?"

The DOD director continues, "We don't believe they can pull this off by themselves. Like the Chinese, they will manipulate, steal and even kill to procure everything and anything needed to accomplish their goals. Madam President, please don't think for one minute that we don't have countermeasures. We have worked up every possible scenario throughout the years and they are updated and reevaluated constantly. There is nothing they can do that we haven't planned for. This plan of theirs is a bit out there and very extreme, but is also in our planning mix."

*   *   *

Meanwhile, back in Anchorage, Air Force Chief Master Sergeant Jessica McWain is leaving the military hospital at Joint Base Elmendorf-Richardson followed closely by Biggin and his half-brother, Special Agent Jennings Sanders. With the interview finished, the only living member of the Belarusian hit squad, officer Artsyom Kavalyow, can now get some rest. Sanders, Biggin and

McWain have kept him up answering tough questions, wayyyy past his bedtime, as they now take their seats on a bench near the hospital entrance.

Sanders asks Chief Master Sergeant, "Do you have any Air Force Special Forces at your disposal? I'm asking you before I place my call to the FBI Director. I'll need to have some answers ready for the many questions he'll be hitting me with. It shouldn't take us long to find the underwater submersibles he described and we need to let the director know that they were dropped off here by a Russian submarine."

McWain answers very enthusiastically, "Yes! As a matter of fact, we do! The 24 SOW D-Cell is on station now. The Airmen of the 24th Special Operations Wing (SOW), Detachment 1, also known as Deployment Cell or 'D-Cell,' consists of 54 members across 15 career fields forming four agile teams." Chief Master Sergeant McWain continues... "These teams of multi-capable Airmen are trained in 49 cross-functional tasks including Survival Evasion Resistance and Escape, or SERE, training, advanced shooting, scuba diving and skydiving. The unit is based at MacDill Air Force Base in Florida but teams come in every year to Joint Base Elmendorf-Richardson. Twenty-seven men from D-Cell arrived last week and will be with us for 3 more weeks."

Special Agent Sanders smiles and remarks, "Give me a minute..." Sanders stands and walks away from Biggin and McWain while removing his GSMK Cyptophone from his pocket and flipping up the antenna before saying, "Special Agent Sanders for the director."

* * *

About a half hour before nightfall, Master Chief O'Malley gathers us all together.

"Mr. Krogh, Big Al, Hulk and Pistol Pete, Dolph and Chucci, I'd like to introduce you gentlemen to Kira and Mira. These

139

two sisters are members of BYPOL, better known as the Belarusian Resistance. They plan to help coordinate an uprising to overthrow Lukashenko and put the true winner of their election, opposition leader Sviatlana Tsikhanouskaya, into power."

We all shake hands with the two sisters. They might only be 5-foot 3-inches in height, but their handshake is firm and they look you straight in the eyes. The Master Chief continues to speak… "Don't let their size fool you...they are both experts in Luta Livre, a free-form Brazilian martial art that incorporates Jiu-Jitsu. They both wear the red and white belt which is the tenth level of black belt in the advanced den black belt. Let's just say, it doesn't get any higher than that. In other words, they can kill you ten different ways with their bare hands or blow you up with their field of scientific knowledge as explosives engineers. They're our backup plan to get out of here. As well as covering us before takeoff, the second we're airborne their team will be turning this airbase into the next 'Breaking News' segment on CNN."

Kira and Mira thank the Master Chief and say their goodbyes to us as O'Malley picks up his radio and asks, "How are we looking Skids?"

" Coast is clear Master Chief." With that, Master Chief O'Malley comes to attention and salutes the two sisters...this brings us all to our feet and to attention as we also salute these two strong women. O'Malley finishes his salute and brings his right hand back down to his side before continuing, "Good luck to both of you ladies and your team this evening. May you give dictator Alexander Lukashenko the striking blows from your hands, feet, knees and elbows needed to finish this bastard off." They both walk over and hug the Master Chief, then turn to us and wave as they head out into the darkness.

The Master Chief is standing still for a few minutes as he's taking it all in. Then he turns and says, "We plan to return here with the package an hour before sunrise. While we're gone, your mission is to plant the explosives you've brought along. However, we've expanded your arsenal by transporting a few extra blocks of Composition four (C-4) to help you with your sabotage and destruction plans." DJ brings out five blocks of C-4 and hands them to Hulk before the Master Chief continues to speak, "We've seen the photos of your work at the Ugolny Airport...nicely done gentlemen! For all of us to get out of this place in one piece, you'll need to do the same thing here. We've brought with us a targeted plan for this installation." O'Malley unfolds a piece of paper the size of a legal pad with Xs on every place he wants to go BOOM! Then he hands us timers already set to the exact time he wants each location to explode. He then asks, "Do you old PSYOPers understand the plan?"

We all shake our heads in unison before Lieutenant Pistol Pete says, "Those large above ground storage tanks hold 320,000 barrels of AV fuel. That's 3.3 million gallons! When they go up, we better be quite a distance away. If this doesn't get their attention, nothing will. Every fire unit on this base, along with anything with a flashing light, will be headed to the flames."

O'Malley remarks, "That's correct! Also, the underground storage tanks will blow minutes later from the heat. They simply put the two tank systems way too close together. Wherever we are, we will hear the explosions. Everyone for miles will feel and hear the blast and that sound will let us know we have 30 minutes to get ourselves and our package back to the airfield and aboard this aircraft before the next group of preset explosions. Once they receive the second set of detonations, they may quickly understand something's amiss, or in all the confusion, we may be able to slip out of here undetected. Either way, we will need to be airborne within minutes. Any questions?"

I remark, "We're good, Master Chief. Thank you and your men for all you do and we look forward to seeing you all back here

141

before daybreak. It looks like we also owe a debt of gratitude to the BYPOL, Belarusian saboteurs. You certainly know how to put a plan together Master Chief."

O'Malley quickly replies, "We're just a moving part like you and your team and Kira and Mira's team."

With that being said, Master Chief calmly continues, "Your uniforms and vehicle should help you all move effortlessly around the airbase. We are all working as one team to complete this mission. We will return with our package and we're sure you'll take care of your end. Your prisoner has finished up his pack of smokes, he's eaten and has been hydrated and he's presently secured in the rear of the building. He won't need any of your attention. They will find him at some point in time, but we will be long gone. We will see you well before sunrise. Good luck gentlemen…"

Having made that remark, Chucci takes up his sniper position on the crumbling wall outside the dilapidated maintenance building and the six SEALs along with Dolph Jet Coley disappear into the evening mist.

*   *   *

Chapter 19

Back inside the Pentagon, General Johnathan Stanley has an idea that is going to take him through some CRYPTO (cryptographic) files at the Top-Secret level. He has an idea, a sick idea for sure, but one he wouldn't put past either Xi or his counterparts, Kim Jong-un and Gray Cardinal.

His first thought is to find out if it's possible and if so, who's already done it? The general finds himself a secure room and opens his first Top Secret file.

Nuclear explosions in the atmosphere:

Type of Test	United States	USSR/Russia
Atmospheric:	215	219
Underground:	815	496

Total: 1,030 Not including Hiroshima and Nagasaki

General Stanley places that file on the desk to his right as he opens the next Top Secret file.

Nuclear explosions detonated in space:

This is the exact file the general was looking for. He relaxes into his chair and begins to read.

Launched from Johnston Atoll on July 9, 1962, this was the largest nuclear test conducted in outer space, and one of five conducted by the U.S. in space.

Starfish Prime:

Country:	United States
Test series:	Operation Fishbowl
Test site:	Johnston Atoll
Date:	July 9, 1962

Starfish Prime was a high-altitude nuclear test conducted by the United States. This was a joint effort of the Atomic Energy Commission (AEC) and the Defense Atomic Support Agency. It was launched from Johnston Atoll on July 9, 1962, and was the largest nuclear test conducted in outer space and one of five conducted by the U.S. in space.

The Thor rocket carrying a W49 thermonuclear warhead (designed at Los Alamos Scientific Laboratory) and an MK-2 reentry vehicle was launched from Johnston Atoll in the Pacific Ocean about 900 miles (1,450 km) west-southwest of Hawaii. The explosion took place at an altitude of 250 miles (400 km) above a point 19 miles (31 km) southwest of Johnston Atoll. It had a yield of 1.4 Mt (5.9 PJ). The explosion was about 10 degrees above the horizon as seen from Hawaii at 11 PM Hawaii time.

Operation Fishbowl:

The Starfish test was one of five high-altitude tests grouped together as Operation Fishbowl within the larger Operation Dominic. A series of tests in 1962 began in response to the Soviet announcement of August 30, 1961, that they would end a three-year moratorium on testing.

In 1958, the United States had completed six high-altitude nuclear tests that produced many unexpected results and raised many new questions. According to the U.S. Government Project Officer's Interim Report on the Starfish prime project:

Previous high-altitude nuclear tests: YUCCA, TEAK and ORANGE, plus the three ARGUS shots were poorly instrumented and hastily executed. Despite thorough studies of the meager data, present models of these bursts are sketchy and tentative. These models are too uncertain to permit extrapolation to other altitudes and yields with any confidence. Thus, there is a strong need not only for better instrumentation, but for further tests covering a range of altitudes and yields.

144

The Starfish test was originally planned as the second in the Fishbowl series, but the first launch (Bluegill) was lost by the radar tracking equipment and had to be destroyed in flight.

The initial Starfish launch attempt on June 20 was also aborted in flight, this time due to failure of the Thor launch vehicle. The Thor missile flew a normal trajectory for 59 seconds, then the rocket engine stopped and the missile began to break apart. The range safety officer ordered the destruction of both the missile and warhead. The missile was between 30,000 and 35,000 feet in altitude when it was destroyed. Parts of the missile as well as some radioactive contamination fell upon Johnston Atoll and nearby Sand Island and the surrounding ocean.

Explosion:

On July 9, 1962, at 09:00:09, Coordinated Universal Time (July 8,1962,11:00:09 p.m., Honolulu time) the Starfish Prime test was detonated at an altitude of 250 miles (400 km). The coordinates of the detonation were 16 degrees 28'N 169 degrees 38'W. The actual weapon yield came very close to the design yield which various sources have set at different values in the range of 1.4 to 1.45 Mt. The nuclear warhead detonated 13 minutes 41 seconds after lift off of the Thor missile from Johnston Atoll.

Starfish Prime caused an electromagnetic pulse (EMP) that was far larger than expected, so much larger that it drove much of the instrumentation off scale causing great difficulty in getting accurate measurements. The Starfish Prime's electromagnetic pulse also made those effects known to the public by causing electrical damage in Hawaii, about 900 miles away from the detonation point, knocking out about 300 street lights and setting off numerous burglar alarms as well as damaging a telephone company's microwave link. The EMP damage to the microwave link shut down telephone calls from Kauai to the other Hawaiian Islands.

A total of 27 small rockets were launched from Johnston Atoll to obtain experimental data from the Starfish Prime detonation. In addition, a large number of rocket-borne instruments were launched from Barking Sands, Kauai, in the Hawaiian Islands.

A large number of United States military ships and aircraft were operating in support of Starfish Prime in the Johnston Atoll area and across the nearby North Pacific region.

A few military ships and aircraft were also positioned in the region of the South Pacific Ocean near the Samoan Islands. This location was at the southern end of the magnetic field line of the Earth's magnetic field from the position of the nuclear detonation, an area known as the "southern conjugate region" for the test.

An uninvited scientific expeditionary ship from the Soviet Union was stationed near Johnston Atoll for the test and another Soviet scientific expeditionary ship was in the southern conjugate region near the Samoan Islands.

After the Starfish Prime detonation, bright auroras were observed in the detonation area as well as in the southern conjugate region on the other side of the equator due to the detonation. According to one of the first technical reports:

The visible phenomena due to the burst was widespread and quite intense. A very large area of the Pacific was illuminated by the auroral phenomena, from far south of the south magnetic conjugate area (Tongatapu), through the burst area to far north of the north conjugate area (French Frigate Shoals). At twilight after the burst, resonant scattering of light from lithium and other debris was observed at the Johnston and French Frigate Shoals for many days confirming the long-time presence of debris in the atmosphere. An interesting side effect was that the Royal New Zealand Air Force was aided in anti-submarine maneuvers by the light from the bomb.

After effects:

While some of the energetic beta particles followed the Earth's magnetic field and illuminated the sky, other high-energy electrons became trapped and formed radiation belts around the Earth. There was much uncertainty and debate about the composition, magnitude and potential adverse effects from the trapped radiation after the detonation. The weaponeers became quite worried when three satellites in low Earth orbit were disabled. These included TRAAC and Transit 4B. The half-life of the energetic electrons was only a few days. At the time, it was not known that solar and cosmic particle fluxes varied by a factor of 10 and that energies could exceed 1 MeV (Megaelectronvolt – The energy of ionizing radiation is measured in electron-volts. One electron-volt is an extremely small amount of energy.) (0.16 pj). In the months that followed, these man-made radiation belts eventually caused six or more satellites to fail. Radiation damaged their solar arrays of electronics including the first commercial relay communication satellite, Telstar, as well as the United Kingdom's first satellite, Ariel 1. Detectors on Telstar, TRAAC, Injun and Ariel 1 were used to measure distribution of the radiation produced by the tests.

In 1963, it was reported that Starfish Prime had created a belt of MeV electrons. In 1968, it was reported that some Starfish electrons had remained in the atmosphere for 5 years.

After reading this information, General Stanley is quickly on the phone with Ms. Bikowsky, "I have an interesting hypothesis I'd like to pass by you. I'm in the National Military Command Center (NMCC), just a couple of floors down."

Ms. Bikowsky replies, "I'm on my way General."

As Ms. Bikowsky is making her way to NMCC, the general

is doing some more homework. Of the 30 counties with satellites in low Earth orbit, the United States has just under half with 2,804. The closest to us is China with 467 and in last place we have Kazakhstan with six. More than half of these satellites are for communications, with 63%. Earth observation (mostly spy satellites) is second with 22.1% and technology development is a distant third with 7.8%.

As Ms. Bikowsky arrives, she's met by a United States Marine sergeant who opens the door and closes it after she's stepped in. "What do you have General?"

"Come sit!" he says as he points to a seat across from his, "I want you to look at these and give me your opinion."

General Johnathan Stanley stands up and begins pacing the floor. He understands the gravity of what's happening in this very room because these walls are a product of the early nuclear age. This Joint War Room, right where he's walking, directly supports the National Command Authority and its ability to rapidly order up nuclear attacks. If his calculations are correct, the Joint Chiefs of Staff will soon be in this conference room (commonly nicknamed "The Tank") and it will also be filled with crisis management personnel, wartime tactical command, intelligence officers, the Secretary of Defense and the DOD.

Ms. Bikowsky has a disturbed look on her face as she finishes reading these "Top Secret" files. She looks up, all the while understanding his thought process as she says, "Sir, this is a very plausible theory, one that I'd put extremely close to the top of the list. An explosion in our atmosphere with the megaton warhead they have at their disposal would easily take out most of our communication and navigation satellites. They would also be taking down the International Space Station and the Hubble Space Telescope, not to mention the lives lost immediately and for many years down the road. We'd be vulnerable on so many levels, it's unfathomable to think of them all."

The general has his elbows on the table and his hands clasped tightly under his chin as he asks, "If you concur, I believe it's time to call the President."

Ms. Bikowsky is shaking her head slowly to the left and right as she lets out a slight sigh before saying, "Yes General... This can't wait!"

*   *   *

While Agent Sanders is chatting away with FBI Director Cole Michael, Air Force Chief Master Sergeant McWain is on her phone looking around the hospital grounds for some wheels. Once Sanders has brought the director up to speed, he and his half-brother go back into the hospital and up to the Belarusian hit squad commanding officer's room. Sanders tells the guard at the door to take a break as they have more questions for their prisoner and will be there for a while. Artsyom Kavalyow was fast asleep when Biggin gave him a rousing slap across his head, "Get up and get dressed!" Agent Sanders takes out his key and unlocks the handcuffs while Biggin, without giving a rat's ass about Mr. Kavalyow's wounds, rips out his IV and throws him his pants and shirt. After helping him with his socks and shoes, Biggin continues, "You're taking us to your underwater submersibles at Pilot Point."

While Biggin and Agent Sanders are dragging their prisoner out of the hospital's back door, Air Force Chief Master Sergeant Jessica McWain is rounding the corner in a military ambulance. Biggin shoves the Belarusian officer into the back and joins him there while Sanders enters the passenger door next to Jessica as she fills him in, "I've got six airmen of the 24th Special Operations Wings D-Cell meeting us at the airfield. They'll be driving a Humvee and bringing along a pilot."

149

Sanders asks, "What's our mode of transportation?" Sergeant McWain replies, "The Sikorsky MH-60G/HH-60G Pave Hawk. It'll be a tight fit, but we can do it."

As they're driving up the tarmac of Elmendorf Air Force Base, they see that the four-blade, twin-engine, medium-lift utility military helicopter is warming up. The six airmen from D-Cell are standing just outside the chopper's doors as the military ambulance parks next to the Humvee.

Biggin glances at his prisoner and says, "You don't look so good!" The look on Artsyom Kavalyow's face shows that he doesn't feel too good either. It doesn't help that Biggin had purposely put his large foot on Kavalyow's wound and pushed as hard as he could for the entire five-minute drive to the airfield.

Special Agent Sanders asks, "If there's anything else you'd like to add to your story, we can end this trip right here and now."

The Belarusian officers says, "Like what?"

Sanders continues, "Like why a Russian BS-64 Delta-IV-class nuclear-powered ballistic missile submarine departed navy base Gadzhievo outside of Murmansk weeks ago and traveled all the way to the estuary of Onemen Bay? Then this nuclear sub picks you and your team up and drops you off the Alaskan coast at Pilot Point? In our country, we call that, 'Overkill!' What is the real mission of this Russian sub and who else is onboard?" Kavalyow's facial expression gives Agent Sanders the opening he needed, "Biggin, put him on the chopper."

"No please, I'll tell you what I know!"

With their deception complete and the questions they had for Kavalyow answered, Agent Sanders walks over to the chopper and thanks Air Force Chief Master Sergeant Jessica McWain along with the six airmen of the 24th Special Operations Wings D-Cell and the chopper pilot. He takes Sergeant McWain aside and makes a remark to her.

"I'm sorry I couldn't let you in on our deceitful little scheme. Kavalyow had to take the bait...hook, line and sinker. The director informed me that we have the Russian sub boxed as well as and custody of the two underwater submersibles. Our job was to get a better understanding of this sub's mission. The powers that be also needed the submarine commander's name and the names of any other officers or commanders on board. I didn't want to deceive you, but you did very well and the director will hear all about that. Please let these airmen know they too have the thanks of the director and many others a lot higher up on the food chain. All of us are playing a role in finding out what exactly is going on."

Air Force Chief Master Sergeant McWain smiles and shakes her head before replying, "Well played Agent Sanders. Glad we could all be of service. If that's all, I need to get back to the safe-house and finish up my report."

They both shake hands before the sergeant remarks, "Jump in and I'll give you a lift back to the hospital."

Agent Sanders says, "Thank you...Please give me a minute and I'll take you up on that."

Biggin opens the back door of the military ambulance and gently helps the prisoner back in. They will take Kavalyow back to his hospital bed and make sure he's securely fastened down and the security guard back on station.

While the Sikorsky Pave Hawk's blades are slowing down, Agent Sanders begins walking away from the rotors as he's flipping the antenna up on his sat-phone. "Yes, sir! Ms. Bikowsky was absolutely correct."

The Director responds..."Ms. Bikowsky actually gives some

151

of the credit to Mr. Krogh. She says they had a one-on-one question and answer session and that she got this from him during their tit-for-tat. I'll call General Stanley and fill him in. I want your full report within the hour."

"Yes, sir!"

*   *   *

The Russian BS-64 Delta-IV-class submarine has been sitting patiently off the coast of Alaska. The captain knows he's been floating a bit with the currents but feels he is still in international waters. However, Admiral Feliks Gromov also knows that the U.S. intelligence aircraft has an exact fix on his location. What he doesn't know is that his ship's two fixed-pitched shrouded propellers have been slimmed.

A Navy SEAL team was flown in to Anchorage from Coronado and while the Navy's Boeing P-8A was dropping sound-buoys that were emitting acoustic waves underwater. The SEAL team was utilizing the secreted Hagfish gel which prevents the propeller blades from scooping water. While this sub is now literally dead in the water, the SEALs proceeded to jam the VLF radio waves (3-30 kHz) frequency band that is used by submarines at shallow depth for communication. So now she sits here with no eyes, no ears and no propulsion.

That's when the sub's captain hears someone tapping on his ship sail — from the outside. Four dots, pause, 1 dot, pause, 1 dot, 1 dash, 2 dots, pause, 1 dot, 1 dash, 2 dots, pause, 3 dashes. Then it's repeated. The admiral shakes his head because he knows, "Someone is underwater at his sub's conning tower tapping out Morse code and this smart ass is saying Hello."

*   *   *

Chapter 20

With our Russian Tigr 4x4 multipurpose all-terrain vehicle packed with explosives, timers, weapons and four apoplectic 70 year olds, we quickly check our comms. We are using Instant Connect, the JITC-certified tactical radio interoperability system. This allows us to bridge any radio voice nets and connect any radio channel for users of any MANET (mobile ad hoc networks) or combat net radio. It means we can stay in touch with the SEAL Team and Chucci at any time from any location on the Belarusian Air Force Base. "Chucci, how do you read...over?"

All he says is, "LC" (Loud and Clear), as we head out for our first stop...the aviation fuel storage tanks.

The map given to us by Master Chief O'Malley is a miniature drawing of this very complex base. We know which direction to go, but have no idea how many obstacles we may have to traverse. However, it doesn't take long to find out as we make our first right turn and are momentarily stopped by a unit of the Belarusian SSO or Spetsnaz brigade. The SSO run security for the Machulishchy Air Force Base. It was only when they saw General Hulk in the front passenger seat that they saluted and let us pass. I'm thinking, *I don't care who Hulk had to terminate to get these uniforms...they just saved us from having to play our trump card early.*

Then we got lucky and pulled up behind an airport aviation fuel truck and followed it all the way to our first destination. The fuel truck stopped at the front of the fuel depot. Big Al drove around the truck and behind the enormous tanks. Pistol Pete and I exited the rear doors of the Tigr which had seating for up to 7 passengers. The space that was left for the other three passengers are where we'd stored all of the C-4, detonation timers and extra magazines packed with ammo. Pete and I opened the back and double checked that we had the proper timers for aviation fuel tank number one. Then I grabbed a thick block of Composition C and we molded it into our desired shape so as to make it almost impossible for anyone to see. We both looked it over and gave each other a nod. When we got back to our seats and closed the door, General Hulk ordered, "OK, General-Major Big Al, on to stop number 2!"

*   *   *

The Belarusian State University (BSU) is a university in Minsk, Belarus. It was founded on October 30, 1921. In 2021, it was ranked the 1,201st of all the universities in the world — at least in the World University Rankings by Times Higher Education. BSU owns buildings at various locations within the city of Minsk. The main campus is located in the city center. The second campus of Belarusian State University is located on the Southwestern outskirts of Minsk. Each of the university study buildings are equipped with classrooms, seminar rooms and reading lounges. There are 70 computer laboratories and 4 media classrooms.

The Military Faculty of the Belarusian State University was established on November 4, 1926, by order of the Soviet Revolutionary Military Council. In 1941, at the outset of the Second World War, military training classes were interrupted only to be resumed in 1943. In the post-war years, the military department continued to train reserve officers in accounting specialties. In 2003, the military department was reorganized into the modern military faculty of BSU.

Belarusian dictator Lukashenko, often referred to as "Tarakanishche" or in English (Cockroach) fathered a son, Nikolai, who was born in 2004. Though never confirmed by the government, it is widely believed that the child's mother is Irina Abelskaya – the two had an extramarital affair when Irina was the tyrant's personal doctor. There have never been any public

154

statements about who Nikolai's mother was, Nikolai was raised solely by his father. It has been reported by Western observers and media that Nikolai, nicknamed "Kolya," is being groomed as Lukashenko's successor.

Referred to as "Little Prince" by his dad, Kolya wasn't seen in public until April 2008, when the Dictator and his son worked side-by-side on the construction of a huge sport hall, helping to mix and pour concrete. The next day, a photo of them was on all the front pages of the Belarusian newspapers, accompanied by the the headline, "Who is the boy?" The presidential press office denied knowing anything. A few days later, during a television documentary, the child was seen addressing the dictator as "dad." That is how Belarus learned the existence of the Lukashenko's third — and secret — son.

The BSU has 11 student dormitories. Most of the housing provided by the university consists of rooms shared by 3-4 persons with a common kitchen and sanitary arrangements. However, Kolya, the boy born with a silver spoon in his mouth, isn't a little prince anymore...he's a grown man and studies at the university's advanced adult military training department. He doesn't share a room or a kitchen with anyone and his sanitary arrangements are very exclusive.

Master Chief O'Malley (Charms) has his three shooters, Buddha, Oak and DJ, set the perimeter as Rags and Skids follow him from the roof down a flight of stairs and to a hallway which leads to the 1,200 square foot living quarters of one Nikolai (Kolya) Lukashenko.

Their plan was to get in and out as quickly as possible without leaving a blood trail, but that plan went out the window fast. It seems that instead of a flashy "Luck of the Irish" kind of early morning, Sod's Law was quickly getting in their space. Sod's Law is the United Kingdom's cultural axiom for Murphy's Law —

155

and states — "Misfortune will happen at the worst possible time."

As Charms, Skids and Oak exit the stairwell, the door at the end of the hall opens and out steps two armed bodyguards. In a split second, both men begin the motion of raising their weapons, but it's 0.01 percent of a second too late. All three SEALs already had their weapons primed for attack. Using firing discipline, each man discharged a single taciturn round as both bodyguards fell to the floor. The door quickly slammed and was bolted shut before the three SEALs could close the distance. Skids expended two more rounds into the door handle and the three quickly entered the room as Charms tackled and injected a dose of Propofol into Nikolai's neck.

Skids and Oak dragged the two dead bodyguards back inside the room where their bodies are searched. Charms orders both team members to grab the laptop, all papers and any intel they can get their hands on. While Skids is bagging up the living room, Oak heads for the bedroom door where he hears scratching coming from inside the room and a tentative bark. "Master Chief, we have a K-9." Charms puts his mind on rewind taking it back to this mission's briefing. Then he says (in the form of a question) "Weren't we told Lukashenko has a pet dog, a spitz that spends a lot of time with Nikolai? The youngest son is the only other person Lukashenko lets handle his pet. The dog is named after a 1969 Soviet animated film based on a children's book by Yuri Yakovlev..." Now Charms is thinking to himself, *It means 'polar bear'...what is it? Umka!* Charms makes his way to the door and quietly says, "Is that you Umka?"

Skids makes his way to the kitchen and looks for dog treats. As he grabs a bag with a picture of dog bones on it he says, "Master Chief, take these."

Charms takes the treats and softly say, "Hi Umka," as he opens the door and hands the spitz a few treats before turning back to Skids and Oak remarking, "If having Lukashenko's son doesn't bring him to the table...I'll bet you, Umka, here will do the trick."

Skids and Oak rapidly clean up the floor in the hallway while Charms is making friends with Umka. All the intel, including laptop computer and cell phones are stashed into a backpack as Skids slides it onto his back. Charms is carrying Umka while Oak has 6-foot 3-inches and 190 pounds of dead weight slung over his shoulder as he locks and closes the door behind them.

*　*　*

It's a short distance to our next stop, but as we drive, we're picking up chatter on the radio. We let our Enence instant translator decipher the chatter only to find out that they've basically put out an all-points-bulletin for our jeep and the two missing Russian security personnel. As we're pulling up behind the next set of Aviation Fuel tanks, Pistol Pete and I are again at the rear of the Tigr grabbing our next set of explosives and timers as Hulk and Big Al take the Enence and transform the setting from Russian to English. While Big Al holds the radio, Hulk says, "We saw that jeep at the far north end of the Airbase."

The second Hulk finishes, Big Al keys the MIC on the Russian radio and the Enence sends out a clear voice stating in Russian, "My videli tot dzhip v dal'nem severnom kontse aviabazy."

Big Al quickly transforms the setting back and they hear in English, "All security immediately to the north end of the base." These two old PSYOPers smile at each other while slapping a "high-five."

With the second group of AV fuel tanks wired, we now know we have about fifteen minutes to set up the second phase and get back to our dilapidated hangar. Hulk and Big Al have done us all a solid by sending most of the airbase security as far away from us as they could possibly go. That being said, we have over a mile to traverse as we make our way to our next target. The runway we landed on, 1/19, is filled with truckloads of troops heading north, so we pretty much blend in. Hulk and Big Al give a quick glance at each other and smile. A few minutes later and out of nowhere we hear, "Ostanavlivat'sya!"

Hulk whispers to Big Al, "That means Halt!"

Within seconds our Tigr is surrounded by no less than six security personnel carrying automatic weapons which are pointed at us as we're being asked to step out of our vehicle. General Hulk opens his door first and gives his death stare directly at the Russian sentry who's pointing his AK-47 at our fake Belarusian general. The sentry looks a little shaky and perspiration beads are forming on his forehead as he asks for General Hulk's papers. Hulk keeps the death stare going straight into the sentry's eyes as he puts his left hand out to his side and snaps his fingers as if asking Big Al to miraculously make some papers appear. However, we did get the message and as I'm opening my door, I yell, "Der'mo!" (that's shit in Russian) and that distraction is all it took for us to get off the first shots. This is also the exact same second the six Russian sentries start collapsing on the tarmac, each with a single hole in their forehead.

Pistol Pete looks at Hulk and asks, "So, now you can just snap your fingers and every bogey falls over dead?"

That's when we hear, "Quickly, you must plant your explosives and leave here!" I look to my right and see two angles...Kira and Mira along with a support team of about fifteen. Most of them are women and all of them are BYPOL – Belarusian underground fighters.

Pistol Pete and I exit the jeep quickly and grab our supplies as Kira says, "We knew they kept extra security at their communications center and we finished our work early. Time is of the essence! Only ten minutes before the fuel tanks explode. We will take care of these bodies. You must hurry!" As Pete and I are heading for the communications tower we notice a few more dead Russian and Belarusian military personnel along the way. We both work expeditiously at both the tower and the communications center. This is the Machulishchy Air Force's communications and brain center — and it's about to have a lobotomy.

Pistol Pete and I promptly take our seats in the Tigr when I notice it's just the four of us. "What the hell...they sure did clean this place up quickly?"

General Hulk says, "They're off to their next job which is making sure we have a safe runway for our exit. How or what that means I can only leave up to your imagination. They did wish us good luck and asked that we come back for a visit once they're a free country. I told them we will look forward to that time."

Before Big Al can even put the jeep in gear, the first aviation fuel tank explosion shakes the entire earth around us. This place has gone from dark to brighter than daylight in a millisecond and the heat is unimaginable. It feels like we're sitting on the sun.

*   *   *

Chapter 21

Madam President is in the Situation Room with all the top brass and the heads of every acronym in charge of intelligence and security in the United States of America. FBI Director Cole Michael's briefing begins.

"The interrogation of the Russian military pilot and crew aboard the billionaire Russian oligarch Alisher Usmanov's Airbus has concluded. The pilot is a highly decorated female Russian colonel named Valentina Stepanovna Grizodubova. Special Agent Favitta is the head of the FBI's High-Value Detainee Interrogation Group (HIG). He's been working with the CIA and DOD interrogators putting her through all stages of interrogation — from isolation, anxiety, fatigue, lack of sleep, uncomfortable temperatures and chronic hunger. She may be tough and well trained, but their report says she only knew that this assassination team was there to kill the Wagner Group deserter Marat Gabidullin. The interrogation of Russian oligarch Alisher Usmanov, who we kidnapped off his super-yacht Dibar in the Bay of Kotor, gave us nothing. He's also the owner of the airbus that transported Colonel Grizodubova and the Wagner Group assassins into LAX. Alisher Usmanov had no idea why they were traveling to Los Angeles. He was only doing a favor for Gray Cardinal. He's an overweight businessman, not a pro, and he caved in and broke quite easily. He knew nothing. The captain of the super-yacht Milliarder Vodka who was stopped leaving Bermuda on his way to the Ocean Reef Club in Key Largo, and the Wagner Group assassins that were onboard all had the same story. They were on their way to kill three enemies of the Russian State. They were told that these three oligarchs had stolen over a billion dollars in gold and rubles, not to mention that two of the three super-yachts belonged to Vladimir Putin and are now considered the property of the Soviet Union. Their mission was to abduct all three oligarchs and the yachts, head back out to sea, kill the three traitors and feed them to the sharks. Then they were to return the super-yachts to Russia and if they found the gold and rubles, they'd all split a 10% bounty while the rest of the loot would be handed over to Gray Cardinal. Our best government interrogators put them all through the wringer, Madam President. It's now our belief that this entire plan is compartmentalized. It's our conclusion that only Gray Cardinal, President Xi Jinping and Kim Jong-un are privy to the particulars of this entire operation. The only person that gave us useful intelligence was the Wagner Group deserter Marat Gabidullin. He came to us while seeking asylum through the Los Angeles field office. He was flown to FBI Headquarters here in D.C. and was thoroughly scrutinized using some very uncommon interrogation techniques. We phrased questions differently — we used every mind tool in the kit — and everyone has concluded that he was very credible. Wagner Group personnel are usually retired military but rarely are they trained in navigating their way through sophisticated interrogation techniques. We've concluded that he deserted his unit. The assassination team who landed at LAX was sent here to eliminate him and to videotape the killing to show other Wagner Group soldiers what happens if you try to desert the unit. We also believe he was truly seeking asylum and that his very credible and disturbing blurb about an above ground nuclear explosion is very cogitable. A very elaborate lie detector evaluation backs all this up."

Madman President stands and thanks the director before remarking, "Some of you already know that I've tried several times to call both President Xi Jinping of China and Gray Cardinal of Russia, neither one is picking up the phone. The NSA informs me they are both in their respective countries and not far from their desks. That being said, we've come to the conclusion that whatever their plan is, it will be happening soon. General Stanley and Ms. Bikowksy have come up with some very disturbing analysis of what this plan could entail...General Stanley, Ms. Bikowksy, the floor is yours."

Major General Johnathan Stanley and Ms. Alfreda Frances Bikowksy both stand as General Stanley begins to speak.

161

"Thank you Madam President. We both concur (as he turns to Ms. Bikowksy before turning back to face the President) with the director. From the Chinese spy balloon incident, to the assassins hunting down oligarchs, to the Russian/Belarusian troop buildup along the Ukrainian border, and the Russians sending a nuclear-powered submarine complete with assassins to kill that PSYOP team in Alaska – though all of these are real and taking place, it's our belief that this is all a misdirection from their real plan. As we've specified, all of the intelligence gathering points us to an atomic explosion between 80 and 150 miles into outer space. We must ask the question...where will this explosion take place — certainly not above their country...so where? Will it only be one rocket with one warhead or will it be multiple rockets with multiple warheads? A nuclear blast anytime over the next few weeks would create dangerous fallout — residual radioactive material that would travel in the jet stream straight over the U.S. and settle back onto our fields, streams, cities, towns and countryside for weeks on end. Most fallout takes anywhere from one day to a week to return to the ground but if the blast is high enough, it will travel further and take longer to return to Earth. We must be prepared for anything. Thank you, Madam President."

The President stands and replies, "I thank you all for your time and fortitude." Then she turns to the Joint Chiefs and continues, "I've been informed that we are moving this operation to Raven Rock. Is that your understanding General?"

Chairman of the Joint Chiefs, General Adams stands and replies, "Yes, Madam President...we are wheels-up in thirty minutes."

The primary backup operations site for the Pentagon is known as Raven Rock or Site-R. It's buried very deeply under a mountain near Blue Ridge Summit in Pennsylvania and is nicknamed the "Underground Pentagon." This is where the DOD's Alternate National Military Command Center (ANMCC) is located.

This installation duplicates the NMCC's capabilities as well as other Pentagon functions. The bunker has emergency operations centers for the United States Army, Navy, Air Force, Space Force and Marine Corps. It remains semi-operational at all times, ready to take over at a moment's notice for its far higher profile cousin. This is one of three core bunker complexes for the U.S. Continuity of Government programs should there be a need to survive a nuclear strike or be forced offline in any other catastrophe.

Site-R is a 265,000 square foot bunker located 650 feet beneath the 1,529-foot summit of Raven Rock Mountain. If you live in Washington, D.C. you'll know that every day that ends in a "Y," you will witness the blue-and-gold U.S. Air Force UH-1 (call-sign Mussel) from the 1st Helicopter Squadron flying over the Potomac River. This unit exists to evacuate high-ranking officials to secret bunkers in the event of a terrorist or nuclear attack on the Capitol. This massive multibillion-dollar complex is located just miles from Camp David.

The Pentagon's elaborate command and control capabilities are duplicated multiple times over in various formats and for good reason. Any bunker isn't likely to survive a major nuclear exchange. NO place is truly safe if the enemy wants to dedicate enough megatonnage to a specific target. However, any enemy would know that a counter-strike would be imminent. The U.S. would execute the Single Integrated Operations Plan (SIOP).

The SIOP is one of the most highly classified of all U.S. government documents. Many details about it remain shrouded in mystery. From its inception it holds an historic classification, a special information category—extremely sensitive information (ESI)—has been attached to the SIOP.

*　　*　　*

Master Chief O'Malley has outfitted Umka with a vest that includes a Kevlar D-ring. They are used to parachute and rappel K-9s that support SEAL teams. DJ's in charge of bringing all the little things on missions that no one else thinks of and he has brought a Kevlar D-ring along. With the entire team now on the roof of the BSU student dormitories, Skids and Rags toss out their ropes and rappel the five stories to the ground. As they're setting the perimeter, Oak straps a harness onto Nikolai and they are the next two over the side. Once they touch the ground, it's time for Charms (with Umka strapped to him) and Budda to go over while DJ provides cover on the roof. While they're rappelling, they hear the explosions coming from the airbase. Skids keys his mic, "We're on the clock...30 minutes Master Chief," as DJ quickly slings his weapon over his shoulder and heads over the side.

With the team safely on the ground, they slowly and meticulously make their way to the stolen UAZ-452A ambulance, aka Sanitarka or "the medic lady."

Skids keys his mic, "Dolph, we are eight minutes out."

Dolph replies, "10-4." The ambulance seats up to 4 stretchers, enjoys four-wheel drive and has off-road capability.

Once they have Nikolai strapped down with Umka in his lap and Dolph behind the wheel, DJ says, "Take us home Jet" as the team takes off for the return trip to Machulishchy airbase.

Dolph Jet Coley has the sirens blasting and the flashing lights revolving as their ambulance is waved right through the Machulishchy Air Force security gate. With all the chaotic activity happening at the base, the next round of explosions just adds to the frenzied atmosphere as the communications building and tower are leveled. The medic lady turns the corner and is on her way to the abandoned, dilapidated maintenance building.

*   *   *

We've been preparing our getaway aircraft while waiting for the SEALs to return and now we see the flashing lights heading our way as we hear Skids come on the radio, "We are inbound with the package. Master Chief wants to be wheels up in 5 minutes." Captain Hal already has the engines fired up and our Russian Ilyushin Il-112 V, military transport aircraft is pointed in the proper direction... toward runway 15/33. We had received word that runway 1/19 would soon be out of commission, thus thwarting any Russian Mikoyan MiG-29 aircraft from trying to leave the airbase and possibly chase us down.

The MiG was produced by a design bureau founded in 1939 by Artem Mikoyan (M) and Mikhail Gurevich (G). The letter "i" in MiG is the Russian word meaning "and." From the MiG-9 in 1946 to the MiG-25 designed around 1960 and introduced in 1970, this twin-engine interceptor was considered the fastest combat aircraft ever in active service with registered speeds at Mach 2.8 and an operating ceiling above 80,000 feet. The MiG-29's first flight was in October of 1977 and has several variants which make it a little slower, but it can still hit Mach 2.3.

Dolph turned off the flashing lights about two hundred yards before reaching the getaway plane. We quickly transported the unconscious future tyrant into the aircraft along with Umka. Chucci is heard on the radio, "One vehicle coming our way. I have them in my crosshairs."

Master Chief says, "10-4" then tells his team to fan out as Hulk, Pistol Pete, Big Al and I are moving the rest of our weapons, ammo & C-4 into the aircraft.

As the vehicle is getting closer, it starts flashing its lights. Master Chief shouts, "Stay alert!" The SEAL team has their weapons at the ready as the vehicle pulls up to the getaway aircraft.

Kira jumps out along with three other women from the BYPOL underground as these fighters are yelling above our aircraft's noise, "Mira is severely wounded along with two other fighters...we can't take proper care of them...please take them with you!"

Master Chief keys his mic, "DJ, go to the ambulance and snatch everything you can get your hands on! Chucci, get that POW of yours out of the hangar...he's going with us!" Then the Master Chief yells, "Get everyone onboard pronto!" Next he looks at Kira and says, "We'll take good care of them and get them the help they need. You need to get the hell out of here."

Kira yells while trying to hold on to her hat, "Thank you Master Chief...you need to know that no runway is safe. You'll need an alternative." Kira goes and hugs her unconscious sister then turns and runs back to their truck. With the other three ladies already aboard, Kira speeds off back into the mayhem.

Master Chief O'Malley jumps into the plane and works his way into the cockpit and says to Captain Hal, "All runways are closed. What do you need to get us out of here?"

Capt. Hal says, "The specs on this aircraft with a light load is around 4,000 feet. We'd need to turn around and grab the 300 - 400 feet behind us. This parking area might be 2,000 feet and then we have the crossroad at the end of our parking area. With a little luck, which would mean that there are no vehicles crossing in front of us at the same moment we arrive at that intersection, we can cross into the parking lot on the other side. It looks clear from here, but very quickly buildings at the end of the other parking area come into play. I'd give us a 50/50 shot!"

Charms rubs his four-leaf clover before saying, "Let's do it!"

With all wounded personnel strapped down and those needing immediate medical attention being looked after, Chucci pushes the POW through the door, pulls it shut and locks the handle. Charms, seeing how everyone is safely onboard and secured, taps Captain Hal on the shoulder letting him know that it's his time to pull off some magic.

*   *   *

Chapter 22

With the President now safe at the backup operations site in Raven Rock (Site-R), better known as the Underground Pentagon, helicopters from the U.S. Air Force UH-1 1st Helicopter Squadron are still ferrying in the military staff and the intelligence officers needed for our nation's security. The first to arrive, however, is the Missile Defense Agency (MDA). It's their job to test and demonstrate the capability of a ballistic missile defense (BMD), inclusive of configuring Aegis modified ships (The Aegis Combat System is an American integrated naval weapons system that uses computers and radar to track and guide weapons). The Aegis system communicates with the standard missiles through a radio frequency (RF) uplink using the AN/SPY-1 radar for mid-course update missile guidance during engagements, but still requires the AN/SPG-62 fire-control radar for terminal guidance. This means that with proper scheduling of intercepts, a large number of targets can be engaged simultaneously.

The Aegis Combat System was developed by the Missile and Surface Radar Division of RCA and it was produced by Lockheed Martin. This system is aboard 110 Aegis-equipped allied ships from the United States to Japan, Spain, Norway, South Korea, Canada and Australia. With everyone on edge, each of these countries has ships deployed in seas and oceans around the world.

While Navy Vice Admiral Hill, Director of the Missile Defense Agency, Army Lt. General Barber, Commander of the Army Space and Missile Defense Command and Space Force Major General Miller, Director of Operations of the U.S. Space Command are setting up for their briefing with the President and the Joint Chiefs, the Chairman of the Joint Chiefs, General Adams, approaches and hands a note to Madam President. It reads in part: Satellites have picked up large explosions at the Machulishchy Air Force Base in Minsk Region, Belarus.

The President looks at General Adams and says, "They've done it! Now we need to pray that they get out of there with the package intact. The Soviets have yet to cross the border into Ukraine and this may be our last hope on that front."

*　　*　　*

With his foot on the brakes and his right hand pressing the throttle forward, the two Klimov TV7-117ST turboprop engines, each powering six-bladed AV-112 pitch propellers, are screaming to be freed while quickly drinking all the aviation fuel they can handle. As Captain Hal takes his foot off the brakes, the Ilyushin II-112V Military Transport Aircraft instantly begins picking up speed. We can all hear Captain Hal's singing and it's gradually getting louder and louder until he's singing at the top of his lungs, "This ain't no party...this ain't no disco...this ain't no foolin' around!" He repeats the verse over and over again as he tries to muster every bit of power out of this aircraft's engines. As we are getting to the end of the old vacant facilities parking area, our fleetness has taken us up to 80 mph. This is when we must meet the crossroads which, by definition, are going in the opposite direction. One truck almost meets us at this intersection but instead it slams on its brakes and turns sideways. It comes to a stop just as our right wing goes directly over the vehicle's cab. With maybe 200 yards left until we smash into a building, Captain Hal pulls back on the yoke which raises the elevators on the wing. This changes the lift characteristics of the stabilizer, deflecting air up and pushing the tail down. Our aircraft is lifting off... but can we defy enough gravity to clear the building? With both engines screaming, Newton's 2nd law, $F = ma$, the law of motion, has added quantum mechanics and relativity into play. As the landing gear is tucking the wheels away and the roof of the building is quickly growing larger every millisecond, I'm left to wonder if closing my eyes might be the way to go. However, Captain Hal's singing pitch has just quieted down and the aircraft is still intact. I can only imagine that any amoebas perched on the top corner of that roof had to be crushed...that's how close we were to a fiery ending. Instead, we are airborne and sharply banking to port — we are on our way to Kyiv International Airport (Zhuliany), Ukraine. Captain Hal may have quit singing, but you couldn't rip the smile off his face.

*   *   *

DJ is very busy leaning over Mira. She seems to be the patient with the most serious wounds. All tourniquets seem to have been applied quickly. When under fire, tourniquets are usually tied over a person's clothing high and tight, which is how all of these were applied. Now that these warriors are out of danger, DJ is quickly doing his evaluations. The military loves acronyms to help personnel remember the proper order of treatment for causalities and the first one is MARCH – Massive hemorrhage, Airways, Respiration, Circulation, Head injury/hypothermia.

All three patients have had their airways cleared and oxygen masks placed over their nose and mouth. All the clothing around their wounds was cut away and a saline solution (salt water) was slowly poured onto the wounds. Next, they tried to remove all drainage and any dried blood or other matter that may have built up on the skin. Finally, they covered the wounds with sterile dressings and secured the bandages into place.

The two wounded men were conscious and able to verbally tell Oak and Rags about their pain level, etc. On the plus side, their coloring looked good…Not so good with Mira.

The look on DJ's face and the concern in his voice says it all, "Master Chief...we need blood or she won't make it!"

Charms looks to the rear of the aircraft and yells, "Anybody have Type O blood?" We all look at each other but no one says anything, so he yells it again, "Does anyone have Type O positive blood?"

We are all shaking our heads in the negative as the Master Chief is heading to the back of the aircraft where he grabs the dog tags of our prisoner and gives a quick look before he rips the dog tags from his neck and yells to DJ, "I've got your donor." Although the Master Chief doesn't seem very pleased with the prisoner, he grabs him by the back of the neck and quickly walks him over to the gurney located right next to Mira.

DJ tells the Master Chief, "We need to do this quickly or we're going to lose her."

The Master Chief looks the prisoner straight in the eyes and tells him, "You're going to sit here and be very still. We're not going to harm you or take out too much blood. We are going to keep this woman alive and you are going to help. Do you understand?" The prisoner shakes his head in the affirmative and sits down next to Mira. DJ uses an alcohol wipe on his right arm and begins the process. The second DJ has the IV bag filled, he pulls the needle out of the prisoner's arm, wipes it once again with an alcohol wipe, puts a piece of cotton on it telling him to hold it tight as he tapes it down.

DJ has Big Al taking Mira's vitals while he's extracting the blood. Big Al has yelled the vitals to Hulk in the hopes that between the two of them they'd remember them for later.

The Belarusian ambulance only had #18-gauge needles and DJ is now inserting one into Mira's arm and taping it down before he begins to slowly release the blood flow from the bag that I'm holding a few feet above her body. As the blood makes its way to the intravenous (IV) catheter, it begins the process of returning oxygen to and carbon dioxide from the tissues of her damaged body. DJ looks at me and says, "Just keep it steady Sid-the-kid...we should know within the first 15 minutes if she's going to have a bad reaction or not." Then he yells over to Oak, "How's your patient?"

171

Oak gives him a thumbs up as does Rags who's been tending to the other wounded warrior. Then DJ yells to them both, "Keep up the good work gentlemen!" He then looks at me and lets out a deep breath while keeping himself cool, calm and collected.

I remark to DJ, "You sure know how to maintain an even strain!" He gives me a smile as he's checking Mira's IV. Trying to keep things on a lighter note I ask, "Since we have a few minutes to kill...oh sorry...bad use of words. Since we have a few minutes, I was wondering how you guys got your nicknames?"

As DJ stays focused on Mira, he makes a comment, "I spin all the songs at our after-mission parties at Young Veterans Brewing Company in Virginia Beach. They brew green beer for Master Chief O'Malley. I'm sure you can guess how Charms got his nickname. Upon our return from any mission, we all spend time with our families and then two or three days later, we meet up and get a little crazy at Young Veterans Brewing." DJ gives me a quick look and smiles before continuing, "Buddha didn't get his name because he's attained enlightenment. At 6-foot 5-inches and 210 pounds of solid muscle, I can attest to the fact that he has been awakened, however, he was given his nickname from a Siddhartha Gautama (Buddha) quote — 'He who achieves his aim.' You see, Buddha can shoot a penny out from between two of your fingers from 50 yards while free-falling through space. He's the best there is...or ever was!"

Just then, Captain Hal yells out on the onboard comms, "We got company! MiG coming across my bow!"

Within seconds we hear the roar of this jet fighters engine and before we bounce through the shock wave we hear DJ yell, "Hold your patients down tight." He quickly leans over Mira and pins her to the gurney a half second before the left behind high pressure combustion bounces our aircraft like a toy. Then Capt. Hal continues, "That, my friends, is called a threat gesture in the animal kingdom."

* * *

At the control tower of the Antonov/Hostomel Airport on the outskirts of the Ukrainian Air Force Base, two U.S. Air Force air traffic controllers have been monitoring the escape flight and quickly radio their superiors, "Our friendly flight has a bogie. Do we break radio silence, over?"

They hear back, "Negative...Do NOT break radio silence... they'll already know there's a bogie present. Just keep an eye on them and let's scramble some friendlies to meet them at the border."

* * *

The Master Chief yells, "Buddha get up here and bring our prisoner and Lulu with you."

I look at DJ and quietly ask, "Who's Lulu?"

DJ whispers back, "Lulu is not a who, it's a what. Buddha only uses a custom-built and modified Remington M40 he calls 'Lulu.' It has a Remington 700 receiver, Bespoke fluted-bolt with custom trigger. MDT TAC 21 Chassis with Harris Bipod Modified PRS stock that includes a Monopod. The scope is a Bespoke titanium 20X50X75mm with 3 in-glass reticle data points. One is the BDC (bullet drop and wind deflection compensation). Two is inclination (elevation of target) and the third is speed of moving target. A weapon as powerful as they come. Lulu has been modified over the years. Any time there's new advanced technology for weapons systems Buddha has it quickly intergraded into the soul of his weapon. It unleashes custom rounds made by a Black Ops., Armorer only known to Buddha. With 260 caliber A/P rounds that are much heavier (tungsten) at 140 grams they hit you like a freight train. Buddha calls his M40 Lulu because he loves the singer's 1969 hit song Boom Bang-A-Bang."

173

As I shake my head I ask, "Who customizes his weapon?"

DJ puts his finger to his lip as if to shush me. "He only refers to him as Ghost."

The prisoner is still holding the band-aid down on his arm when Charms puts his trigger finger hard up to the prisoner's forehead. "I'm putting you on this radio to talk to the MiG pilot. Your life depends on what you say. That MiG just might kill us all. You save us...and you save yourself. Do I make myself clear?"

Our prisoner says, "Yes sir…" in perfect English. Charms then yells to Big Al, "Bring your portable translator up here fast!"

Big Al grabs the translator and quickly makes his way to the cockpit as Charms continues, "You stay on top of everything he says. Do you understand?"

Big Al answers, "Perfectly!"

With that, the Master Chief puts the prisoner into the co-pilot's seat and changes our radio frequency. Buddha enters the cockpit and asks, "Where do you want me Master Chief?" Charms looks at Captain Hal and asks, "How fast can you descend to 10,000 feet?"

Captain Hal answers, "I can have us there in 4 minutes."

Charms replies, "Do it!"

As the aircraft is descending, Master Chief looks at Buddha and says, "I want you watching this MiG from the co-pilot window. I need you to find any vulnerabilities in this MiG pilot's pattern."

Then the Master Chief looks at our prisoner and Big Al before asking loudly, "ANYTHING?"

The prisoner says, "He's not answering us."

Just then the MiG blasts a salvo from her twin 23-mm Nudelman-Rikhter NR-23 canons across our bow and Charms looks at the prisoner and asks, "What's this threat gesture all about?"

He answers, "I have no idea."

Charms quickly remarks, "Tell him we have wounded personnel from the explosions at the Belarusian airbase and they need immediate medical help. We're transporting them to Ukraine and that we had no other options." The prisoner quickly repeats the message Charms gave him and Big Al shakes his head in the affirmative. Charms takes that to mean that his message was sent.

Captain Hal says, "We're at 10,000 feet and leveling off."

Buddha responds, "Master Chief...the MiG is circling us now and will be coming up on our starboard side in a few seconds. When he does that it gives me less than a second, but he seems to be coming right at me...that's when he's the most vulnerable — your call."

We can all see Master Chief O'Malley's brain quickly calculating our options. He knows he has to make a quick decision...did the MiG pilot get the message or will he try to blow us out of the sky on this pass? That's when the light goes off in his head as he says, "Big Al, get the prisoner out of here now! Buddha, take a seat and let's get this window open." Then he yells out, "Hold on tight we're opening the co-pilot window. Things will get a bit bouncy for a few seconds." He then looks at Buddha and says, "This is why they pay you the big bucks. What are the odds?" As Buddha opens the cockpit window and places Lulu's barrel out into the turbulence, he slowly puts his eye to the scope and says, "Master Chief, I'd say the percentages are 90 – 10." He looks at

Captain Hal and continues, "Captain, you hold her as steady as you possibly can." He continues to wait for the MiG to enter his crosshairs.

*   *   *

At the airbase in Ukraine, the two U.S. Air Force air traffic controllers are back on the radio to their superiors, "Sir, they've descended to 10,000 feet and throttled back."

Their reply is, "10-4, keep us posted. We have two F-15E Strike Eagles on an intercept course."

*   *   *

Master Chief O'Malley tells Buddha, "He's coming around now..." Two-seconds later, Buddha is all smiles as Lulu discharges a high velocity anti-material A/P 60,000 psi cartridge.

Buddha looks up at Charms and says, "Bombs away!"

After a few seconds, Charms lets out a sigh and says, "Looks like a miss! Well, you only had a 10% chance of hitting the MiG."

At that moment, the MiG explodes in a ball of fire and aircraft parts that are coming straight at our aircraft. Charms yells, "Pull-up quick Captain Hal! Simultaneously, Buddha pulls Lulu's barrel back into the aircraft and closes the window while holding on for dear life. The airplane's nose lifts as the throttle is pushed completely forward.

It's only then that Buddha looks at Charms and says, "I meant the MiG only had a 10% chance...piece of cake Master Chief."

DJ looks at me with a very BIG smile on his face and says, "What did I say? He's the best there ever was...or is! Who the hell do you know that could pull off a shot like that?"

Then he hears Charms yell, "DJ, how is she?"

"She's gonna make it Master Chief," before he continues with an afterthought, "Hell, I believe we're all going to make it Master Chief." As I look around the fuselage, it's all smiles.

*   *   *

Back at the Ukrainian Air Force base the two U.S. Air Force air traffic controllers are back on the radio, "Sir, the MiG showed up as a flash on our radar and disappeared, and the Ilyushin Il-112 V getaway aircraft has throttled-up and is climbing,"

"How could that have happened?"

"We don't know sir, but it did."

*   *   *

With Buddha and Lulu on their way out of the cockpit, Master Chief O'Malley takes a seat in the co-pilot seat and changes the aircraft's radio frequency before breaking radio silence, "This is Cutpurse, over."

The voice on the other end sounds happy as he says, "We've got you on radar Cutpurse...no more bogies on your tail and two friendlies are inbound." Just then, two F-15E McDonnell Douglas Strike Eagle high-speed interceptors' blast past us on our port and starboard sides. That was all that was needed to totally lift our spirits. Even knowing we're not safely on the ground as of yet, we know that our chances of arriving in one piece have just gone up exponentially.

O'Malley remarks, "Ground, I'm being hailed on another frequency, be right back."

177

As Charms changes the radio's channel he says, "Nice of you both to join the party. However, you're a bit late."

The Master Chief hears, "Sorry about that Cutpurse...we'd sure like to know how the bogie disappeared from our radar, but that's a story for another time. I'm Major David Harris, call sign, Thumper. You enjoy the rest of your flight home. Your safety is guaranteed."

Charms replies, "Our thanks Thumper. Cutpurse out..."

Quickly, Master Chief O'Malley switches back to his ground communications net and hears, "Cutpurse, this is ground, you've crossed into friendly airspace, over."

O'Malley stays totally focused as he replies, "Ground, we need three ambulances ready at touchdown. Three wounded BYPOL fighters on board...one critical but stable. We have the package plus K-9 and a POW the PSYOPers picked up from Ugolny Airport, over."

Now the communications between O'Malley and his friend on the ground have gone stealthy, I can only hear O'Malley saying, "Uh huh...uh huh..." several times over and over before he ends the conversation with, "Got it, Sir!" As he's putting the mic back in the cradle, he's signaling me to join him. He whispers to me, "President Lukashenko has received the message I left on his son's kitchen table. He knows we have his youngest son, plus his pride and joy...his dog. What we didn't know was that the Belarusian officer you gentlemen kidnapped at the Ugolny airfield happens to be Dmitry Aleksandrovich Lukashenko, the 43-year-old middle son of President Lukashenko. Can you believe that shit? That's a bonus score if there ever was one. It seems that two of the Lukashenko sons are comfortably stowed in the fuselage of this aircraft. Their dictator dad will soon be on the phone with the President negotiating a trade."

*   *   *

178

As that conversation is going on aboard the aircraft, the president's private secretary rushed up to her and said, "Excuse me Madam President...you have a call on the red phone. It's Alexander Lukashenko from Belarus."

As Madam President takes the phone, she places her hand over the mouthpiece before saying, "Thank you Lesley." She then turns her attention to the dictator, "Mr. Lukashenko, this is the President."

Alexander, already pissed-off replies, "I am called President Lukashenko, Madam President - not mister Lukashenko and it seems that you're now sending your SEALs into my country to blow up my Air Force base and kidnap my children and dog. Is this your new pastime?"

With the U.S. National Security Council (NSC) listening in and General Adams by her side, the President says, "I know nothing about your Air Force base. However, we are in possession of two of your children and one K-9. While we are on the subject of kidnapping, let's speak about that for a minute. I believe Belarus is responsible for a state sponsored hijacking of Ryanair flight 4978 that carried 126 souls on board, four of which were Americans."

An aggrieved tyrant butts in, "No one was hurt in that incident and all passengers except two were released and sent safely on their way."

Madam President continues, "Both of your sons and your dog, Umka, are unharmed and being watched over at the Kyiv International Airport."

The irritated tyrant continues, "Your team killed my son's bodyguards and left their bodies piled up in his kitchen."

The President calmly continues, "The bodyguards were combatants who drew down on the wrong people and paid the price.

Let's get to the point of your call shall we!"

With condemnation in his voice, the tyrant replies, "I want my boys and my dog returned immediately."

Madam President is quickly growing tired of the dictator's attitude and says, "Here's my one and only offer Mr. Lukashenko – you will personally fly into Kyiv International. You will bring with you Leonid Mikalaevich Churo, your director general of the state air navigation authority, his deputy Oleg Kazyuchits and two officers of the state security services, Andrey Anatolievich Lnu and Fnu Lnu. These four will be turned over to FBI officials for federal prosecution in New York on charges of aircraft piracy. The only other person on board your aircraft, besides you and your pilot, will be your Lieutenant General Alexander Volfovich. You have a deadline of 4 hours from now to be there. Do you understand?"

The tyrant tries to reason with the President, but she has already hung up.

The head of the Joint Chiefs, General Adams, looks at the President and says, "Well done Ma'am! I'll contact the team in Ukraine and let them know to be expecting guests within the four-hour time frame."

Madam President smiles as she heads down the hall for her meeting with the heads of the Missile Defense Agency (MDA) and the U.S. Space Command.

*   *   *

Chapter 23

As soon as we'd landed at Antonov/Hostomel Air Force Base just on the outskirts of Kyiv, the ambulances and staff got to work immediately helping Master Chief O'Malley, DJ, Skids, Oak, Rags and Buddha extricate the wounded BYPOL fighters from our aircraft. There seemed to be a mix of Ukrainian and American doctors and nurses on the scene. Hulk, Big Al, Pistol Pete, Chucci, Dolph, Capt. Hal and I stayed out of the way. As soon as the ambulances sped off, we went over to help the SEAL team unload the leftover explosives and weapons from our battered aircraft. A vehicle I hadn't noticed before had arrived to pick up the SEALs along with all the gear and the two prisoners. We took charge of Umka.

I thought it would be a quick goodbye but they spent a good bit of time thanking us as Master Chief O'Malley remarked, "I can honestly say that for a group of 70-year-olds, you've all still got a lot of fight left in you. It's been a unique pleasure working with the four of you and hearing those terrific stories about Whoman. I know how you feel about losing a teammate, brother and friend. I'm sure he's smiling down on us all right now."

The Master Chief then sticks out his hand and we each take it one at a time — along with a powerful, meaningful hug. Each man on his team does the same. We've all gained that mutual respect for each other that comes with sharing time together in combat. We pulled off a special mission together. We did it on the fly so to speak and it came out rather well.

Then Charms smiles and comments, "I look forward to seeing you Army boys around some time. It's been a pleasure doing business with you too Chucci, Dolph and Capt. Hal. Great flying by the way!" He waves before boarding the vehicle along with his team and proceeds to drive away.

I looked around and noticed that everyone was gone except for us and some airport crew. Big Al had the same look on his face and comments, "What are we, chopped liver?" We all started laughing, mostly because that's exactly how we felt, but partly because it broke the tension of the moment. Once again we had beaten the odds and returned relatively unscathed.

That's about the time a U.S. Embassy van pulls up and we are met by William B. Taylor, Jr., a political appointee from the embassy. He seems very pleased to meet us and remarks, "Ambassador Brink is looking forward to meeting you all. The President was in touch with her just over an hour ago and we've been given orders to take exceptionally good care of you men." Then he asks, "Who are Chucci, Dolph Coley and Captain Hal?" They each identify themselves as the political appointee Taylor continues, "You three will be on a flight back to the U.S. later today." Then he looks down at a piece of paper before continuing, "Mr. Krogh, where are you sir?" I put a finger in the air to help identify myself as he keeps going, "You and your team will be staying at the Embassy for a couple of days for debriefing and then you'll be off to Alaska to be reunited with family members. Mr. Chucci, Dolph and Captain Hal, you three will be debriefed on your flight back to the states. Any questions?"

Hulk is quick to respond, "Yeah, when can we get some ice-cold beer and a steak?" Hulk then quickly looks over at me and continues, "And a couple of lobster tails for Sidney?"

Then I ask, "Mr. Taylor, we'd all like to call our loved ones as quickly as possible to personally let them know that we're OK and just to hear their voices once again."

Her replies, "We are on our way to 4 A. I. Sikorsky St. which is the residence of the United States Embassy here in Ukraine. I assure you there is very cold beer, steaks, lobster tails and anything else you'd like to eat being prepared as we speak. Your wives and girlfriends have already given the embassy chef the entire lowdown on your eating habits. Phones are also available and you'll be given time to make those calls anytime you like. So, sit back and enjoy the ride."

We all enjoyed hot showers, delicious food and drink, plus those phone calls to Alaska. It's always great to hear Marty's voice. We laughed (cried a little) and generally got caught up on what our ladies had been up to while we were away. I was grateful to hear about the security bubble that was protecting them. We had no idea that the President had pulled a rabbit out a hat and had stamped us with a "do not touch" classification with Russia. She's one sophisticated, classy woman.

*   *   *

Seconds before the President enters the room for her briefing, NORAD sends an encrypted message to the Pentagon's underground communications center that reads: "Three missile sites in North Korea have gone HOT! Satellite images show lots of movement in and around launch sites. Recommend going to DEFCON 1 immediately!"

Word gets to the President within seconds and then to all NATO countries and U.S. military installations worldwide seconds later, along with the words — "All base commanders – GO to DEFCON 1 immediately. This is NOT a drill!"

The President looks at General Adams and says, "General, please give President Xi and Gray Cardinal one last call and see if they pick up. If not... let the show begin."

*   *   *

Madam President takes her seat at the head of the table and says, "Things are getting a bit dicey and we may have to cut this short, so give me the skinny."

Navy Vice Admiral Hill, Director of the Missile Defense Agency, stands and begins speaking, "Madam President, if you'll turn your attention to the screen." Pictured here is a full-scale mockup of a rocket with a warhead. There are four major components to any full-scale rocket: structural system or frame, the payload system, the propulsion system and the guidance system. The guidance system of a rocket includes very sophisticated sensors, on-board computers, radars and communication equipment. The guidance system has two main roles during the launch of the rocket — to provide stability for the rocket and to control the rocket during maneuvers. There are many different methods developed to control rockets in flight. However, we will only talk about what we know to be true of the Chinese/North Korean rockets which are on the pad as we speak. This is an inertial navigation system (INS) which is comprised of an IMU, a global navigation satellite system (GNSS) receiver and sensor fusion software. These components work together to calculate position, orientation and velocity in order to deliver critical navigation information."

General Adams enters the room saying, "Please excuse me Admiral Hill, but we have three missiles in the air." The room goes dead quiet as the General continues, "Madam President, I believe Admiral Hill can explain in detail what's going to happen next...Admiral."

"Thank you General. Madam President, the skinny on this is that we are going to take control of all three rockets that have launched. I'm very certain we are already are in charge of their trajectory, plus the arming and disarming of any and all nuclear warheads."

The President has a whimsical look on her face as she asks, "How the hell did we do that?"

"Ma'am…that's Top Secret/Sensitive Compartmented Information (TS/SCI), however, I believe I can disclose this to you. You may remember that on December 5, 2011, an American Lockheed Martin RQ-170 Sentinel unmanned aerial vehicle (UAV) was captured by Iranian forces near the city of Kashmar in northeastern Iran. The government of Iran announced that the aircraft was brought down by its cyber warfare unit stationed near Kashmar and 'brought down with minimum damage.' This, of course, is exactly what we wanted them to think. According to unnamed U.S. officials, a U.S. UAV operated by the Central Intelligence Agency was flying on the Afghan side of the Afghanistan-Iran border when its operators 'lost control' of the vehicle.

Five days later, on December 10, 2011, Iran announced that it intended to carry out reverse engineering on the captured RQ-170. A few months after that, in April of 2012, the Islamic Revolutionary Guard Corps claimed to have succeeded in extracting the entirety of the data collected by the drone and that they were currently in the process of building a replica of the aircraft. This information made a small group of men and women residing in an even smaller room at CIA headquarters in Langley very happy. This drone was not only a Trojan Horse, but all its hardware was completely outdated, except one. The CIA had planted a back door in the drones software which Iran gladly shared, for a price of course, with other countries. Let's just say the stealthiness of that initial 'rootkit' back door still has not been found by any of our adversaries and can be accessed whenever we want in. Russia won the bidding war but a few years later, China stole it from Russia and then later gave the information to North Korea to help their puppet state on their mission to be a thorn in our side. It's like the gift that keeps on giving…kinda like today, for instance. We've always known that sooner or later something like this would happen. For the next few years every adversarial government will be second guessing every bit of software they've ever stolen from us and put to use. It's going to drive them absolutely bonkers. So, the capture of RQ-170 has now given us the ability to change the course of these would be ferocious warheads by putting each of them on different trajectories. For instance, I could send one each to China, North Korea and Russia." This is when the so- called red telephone begins lighting up. The President looks at General Adams and says, "Let the fun begin," as she gestures to the General to answer.

* * *

Chapter 24

Madam President receives her first call from Chinese President Xi Jinping and General Adams fields the call, "How may I help you Xi?"

Xi Jinping replies, "First…I wanted the President to know I've heard she's called me several times, but I've been out of the office. Please let her know that I'm back now and I need to speak with her immediately."

"Sure…one minute, President Xi…"

After a pause, for effect, the President says, "President Xi, I've just heard from my commanders at NORAD that you have a missile heading toward China that was fired from North Korea."

Xi quickly replies, "Madam President, as you Americans say, let's cut to the chase. What is it you want? We need to end this now!"

"Excuse me…I didn't do anything. I've seen what you've been up to and I've tried to call you several times over the past few days to try to have you put an end to this treachery. Don't think for one minute that you can call me now and blow smoke up my ass by telling me you weren't anywhere near your phone, or that you didn't have anything to do with this fiasco!"

Xi, with a serious and earnest voice, asks again, "Madam President…what do you want?"

The Presidents says, "Xi, I only want what the President of Taiwan, Tsai lng-wen, wants and that's independence for her island…full autonomy and nothing less. And…no fly overs or intimidation of any kind. Also, you know over the past few years, I've tried very hard to have you reign in those two chemical companies, Wuhan Shuokang Biological Technology and Suzhou Xiaoli Pharmatech. Their chemical supply chain has added fentanyl to the lucrative cocaine distribution of the Sinaloa and Jalisco Cartels in Mexico which has been killing thousands of American citizens. That ends today! Am I getting through to you Xi?"

"Yes, Madam President!"

"Good! Because now we are moving on to America's farmland. It seems you've been purchasing thousands of acres. Well, we want it all back. Every single acre, including any and all office buildings, shopping malls, golf courses — hell, we even want every putt-putt golf course you may own back in the possession of the United States. All of it returned...every deed...lock, stock and barrel."

Xi says, "Done!"

The President continues, "I wasn't finished! Lastly, it seems China owns $1.1 trillion of the United States debt — that debt is now zero. You will sign and stamp an official document within 5 minutes and I better have it in my hand within six. Am I clear!" The Chinese President knows that once again he's been outplayed by the U.S. President as he finds himself in checkmate on the chessboard of global politics.

"Yes, Madam President!"

*   *   *

The second she hangs up; the phone is ringing again, but this time it's the Russian President known as Gray Cardinal on a teleconferencing call. "Madam President, I see that the U.S. and all of your allies have gone to DEFCON 1. This is very serious! What can be done to bring the temperature down?"

Madam President is shaking her head and half smiling as she looks at General Adams. "Firstly sir (small 's' in sir) we know all about your BS-64 - Delta-IV-nuclear submarine. I know they haven't been in touch with you for a while. That's because their comms have been compromised. We have them in custody and your Naval personnel are fine and being well treated. It's our thought that we might make an exchange...your submarine and crew for pulling all of your troops back from the Ukrainian border and sending everyone home. The oligarchs that we have in custody will remain on U.S. soil and we will be confiscating all the gold and rubles they seem to have absconded with, as well as the super-yachts. I'm not just talking about the super-yachts in our possession...I'm talking about all super-yachts anywhere and in any port worldwide in which they've been detained. They are no longer yours. We have some Wagner Group mercenaries detained in Jacksonville along with a super-yacht captain. They will be released along with a number of bodies belonging to the Soviet Union and Belarus. I've tried for years to get your government to release Paul Whelan and Marc Fogel. Now you've imprisoned American journalist Evan Gershkovich. They, along with all other Americans being detained, for any reason, will be flown back to the United States immediately. On your home front, I want to see Alexei Navalny freed at once. It's time he and his wife Yulia Navalnaya are able to spend some time together. It's also time for some opposition to your autocratic government. One more thing — I want you to listen and listen carefully...whatever problem you or Wagner Group have against that old PSYOP team ends now! Period! Do you understand?"

Gray Cardinal shakes his head in the affirmative before he frantically asks, "What about the missile with the nuclear warhead heading toward Russia?"

Madam President says, "That should be between you and North Korea."

Gray Cardinal replies, "Madam President, you know I had nothing to do with those launches."

The President breaks in rather abruptly, "sir (again with the small 's') your nuclear sub dropped off the Belarusian killers that you sent to murder U.S. citizens on American soil. Then your nuclear sub was to pick them back up and head south into the Pacific Ocean and join in this nuclear fiasco. You were going to launch a nuclear warhead into the atmosphere where it would join three others and explode in the atmosphere over U.S. soil, thus sending fallout residue that would cripple America for decades. You better fess up now or quickly run and hide under a desk."

Knowing he's been defeated again and that he must come clean, Gray Cardinal says, "You are correct Madam President. I accept all of your terms unconditionally."

Madam President says, "I want it in writing and in my hands with your signature within minutes. Do you understand?"

"Yes, Madam President!"

With NO line of communication to North Korea, Madam President decides to let them all just sweat, even after she received the correspondence she'd asked for from the two world leaders. Then she asks Vice Admiral Hill, "Excuse me Admiral, you said we would be able to switch off these nuclear warheads from exploding when they hit the ground didn't you?"

"Yes, Madam President, that's correct. I assure you they are already switched off. I hadn't gotten to that part of my presentation when we were interrupted by the three missiles being launched. As I've mentioned, we are in complete control of their guidance systems. Is there anywhere specific that you'd like them to land?"

*   *   *

As the Belarusian President's Boeing 737 touches down at Kyiv International Airport, his jet is followed to the terminal by 20 Ukrainian

190

military trucks, each loaded with armed Ukrainian soldiers. The second the engines shut down, the trucks surround the jet and the soldiers exit. This show of force was mandated by Madam President.

With the stairs in place, the aircraft's exit door opens and the first person down the stairs is Leonid Mikalaevich Churo, the director general of the Belarusian State air navigation authority, his deputy, Oleg Kazyuchits, and two officers of the state security services, Andrey Anatolievich Lnu and Fnu Lnu. These four have been charged with conspiracy to commit aircraft piracy. Churo personally communicated the false bomb threat to the staff at the Minsk air traffic control center and directed controllers to instruct the flight to divert while Kazyuchits directed air traffic authorities to falsify incident reports. Once they set foot on Ukrainian soil, they were handcuffed by FBI agents along with agents from Interpol. They were then escorted to a van which drove them 200 yards to a waiting jet that would transport them to the BIG Apple where federal prosecutors awaited their arrival.

Lieutenant General Alexander Volfovich is next out the door, followed closely by the dictator himself, Alexander Lukashenko. Once their feet hit the ground, the U.S. Ambassador to Ukraine, Bridget Brink, steps up and says, "Gentlemen, please follow me." She then turns and slowly walks into the airport terminal and into a private office. They are followed by five heavily armed Ukrainian soldiers. As they enter, they all see a seated Ms. Sviatlana Tsikhanouskaya, the Belarusian political activist who actually won the Belarusian Presidential election in 2020.

The dictator Lukashenko is totally outraged, "What is she doing here? I just want to get my two sons and my dog and then get out of here."

Ambassador Brink says, "If you'll take a seat sir (another small 's') and General, please sit here." As the general and the tyrant take their seats, the ambassador's staff is bringing in video equipment and setting it up.

Lukashenko is beside himself, "That's enough! I was told to come here and pick up my sons and dog. I want them here NOW!"

Ambassador Brink smiles as she says, "You will shut your mouth until I tell you to open it...and when I tell you to open it you'll say only what is on the prompter in front of you. Do you understand?" As she says this, a Ukrainian soldier takes the butt of his weapon and smashes it into the back of the tyrant's head. General Volfovich tries to protest but four weapons are instantly pointed at his head and he calmly sits back down.

Ambassador Brink nods to a member of her staff and she quickly turns on the prompter and smiles back to the ambassador who says to the tyrant, "You will smile as you read this statement and you will say every word as if it's coming from your heart and soul. Should we have to do this reading a second time because of your attitude...well...I have no idea what these soldiers might do, and, as you know...this is their country and like you, I am only a guest." The ambassador then looks at the person operating the camera and continues, "Will you please start the video?"

Less than an hour later, the citizens of Belarus are buzzing with the news that is being broadcast throughout the country. "The Presidency has been peacefully handed over to the already elected president...Sviatlana Tsikhanouskaya."

Lieutenant General Alexander Volfovich has told the military that they are to listen to their new commander-in-chief. PresidentTsikhanouskaya has made her first public remarks to her nation and the world as she condemns the buildup of Soviet forces along the Ukrainian border, noting that NO Belarusian military units will be available to Russia and there will be NO staging of Russian military forces in Belarus. Then she hugs the U.S. ambassador before boarding her Boeing 737 which will take her back to Belarus.

U.S. Ambassador Brink comes to attention, salutes her and remarks…"President Sviatlana Tsikhanouskaya, may you enjoy a safe flight home and may God be with you and protect you and your countrymen and women."

The new President salutes the U.S. Ambassador and smiles, "Thank you Ambassador Brink, and may God bless you and the United States of America." Then she turns and makes her way up the steps. She is on her way to lead her country out of the tyranny that has lasted far too long.

Alexander Lukashenko and Lieutenant General Alexander Volfovich are soon-to-be carted off to the Hague in the Netherlands to face the International Court of Justice. Lukashenko's two sons, Dmitry and Nikolai, will both be detained in a Ukrainian prison until Belarusian President Sviatlana Tsikhanouskaya says differently. Umka is also enjoying her freedom, as she roams around the U.S. Embassy in Ukraine.

*   *   *

So where did the President have the three nuclear warheads land? Well, the one that traveled to Russia had its parachute open at 7,000 feet as it crashed through the roof of the Russian Ministry of Defense's fairly new, three-tiered, multibillion-dollar control center. This facility looks like a scene straight out of "Dr. Strangelove." The Russian State news agency noted in its headlines, "Russian Defense Data Center Outperforms U.S. Facility Threefold: Official." The center, is said to be fortified and sits on top of a maze of underground tunnels, which is located in Frunze Naberezhnaya on the bank of the Moscow River, a little over two miles from Red Square. The center employs over 1,000 officers working on a rotating watch system. The Russian armed forces select their best officers for these posts. Many with skills not previously taught to officers of the Russian military until recently. This facility comes complete with color-coded rows with matching headsets and water bottles bearing the Russian army brand. Today, however, there will be lots of cleaning up to do as the 290 pound nuclear warhead enters the roof of this Russian military nerve center which has obviously shown design flaws in its fortification.

The second nuclear bomb's parachute opened at about the same distance from the ground only to crash through the roof of the Chinese chemical company Wuhan Shuokang Biological Technology Co., Ltd. One of two Chinese businesses supplying fentanyl to drug cartels in Mexico. Shuokang Biotechnology Company Ltd. is located in Wuhan, China, and states in its company's marketing statement that its management policy is to carry out a customer-oriented business philosophy. It also claims to advocate the spirit of excellence, pioneering and innovative work and to provide customers satisfaction of chemical products through the company's hard working and honest staff who have won the praise and trust of customers at home and abroad. It's proud to have established long-term stable business relations both foreign and domestic, with fabulous after-sales service. They go on to promise to continue to adhere to the tenet of "quality first, user first, reputation first, service first" and will provide high quality products and excellent service to customers at home and abroad. I know their statement sounds and is redundant. They sure want a good pat on the back for quality and service, but nowhere in their statement does it say anything about the 53,000 fentanyl deaths in the United States in 2020, or the 67,000 deaths in 2021. The death toll keeps rising each year. In 2022 we hit a record 109,000 deaths and so far in 2023 we've lost 79,000 Americans to this drug.

The third nuclear device didn't open until it was 1,000 feet from the ground. It smashed right through the roof of Rocketman's massive seaside estate in Wonsan, North Korea. It did so with such velocity that it made its way through all three floors and landed in the fat man's living room, where it's rumored, he was sitting in his soiled pants.

*   *   *

194

Chapter 25

The old PSYOP team spent the past two days being debriefed, housed and fed at the United States Embassy in Kiev. We were given a ride over to the hospital with permission to check in on Mira and the other two wounded BYPOL fighters from Belarus. All three were awake, alert and in really good spirits. I had no idea BYPOL stands for Union of Security Forces of Belarus and includes among its ranks, police officers and former Soviet spies who joined in to oppose the dictator Lukashenko. We were also able to catch up on all of the international news. With few exceptions, we had no idea what had been going on in the world.

There is a constant stream of "Breaking News" as reporters from around the world are piecing together the last few days. For instance, who knew those BYPOL fighters could make such a mess out of the Machulishchy Air Force Base? It's beyond recognition! Not to mention the saboteurs who destroyed the Ugolny Airport in Eastern Russia the day before. We all got a kick out of hearing a Russian nuclear-powered submarine had been detained in the shallow waters off of the Western coast of Alaska. Exactly how does one capture a nuclear-powered submarine? I can't wait to get the whole story on that.

Instead of a major conflict (better known as war) between Russia (the aggressor) and Ukraine (the independent free country) the Soviets had pulled back, stuck their tails between their legs and gone home without so much as an "oops sorry."

Of course, who could forget the headlines about North Korea sending up three of its newest long-range missiles, topped with nuclear warheads, and three going haywire at the exact same time. Instead of splashing down into the Sea of Japan (like usual), one had fallen somewhere in Russia while another made it all the way to Whohan China. The third one landed where it began, somewhere on the coast of North Korea. Coincidence? I don't think so!

But the fun filled fact that the Belarusian scumbag Alexander Lukashenko had been tricked into flying from Belarus to Ukraine to pick up his sons and dog was a story right out of a comic book. To know that the rightful winner of the the Belarusian election was now at the helm of her country and that Lukashenko was sitting behind bars in the Hague awaiting trial brought the loudest laughter and applause from the crowd of four 70-year-old PSYOP warriors. The world events were piling up faster than a flash of lightning, a speeding bullet, or disappearing turkeys in November. But, as my mind was enjoying the moment, the embassy's political appointee, Mr. Taylor, approaches me with a Sat-phone saying, "This is for you Mr. Krogh."

I thanked Mr. Taylor before saying, "Hello this is Sidney Krogh."

The voice remarks, "Hello yourself, Sid-the-Kid! Do you know who this is?"

"This sounds like the voice from my very recent past."

The Master Chief continues, "I'm sending you a text with coordinates. I've heard from your old PSYOP team that you like to play the GPS game with them. So, let the games begin. Can you be there in four days' time? Is that possible?"

I respond with, "I'm always up for travel, nice surprises and converting coordinates into a destination. If I can get out of Belarus and back to Alaska I'll be there! If I can make this happen, may I bring Marty with me?"

Charms chimes in with, "This has always been a guy event and we'd like to keep it that way."

I respond, "I don't believe you've met Marty, so let me tell you a quick story. She was wounded last year in Whittier, Alaska, but took out two Wagner Group mercenaries. The President of the United States called her and her doctors at the hospital in Anchorage to see how she was doing. (14) Last week at the safe-house in Anchorage, she killed the Chef, whose family, including him, were all Cold War Russian planted KGB intelligence officers. With everyone's life in danger at the unsafe safe-house and three FBI Special Agents dead and one wounded, she broke into the weapons storage cabinet in the basement, loaded three rifles and with the help of two other wives, proceeded to take out five of the Belarusian hit team members while wounding the sixth. I totally understand the territorial boundaries you SEALs enforce and live by, but I'd like to ask for a temporary suspension of the rules. The long and the short of it is, with all due respect, Marty comes or I stay home."

Without even a short pause I hear, "See you both in four days Mr. Krogh. You don't know it yet, but you and your PSYOP team will all be heading back to Alaska shortly. Keep it on the down low."

My phone dings and there it is – 36 degrees 47' 11.67" N by 76 degrees 03' 19.78" W. "I'll be damned... I wonder what this is all about!"

The fact that the world was still in one piece and we were all still alive and in fairly good health means today is a good day. That's when the U.S. Ambassador to Ukraine, Bridget Brink, walks in and says, "I have four brand new United States passports for you gentlemen. The President has a military aircraft that will be landing at the International Airport here in Kiev in 30 minutes. She thanks you for your service to your country and for a job well done! You're to gather your belongings and be ready to depart in 15 minutes."

(14) Book Series II - Bedlamites

197

Pistol Pete breaks out laughing before gaining back his composure. "Firstly, we want to thank you for your generosity and hospitality, but you should know that we have no belongings, no cash, no credit cards, cell phones and until this minute...we had no passports. Pretty much nothing except the clothes on our backs, which we thank you for. You've been most gracious. You and your staff are always welcome around our campfire." His comment gave us all a chance to stand up and give a cheer for our host (hostess). The embassy did take our Belarusian uniforms and dress us up nicely in civilian clothes the day we arrived. I want you to know that it was Big Al who asked the Ambassador to please clean and pack our Belarusian uniforms for us to take home as souvenirs. Kind of an "old time sake" gesture, but I knew he wanted everyone back home to know that he finally outranked Pistol Pete.

With this country's Captain Morgan shortage and no ginger beer anywhere to be found, I figured it was as good a time as any to be wheels up and heading back home to Alaska.

*　　*　　*

Chapter 26

The flight from Kiev to Anchorage seemed short but that's probably because I was sleeping. All of us were fairly quiet the entire flight. I don't know if we were still winding down or wondering what we'd say to our ladies upon arrival.

That thought didn't last long as the flight attendant informed us we'd soon be landing and to put our seats in the upright position and to secure our tray tables. Within a minute or two I heard the rubber meet the asphalt. That's when I realized that we had no flight attendant or trays to put away. We quickly figured out that it was Special Agent Drake messing with our minds as the Gulfstream V was touching down at Joint Base Elmendorf-Richardson. We are at the Elmendorf Air Force Base part of the amalgamation. The Richardson part is a United States Army Base.

We could see our ladies waving as we taxied up to the host units command center before our aircraft's captain, Special Agent Cash, shut down the engines. The airmen of the 673rd Air Wing at JBER (Joint Base Elmendorf-Richardson) came over immediately and helped us exit our aircraft and dive into the arms of our loved ones. It was quite the scene. Marty wouldn't let go for several minutes and when she finally did, she put her face directly in front of mine, looked me straight in the eyes and said, "I love you sweetie," before planting a long and loving kiss on my lips. Then she continued, "We need to make a life changing move. We'll talk about it over cocktails," as she turns and signals an airman to come over. In his hands he holds a tall glass of Captain Morgan with Reed Ginger Beer for me and a glass of wine for her, "My favorite...so you didn't forget!"

"Sweetie, you were only gone for five days." "Is that all...really? It seemed like forever." We touched glasses and enjoyed our first of many sips.

There were two U.S. Air Force vans parked at the command center. After about 15 minutes, all four couples were ready to board the vans and head over to our new quarters, which our ladies had informed us were inside the secure boundaries of Joint Base Elmendorf-Richardson. Not only was the so-called safe-house a crime scene, it was never very safe. The security at the Joint Base was still at DEFCON 1, known as Cocked Pistol – meaning maximum readiness, immediate response, nuclear war imminent (or has already begun). My guess is that Madam President is keeping the screws turned tightly on Mother Russia and her co-conspirator, China. After all, you can see Russia from your porch here in Alaska. My sixth sense keeps playing a Grateful Dead verse over and over in my head, *When life looks like easy street, there's danger at your door.* Why it keeps playing in a loop I have no idea...however, I'm totally listening and very aware that my sixth sense has never let me down or steered me in the wrong direction.

The U.S. Air Force vans dropped us at 7153 Fighter Dr. Our new digs are JBER Lodging (formerly North Star Inn). The vans were to wait for us as we showered and changed before they drove us to our dinner at a restaurant on the base named Iditarod Dining Facility. This is where we will meet back up with Special Agent Jennings Sanders and his half-brother Biggin. It will be great to see them both again and I always enjoy watching Biggin eat (and drink). This man is a monster and he may have a few screws loose but I'm proud to call him a friend.

With everyone spruced up, though a bit lethargic, we boarded the Air Force vans and headed out to the Iditarod Dining Facility. The second we arrived, we were met by the half-brothers and all of us became revitalized — hugs and smiles all around.

It looks as though they put three or four tables together over in a corner to support our numbers as well as to give us some privacy. Open bottles of wine were already on the table along with a Captain and ginger beer. As everyone was beginning to take their seats, Biggin and Agent Sanders called me to the side before Sanders said, "We need a quick sidebar." The three of us walked out of the restaurant and they found a suitable quiet spot before Agent Sanders continued, "I know you don't want to hear this, however, it's not over for you. We want to be completely upfront about this. I know how angry you were with me in Alaska when I left you out of the loop. (15) In my defense, I was under very strict orders to say nothing."

With that disclaimer out of the way I said, "Well then, let's hear it. Please give me the short version now and you can fill in the blanks later."

Biggin didn't look like he wanted to speak so I put both eyes on Special Agent Sanders. "OK...the hit on you is still ongoing. The one Belarusian prisoner we have in custody says that there is an Operator X, who is unbeknownst to him, except for the fact that the Belarusian Ex-President Lukashenko bragged about him during their initial planning session for the botched mission here in Alaska."

With my mouth hanging open I ask, "So, there's an unknown paid assassin — out there somewhere — just waiting for me? Is that really what you're telling me? So...that's why my brain has had the Grateful Dead lyrics spinning in a loop! What the F_ _K!"

Two positives I can take away from this are that I'm certainly glad I wasn't being kept in the dark (again) and also I'm pleased to learn that my every step is being shadowed by professional shooters. When we returned to the dinner table, I had to fake a smile throughout the rest of the evening, even though I did enjoy the company, food and Captain Morgan.

---

(15) Book Series II - *Bedlamites*. Special Agent Sanders kept something secret from me that could have cost me my life.

Knowing that this base is still on DEFCON 1 also gave me a safety blanket of security. But what about telling Marty? She has a right to know...doesn't she? I could sure use inspiration of divine proportion right about now, but my mind is blank.

After tucking an inebriated Marty into bed, I kept thinking about my earlier conversation with Ms. Alfreda Frances Bikowsky. For some reason she keeps popping up inside my poor worn-out brain. Even though it was early morning on the East Coast of the United States, Ms. Bikowsky was about to get a wake-up call.

A yawning, but cheerful voice asks, "Don't you ever sleep Mr. Krogh?"

I reply, "The sun is still shining brightly in 'The Land of the Midnight Sun'. I didn't want to wake you, but I need information quickly. You once told me a story about an FBI woman, a military or CIA interrogator that you've been in recent contact with and she hinted to you that she has a guy..."

Ms. Bikowsky quickly interrupts me, "STOP NOW! Not another word...Are you on a secure line?"

I grit my teeth and contort my face as I realize my mistake, "No Ma'am. Sorry! I wasn't thinking."

"That midnight sun must be baking your brain. I'll text you a number to call me in the morning...1 PM my time. That will give your brain time to cool down."

"Yes, Ma'am...thank you."

I head off to bed, but first I must clean my CPAP machine, fill it with distilled water, strap it on and presto...I said presto. Shit...it's going to be a long night as my brain is still baking and 9 AM is a long way off.

I turn on the TV hoping that my mind will slow down, or at least change it's focus. It worked...and within 15 minutes, I was in La-La Land.

I know I'm only one of the millions of Americans who wear a sleep apnea mask in order to enjoy a good night's sleep. The one thing I don't like about sleep is when I'm entering the REM phase. This is the sleep stage where most of our dreams happen, and it's also where my own personal bout with yin and yang seems to kick in.

Yin and yang is the concept of duality and balance in the Chinese philosophy and culture. Yin and yang are two opposite and yet complementary principles or forces that influence the destinies of creatures and things. Yin is the feminine, passive, dark, cold or damp side, while yang is the masculine, active, bright, warm or dry side. Neither are entirely good or bad but they can change while opposing each other.

Tonight's featured dream/nightmare has taken me back to Vietnam once again. As an HB Combat PSYOP team leader, my team was usually called upon to move out quickly, usually into an immediate combat situation. As psychological operators working in and around the Demilitarized Zone, we weren't called upon to enjoy a cold beer while relishing on a lawn chair and enjoying the sun's rays.

I know this dream/nightmare is taking place between November and April because that's monsoon season in Southeast Asia. The rains are usually relentless and today they are living up to their maximum potential...not by raining cats and dogs, but more like elephants and hippos. This is usually a time when both sides take a break from fighting and strip down for a shower or to pout to your buddies about being soaked to the bone. Nevertheless, that's not what's happening today as the NVA unit that India ¾ Marines

203

had been hunting decide to raise their ugly soaking wet head. I could hear the pops from the Soviet model M-40, 50-mm mortar rounds above the torrential rain. It's a very distinct sound and one you don't forget.

I'd been hanging out in a self-made lean-to with three marines shooting the shit while eating lunch out of a can, when the first tree burst sent debris crashing down upon us. That's just about the exact same time another soviet made weapon began spraying down our LZ (Landing Zone). The Degtyarev-Shpagin, or better known as the DShK heavy machine gun, commenced firing its 12.7x108mm cartridges right through the downpour.

I never saw which direction the three marines took during our instantaneous departure, nor do I know what became of my last sardine, because I was way too busy grabbing my M-16 and bandoleer of magazines packed with ammo and sprinting at full speed toward my foxhole.

My team had arrived two days prior and the NCOIC (non-commissioned officer in-charge) had located us with the 3rd platoon on the northern edge of the LZ. This is where we had dug in with our platoon sergeant designating our field of fire.

That's the area we are personally responsible for should anyone considered unfriendly try to enter our perimeter. Well, all foxholes look alike when you're dodging raindrops, heavy caliber machine gun fire and very angry fast-moving shrapnel...and that's when I met Rabbit. "Get the fuck out of here! My hole ain't big enough for two!" He was absolutely correct. It didn't matter that it was three quarters full of water and had an African-American with the largest ears I'd ever seen on a human being already filling up at least 92.5% of this hole. However, I had no place to go and zero time to get there — much less argue about it. Rabbit and I tried our best to stay low and keep up an effective ground fire for our own section of the perimeter. Our arguing would have to wait. Staying alive took precedence over whose living quarters we were occupying.

There were no natural defensive characteristics for the terrain in front of us, so days before they'd strung concertina wire and had claymore mines laid out every few feet. You can't just blow your claymores because you're feeling alarmed. You must be certain of a perimeter breach before you deplete that line of defense. Should you do it too early, the enemy will know exactly where the weak spot in your boundary is located. One must stay very disciplined at a time like this. That's when Rabbit tells me, "I just took a piss." So much for discipline! It definitely felt as though the water was getting warmer.

Although I had other things on my mind, I blurted out, "Thanks for telling me."

"I'm telling you 'cause I thought it'd encourage you to fucking leave!"

All I did was let out a smiling, "Ahhh," as I let my own stream add to the warmth of our home.

Rabbit could tell I was relieving myself and smiling as he shook his head he said, "Army man...you be what we call an asshole. What do your friends call ya?"

I told him, "I'm Sid-the-kid."

After blasting a few more rounds into the downpour, he says, "I'm Rabbit."

I smiled and said, "Go figure!"

That's when he stuck out his wet, muddy hand and said, "Nice to meet you Sid-the-kid."

It rained for hours and was showing no sign of letting up. I had no idea where my PSYOP team member or my interpreter were. I knew they had to be close by and I was very sure they were both doing their duty at keeping their/our section of the perimeter protected. Every so often Rabbit or I would spray a few of our 5.56x45mm NATO rounds into our field of fire, always sporadically. You simply can't give the enemy a pattern. Over time, I came to learn that Rabbit was from Chicago. Not the first time I'd met someone from the Windy City out in these mountains. He confided to me that he's had big ears since birth. I was fairly certain that this was true because no one would actually do this to themselves on purpose. He was given the name Rabbit by the nurse that caught him leaving his mother's womb. Like almost everyone I'd ever met in the bush, you rarely ever knew someone's real name. I'm sure there are a few reasons for that but the one I believe to be true is that it's a defense mechanism that builds up inside all combat hardened personnel — the one that protects you mentally when a combatant friend doesn't make it.

I really can't remember when the monsoon rains finally subsided and things went back to normal. In most cases out here "normal" is defined as FUBAR (Fucked Up Beyond All Recognition). I do remember that I only had 3 rounds left in my last magazine. Fire discipline and training at its best! At some point in time my team and I caught a chopper off of this mountain and back to the Rockpile for my usual debrief (after action review) before heading back to Dong Ha Combat Base.

Less than a month later, I was heading back to those beautiful mountains in and around the demilitarized zone to be reunited with the same marine unit. Another PSYOP team was up in the rotation but I asked if I could take the mission. I wanted to bring some beers out with me and enjoy a warm one with Mr. Rabbit. Thank God I was protected by that defensive mechanism I had built up inside because I quickly learned that Rabbit had been killed a week earlier. So instead I shared a few beers with his platoon sergeant as we reminisced about the marine with the big ears. Some say that you die twice...the first time is when you're pronounced dead and then buried or your ashes are shared with the wind. The second and final time is when the last person speaks your name. For that reason alone, I keep the Rabbit alive by mentioning his name a lot. And though we only spent about 36 soaking wet, muddy hours together, Rabbit will always be my brother-in-arms and have a place in my heart.

And as for that defensive mechanism we'd built up inside...one day we all figure out it was a fictitious safety valve. Something we needed to believe in it at the time but it was never really there.

Every once in a while, when I enter the REM phase of my nightly sleep cycle one of these old experiences will return and remind me of the yin and yang of my own life.

This is also the time that I remember what my dad told me as a young man, "There's only one person you have to go to bed with every night...and that's yourself. Make sure you get a good night's sleep!"

*   *   *

The next morning came early, way too early...6 AM to be exact, the phone rang — only this time I recognized the number. I turned off my CPAP and took off my mask before saying, "Hello this is..." but before I could finish my sentence I hear, "Please hold for the President." I was expecting an important phone call this morning, just not this one. A minute later I hear, "Hello Mr. Krogh...how are you doing today?"

"I'm just fine Madam President. Thank you so much for asking! If I may say ma'am, you're really great at your job! I don't know all of the in's and out's, but suffice to say you've had yourself a tough week and yet you come out smelling like a rose."

The President lets out a light laugh and I can tell she's smiling as she says, "You got that right! Great work on your end also! I believe it's time for you and the old team to retire...don't you think?"

"I couldn't agree more, Madam President, and I know for a fact that Marty would second that."

Then the President continues, "I wanted to speak with you personally and invite you once again to the White House. I know it's short notice but I have some free time the day after tomorrow. Are you able to make it here by then?"

How does one tell the president that you have other plans, so I offer, "That's very kind of you Madam President. However, Marty and I have been invited to a secret party on that same day — one that we simply can't miss!"

The pause says a lot before I hear, "Well, OK then. My best to you and Marty and I hope your futures are bright and peaceful!"

I smile and say, "Thank you so much, Madam President."

*   *   *

The second we hang up, Madam President calls her press secretary, Lesley, and her private secretary, Caitlin, into the Oval Office. "Find out what 'secret party' Sidney and Marty are going to the day after tomorrow. Keep it on the down-low."

Caitlin and Lesley both smile as Caitlin says, "Yes, Madam President."

*   *   *

I could smell the coffee, so I knew Marty was up. I wanted to go back to sleep, but that option quickly went out the window, "Good morning sweetie," Marty said as she enters the room while handing me a piping hot cup of joe.

I quickly tell Marty about my late-night phone call to Ms. Bikowsky and the reason for it, which was a call I only made after the side-bar with Biggin and Agent Sanders outside of the restaurant last evening. The sad look on Marty's face said it all. I explained everything the best I could and most especially about our safety bubble, hoping that would put her mind at ease. Then, to cheer her up even more I filled her in on our trip to Virginia Beach and the reunion at the Young Veterans Brewing Company. I didn't let on with the Master Chief that DJ had already filled me in on their team's after-action tradition and its location. Marty was beside herself but very proud after hearing the story I told Master Chief O'Malley about her exploits over the past two years. Marty is a true patriot in every sense of the word. With that being said, Marty left me and my coffee and headed out to start packing. That's when I headed over to Special Agent Sanders' room to use his secure CryptoPhone.

* * *

Chief Wayne and Nita drop Marty and me off at Ted Stevens Anchorage International Airport later that evening. We will be flying the 3,502 miles in business class on our way east to the Norfolk International Airport. Marty and I both need the rest, food and endless cocktails that accompany a business class ticket. I'm not sure where our security detail is or who they are, but I was told there would be four people accompanying us and that everyone on our flight had been vetted.

Once we touch down in Norfolk and claim our baggage, we are met by a security detail which will transport us the 18 miles to Virginia Beach. As we enter the Historic Cavalier Hotel and Beach Club, I can see that Marty is in awe. "I love it Sidney!"

I reply, "What's not to love? I'll have you know; I was reading that when construction began on this luxurious hotel back in 1926, there were 225 men on-site who laid a half million bricks over the next 13 months. This building put Virginia Beach on the map. Some of their guests included presidents, movie stars, writers and famous sports figures, including Muhammad Ali. And if you think that's cool, just wait until you see our room!"

As we're checking in, I hear hotel desk manager say, "Oh, I see you've taken the Thompson Suite on the seventh floor which was named for Bruce Thompson, regaled as a man who knew how to throw a party as well as for his love of music! He dedicates this suite to all flappers of the Roaring 20s (flappers were young women who embraced a lifestyle viewed by many at the time as outrageous and immoral. Wearing bobbed hair and short skirts, they drank, smoked and said, "Unladylike" things) and the world-famous big bands that played through the night in the Crystal Ballroom at The Cavalier Beach Club. It's that music that established The Cavalier as the Big Band Capital of America! You're going to love it!"

Marty's eyes grew quite large and her beautiful smile broadened as she grabbed my arm and pulled me close, "This is so exciting...I love you Sidney! Let's change our wearing apparel and hit The Cavalier Beach Bar as soon as possible! I'm sure that you're ready for a ginger beer and its close friend Captain Morgan!"

*   *   *

Retired Special Agent Bennye Wolfe exits her cab at the Enmarket Arena in Savannah, Georgia, and looks up at the marquee that reads: Tonight's Special Guest Jimmy Buffett and the Coral Reefer Band! Just below that in red letters it says – SOLD OUT. Agent Wolfe gives the "sold out" sign a rather large smile as she walks over to the "Will Call" window and up to the young customer service person behind the glass who asks, "May I have your name and photo I.D. please?"

Agent Wolfe hands her government issued I.D. which includes her picture as she says, "Special Agent Bennye Wolfe."

The ticket agent smiles and says, "Aren't you the lucky one! I'm privileged to escort you backstage Special Agent Wolfe. Would you please follow me?"

With the sound check finished, Mr. Buffett is handing over his guitar to his longtime guitar technician, Amber Rose and says, "Sounding good tonight...my thanks!"

As he's patting her on the back he looks up and smiles while saying, "Agent Wolfe...I'm so glad you could make it! I'm going to make you the new Elvis and leave a ticket for you at 'will call' at every concert venue."

Bennye smiles back and comments, "You best be careful...I just might show up at each and every performance. Who knows, I might just turn into a Parrot Head."

Mr. Buffet laughs and replies, "Agent Wolfe, would you follow me backstage?" Jimmy puts out his arm and Bennye takes it as they stroll back into his air-conditioned waiting room behind the stage.

As Jimmy and Bennye enter the room they hear, "Surprise!" All the band members and roadies welcome Special Agent Bennye Wolfe to an event party thrown just for her.

Mr. Buffett takes two champagne glasses from a tray and hands one to Bennye. "Agent Wolfe…we're short on time, so I must keep this brief. We've heard you're retiring from the FBI and we want to make sure that we always know where you are. So we've done a little digging and found that you love South Carolina and have some roots there. Drum roll please..." A masterful steel drum roll from Robert Greenidge ensues — then suddenly stops as sound tech, Amber Rose, unveils a mock-up of a Latitude Margaritaville home. Mr. Buffett continues, "This is from us to you — a 2 bedroom, 2 bath, 2 car garage, 1,507 square foot, Hilton Head Jamaica style home. Your new address is on Latitude Boulevard in beautiful Hardeeville, SC."

The entire room erupts and through the jubilance, Agent Wolfe turns and gives Mr. Jimmy Buffett a very big hug before saying, "You didn't have to do this! A free ticket for every concert for life was enough!" This brings applause and laughter from everyone in the room as she continued, "There's NO way to adequately thank all of you. You are all like family to me now and you will be for the rest of my life. Over time, I will learn all of your names and I will truly enjoy my retirement in Margaritaville." Agent Wolfe turns back to Jimmy as he smiles and continues, "Thank you Mr. Jimmy Buffett. I'm now a Parrot head!"

The room suddenly and spontaneously bursts into song, "Wasting away again, in Margaritaville...before Jimmy shouts, "It's time to hit the stage!" As everyone is filing out, they stop by to give Special Agent Bennye Wolfe a hug or to shake her hand and thank her for her service to our great nation.

That's when the retired Special Agent's phone rings. "Hello Special Agent Wolfe...this is Alfreda Frances Bikowsky."

*   *   *

Fifteen minutes later, retired Special Agent Bennye Wolfe is on her encoded GSMK Cryptophone and turns it to the proper frequency and pushing the squawk button twice before hearing, "This is the MAJOR."

"This is Cobra Venom."

As retired Special Agent Wolfe is collapsing her CryptoPhone antenna she has a concerned look on her face as she's thinking, "A female assassin."

*   *   *

Marty and I awoke this next morning to a beautiful sunrise from our balcony on the seventh floor. The Thompson Suite lived up to its name as Marty turned into a real flapper last night and she continued into the wee hours of this morning.

Again, my thanks to vitamin B1. We both did three set of two B1's throughout the night and I'm wide awake without a hangover. Marty still has that run-over-by-a-truck look. That's when I hear the knock at the door and room service is right on time with coffee and breakfast. Finally, Marty looks like she's coming back to life. I hear my phone ping, so I pick it up and see that I must get down to the lobby pronto. "Hey Sweetie...enjoy your coffee. I'll be back in five minutes."

"OK babe...Hurry back!" As I'm exiting our room, Dolph is standing there with two federal agents. What they tell me is a bit of a mind twister. I let it soak in before I tell them, "I got it! I'll do my part."

An hour later, the Bellman at The Cavalier Beach Club has an Uber driver, friend of his, waiting for us. Our Bellman assures us she's cool as he explains..."I met her yesterday evening and she's new to the area, but she's lots of fun and so I asked her for her card and called her for you." Monique is middle aged, quite stunning and friendly. She also loves to drive fast. Did I mention she can talk? No! Well, let me tell you...she can talk. You could tell she was well educated as well as a world traveler.

Marty and Monique became the best of friends very quickly. I sat back and let the two of them chat away. It's about an hour's drive from The Cavalier Beach Club to 36 degrees 47' 11.67" N and 76 degrees 03' 19.78" W – better known as the Young Veterans Brewing Company on the outskirts of Virginia Beach. As we're getting close, I can't help but notice the local sheriff department vehicles and the barricade blocking the road. Monique pulls right up to one of the sheriffs... the one with his hands out in the 'STOP' position as she explains, "I'm just dropping off two passengers."

The sheriff looks at Monique and then at Marty and me in the back seat and asks, "What are your names?"

I tell him, "My name is Sidney Krogh and this is Marty."

The sheriff says, "I'll need for the three of you to step out of the car." I open the back-passenger side door as Marty slides over and exits next to me.

Monique asks, "What is this about officer?"

"Just a random security check ma'am." As the sheriff reaches to open her door, I notice two golf carts approaching from the sides of the Young Veterans Brewing Company building. Marty is smiling as she sees men waving while holding open beer containers in their hands.

They pull right up to us and Charms takes Marty by her arm while saying, "We'll take good care of her until you can join us."

Marty is laughing as she says, "See you soon Sidney!"

The second they are turned around and heading back to the brewery, from out of nowhere, Dolph Coley has appeared with his weapon pointed directly at Monique's head. With his radio up to his mouth he says, "We've got her in custody. All clear." Then he turns to me and asks, "How was the drive over?"

I reply, "As soon as I got your ping, I kept my hand on my Walther PPK. Marty and the so-called Monique enjoyed getting to know one another. Thanks for the heads up." As the Sheriff Department deputies finish frisking Monique, they handcuff her and place her in the back of one of their cruisers.

Dolph explains, "As the team was diligently scouring the planet for Sylvia Bezukov, it was the human hunter herself, Ms. Alfreda Frances Bikowsky who changed the parameters of our search. Instead of looking for her using her father's last name she began looking for her mother's maiden name Vanilova. Then, bingo...Monique Vanilova had flown into the U.S. from Brazil three days ago and she entered with a Brazilian passport as a Brazilian citizen. We will be holding her here until the interrogation team arrives. You better get your butt inside and start enjoying this beautiful day."

I remark, "Thanks brother," as I give Dolph a BIG hug before savoring my two-minute walk to the Young Veterans Brewery.

* * *

Back in Washington DC, a Sikorsky VH-3D Sea King helicopter with the call sign Marine One has already lifted off from the south lawn of 1600 Pennsylvania Ave NW. Onboard with Madam President and her Secret Service detail is the three-agency High-Value Interrogation Group. This includes the FBI, CIA and the Department of Defense (DOD). The team's leader is Special Agent Favitta and he's bringing along another agent-in-training, Special Agent Todd Rhea. The pilots from Marine Helicopter Squadron One are heading south/southeast and are one hour into their flight as they radio the Special Agent in charge of the Presidential Protective Division that they will be touching down in 10 minutes.

Before Marine One lifted off, Madam President's Secret Service detail had already locked down an entire 2 block radius around the Young Veterans Brewery and had been sitting back while the other agencies took down Monique/Sylvia. Now, with her out of the way it was time for them to shine. The field across the street from the brewery now had four Black SUV's and 16 agents in place. Shooters may have been out of sight, but all were on station, as the distinct sound of Marine One's rotors were growing louder.

Once I entered the brewery there seemed to be an attention shift as Charms yells, "Give that man, Sid the Kid, a green beer."

I looked for Marty, but she had all of her attention focused on her dance steps as DJ was spinning old 45's. I turned my attention back to Charms and said, "Thank you so much for letting Marty join in on this party."

As he's clinking his glass of good-luck green beer to mine he says, "She's your good luck charm, Sidney. I'm sure you know that. I've only known her for ten minutes and I already feel like I've known her my whole life. You're a lucky man!"

Before I even have a chance to talk to Rags, Skids, Oak, Buddha or DJ — in walks the President of the United States. Everything stops as all jaws drop. This is one surprise no one knew about...except for me. I'd just heard about it this morning while meeting Dolph and the agents outside of my bedroom door. They gave me a heads up about two women I'd be meeting today. I wasn't allowed to inform Marty about either.

With the room totally silent Madam President asks, "Which one of you is Charms?"

Master Chief Thomas O'Malley answers, "That would be me, Madam President."

"Well, Charms, I'd love a green beer please." The ICE was broken and the roof of the Young Veterans Brewing Company was almost lifted off of it's foundation, with the cheers from a few of America's finest patriots and fighters from SEAL Team Six. They all knew exactly what Madam President had recently done for our country. They knew she had given their team the green light to join this fight. She had faith in them to do their job and now she'd come to pay tribute and party with them — and they loved it!

Outside of the Young Veterans Brewing Company, Dolph was smiling as he was hearing all the cheering going on inside. He'd loved to have joined in, but he was on the job. After the transfer of Monique/Sylvia from the Sheriff Department to Special Agent Favitta, a Black SUV pulled up and Dolph opened the side door and helped Sylvia into the back seat before joining her. The interrogation team also entered the van before it took off, with a second Black SUV leading the way and a third picking up the rear. All three were on the road heading back to Washington, D.C. The interrogation team quickly ascertained that they needed an FBI team to be dispatched immediately to The Cavalier Beach Club and speak with the Bellman. He'd already delivered a package to our room that had arrived from an outside delivery service. A quick investigation by the feds showed Sylvia dropping off a wrapped present with a card to this delivery company. It read, *To Sidney and Marty...all is forgiven. Please enjoy, Leon Varres (the founder of Billionaire Vodka) ps. This is a gift from Bladislav Surkov (the Gray Cardinal himself) and Dmitry Utkin (the founder of Wagner Group).* A bomb unit was immediately called to the hotel which was quickly emptied and cordoned off. Another FBI team was then sent to Sylvia's hotel room in Virginia Beach, confiscating her laptop computer, cell phones, money and two weapons. Back inside the brewery Marty and I were having wonderful conversations with each member of the Master Chief's team. We soon moved on to speak with the President and then all the veterans that owned the brewery. It was truly a day neither of us would ever forget. It also seemed Madam President was enjoying a break from her role as commander-in-chief and was able to let her hair down (so to speak).

Madam President is looking at me from across the room and gestures for me to follow her. As she's walking to a vacated part of the room, she stops and says something to Master Chief O'Malley and he then begins following her. The three of us meet at a table and Madam President asks, "Please sit." A Secret Service Agent pulls out the President's chair and when she's seated, Charms and I take our seats.

The President smiles and remarks, "I'd like you both to join me on a trip to Minsk, Belarus, for the inauguration of President Sviatlana Tsikhanouskaya. Master Chief O'Malley, you and your SEAL team are all welcome to come, and Sidney...I'd love for you and the old "retired" PSYOP team to join us. All wives and girlfriends are welcome. The celebration of a new democratically elected leader in any part of the world is an enormously positive and refreshing statement to the world."

Among President Tsikhanouskaya's guests will be the BYPOL fighters who helped get you all off the ground from the Machulishchy Air Force Base, including the sisters Kira and Mira, along with the other two wounded BYPOL resistance fighters that you brought with you back from Ukraine for medical treatment.

Looking directly at me, Madam President begins speaking. "Mira and Kira have said that you promised to come visit them when their country was FREE! Well, Sidney...it's time to cash in that chip." We are all smiling as the President continues to speak, "Please give your team members the heads-up and we will finalize the dates. My private secretary, Caitlin, will be in touch." She then scoots her chair back and stands up, shakes our hands and walks right back to the bar, takes a seat and finishes off her green beer.

Like everything in life, this party had to come to an end. The President stood up and the brewery went quiet as everyone's attention shifted to her. As she speaks, she scans the room. "I can't thank you enough for all that you do for our country. America sleeps better each and every night because of you. Most may never know the sacrifices you make day in and day out. But make NO mistake...I know!" As she's patting her heart with her hand she continues, "You are in here 24/7. I want you to know that. I hope and pray for you each and every day. I will end by quoting Ralph Waldo Emerson: 'The only reward of virtue is virtue; the only way to have a friend is to be one.' The brotherhood and comradeship you share is your bond — that which brings you together for life and if I may say, a life well lived. God bless you all!"

With that, the cheers go up as each man and woman walk over to shake Madam President's hand and to say, "Thank you."

Outside you could already hear the Sikorsky VH-3D Sea King helicopter's engines warming up as her Secret Service detail is escorting Madam President out the door for her ride back to the south lawn of the White House. We are all outside waving to our President and as she's smiling out the window, she's waving back. As soon as the Sea King banks to starboard, we see five black SUVs queuing up. The moment the fifth vehicle is in line, the procession begins moving forward in an orderly fashion. Once they are out of sight, we all look at each other and wonder why things are so quiet. That is until we hear DJ putting on Buddha's favorite song by Lulu and everyone headed back inside for another green beer.

*   *   *

Fifteen minutes later, cellphones began buzzing and ringing. The U.S. Navy SEALs were established by President John F. Kennedy in 1962 as a small, elite maritime military force designed to operate in any environment, at any time. These highly trained teams are deployed throughout the world conducting some of our nation's most important missions. Half of our nations SEAL contingent is stationed in Virginia Beach. The Joint Expeditionary Base at Little Creek is home to Naval Special Warfare Group 2 and its SEAL Teams 2, 4 and 10. SEAL Team Eighteen, a reserve unit, and Special Warfare Group 4 are also located at Little Creek. The Naval Special Warfare Development Group (NSWDG), abbreviated as DEVGRU (Development Group) is the United States Navy component of the Joint Special Operations Command (JSOC). This unit is often referred to within JSOC as Task Force Blue – Better known as SEAL Team Six.

Master Chief O'Malley pulls the plug on DJ's musical soundboard and yells, "Listen up! All vehicles are to be left here. We will pick them up in ten! Hit the head and do what you need to do to get your acts together. DEVGRU is sending a vehicle for us from Dam Neck Annex. Make no mistake about it…*we are* Task Force Blue, and when we're called upon, we're ready to move out!"

"Hoorah Master Chief!" they reply in unison.

Marty and I quickly walk up to Charms to say our quick goodbyes. He hugged Marty and then took my hand and looked me straight in the eyes before saying, "I don't believe this is the last time we'll be seeing each other Sidney. Stay safe my friend." In a matter of minutes, it was just Marty, me and the staff at the brewery settling in for one last green beer. I asked one of the owners, "Does this happen often?"

She says, "Only once before. This is a very quick turnaround for these guys. I believe that could only mean that it's not only important, but they've already been brought up to speed on all of the particulars." That gave me pause to think about what the Master Chief just said to me.

Before Marty and I even finish our last green beer, in walks Biggin and Special Agent Jennings Sanders.

*   *   *

Chapter 27

Approximately 7,739 miles east, at the Wuhan Tianhe International Airport, two of Canada's latest version of their Bombardier Global aircraft — the 8000 series are being loaded on the tarmac. Bombardier Aviation is a division of Bombardier Inc. and their latest long-range jet is the fastest business jet in the world. With a price tag of $78 million each (before options) and a top speed of Mach 0.92, this long range, flex wing aircraft seats up to 19 including two crew members.

Onboard each aircraft today is one pilot and one passenger plus fifty boxes. Twenty-five boxes each holding 20 pounds of N-Phenethyl-4piperridinone (NPP) a derivative of 4-piperidinone with the molecular formula $C13H17NO$. It is used as an intermediate in the manufacture of chemicals and pharmaceutical drugs such as fentanyl. The other 25 boxes each carry 20 lbs of 4-nilino-N-phenethylipiperidine (4-ANPP), 4-aminophenyl-1-phenethylipeperidine, or despropionyl fentanyl, is a direct precursor to fentanyl and some fentanyl analogues such as acetylfentanyl.

One of these Bombardier Global 8000 jets is heading East to Culiacan, Sinaloa, Mexico and into the waiting hands of Ismael Zambada Garcia (aka El Mayo) the head of the Sinaloa Cartel. The second Global 8000 is also heading east, but to a small airstrip outside of Jalisco, Mexico. This is the home of the Jalisco (CJNG) Cartel (also known as Cartel Jalisco Nueva Generacion) and its head honcho Nemesio Ruben Oseguera Cervantes (aka El Mencho).

Both of these drug lords have heard from their Chinese counterparts that this could be the last load for some time because of a deal made between the two leaders of the U.S. and China. They also know that the Chinese leader, Xi Jinping, is very tired of being told what to do by the President of the United States. It seems his life can only be made whole when he knows he's undermining

America's democracy. That he's killing our children and thousands of American citizen by shipping fentanyl precursors to drug lords in Mexico never enters his equation.

*   *   *

Biggin orders a green beer but Agent Sanders puts out his hand in a way that signals the bartender, "No thank you." My guess is that he's driving.

Marty and I are escorted over to a quiet corner where the four of us take a seat. Agent Sanders begins by filling us in on the Monica/Sylvia story. This makes Marty's eyes grow quite large as she looks from Sanders to me before asking, "Did you know this?" Then shouting, "*YOU*, knew this...didn't you?"

I quickly fess up, "Yes dear! I was given the heads up by Dolph this morning. They weren't positive until Sylvia's living quarters were searched. The Bellman's information about a package being delivered to our room and the delivery service's video of Sylvia dropping off a package at the distribution center gave the FBI the probable cause needed for a search warrant. Once they knew for sure, my phone was pinged, giving me the heads up on Sylvia. I was always armed and we were never in danger." She may have rolled her eyes at me, but I believe its sinking in that Sylvia is an assassin, not her new BFF and that I had our backs the entire time.

Marty and I walk over say our goodbyes to the wonderful owners and staff at the Young Veterans Brewing Company. Then we head outside to join Biggin and Agent Sanders in the Black SUV they'd driven here to pick us up. On the drive back East, we learn that our living quarters were no longer at The Cavalier Beach Club. We were, once again, on our way to an FBI safe-house. This one is located on the outskirts of Virginia Beach. It seems that our package of Billionaire Vodka has caused quite a commotion at the beach club. Marty's only concern seems to be that we may never be invited back. That's probably a very valid point.

*   *   *

We must spend two days at our new safe haven while the powers that be let the dust settle, while at the same time making sure they've covered every angle of the Monica/Sylvia story. That's when Special Agent Sanders gives me the news, "The FBI bomb unit didn't find any explosives. However, their suspicions about Russian attacks range from the exotic — poisoned by drinking polonium-laced tea, or touching a deadly nerve agent. Or, the more mundane, that of being shot at close range, or taking a plunge from an open window and lately it seems air accidents are in play. Labs from Germany, France and Sweden can all confirm deaths attributed to Russia on a nerve agent known as Novichok and that's exactly what the FBI lab found in your Billionaire Vodka. Whether you inform Marty of this or not is up to you."

My jaw drops as I respond, "Thank you Agent Sanders...and NO we won't say a word of this to Marty. She's been using her free time to catch up on her HGTV shows. I'd like very much for her to stay in that world."

I've been using my free time to check in with my old PSYOP team members and seeing how everyone is doing, while at the same time letting them all know not to drink any Russian Vodka.

On our third morning at the safe-house we finally we get the all clear and are told to pack our stuff. Marty never really unpacked and she's all smiles as we're being driven to the Virginia Beach Airport. It's a private civilian airfield located in Pungo, Virginia, approximately four miles southeast of Virginia Beach. Our driver and bodyguards are our two handlers, Biggin and his half-brother Special Agent Jennings Sanders. On the way we make a stop at Starbucks so Marty can grab us something to eat on the plane. She orders two grande lattes and two turkey bacon and egg sandwiches. As we arrive at the airport, Special Agents Cash and Drake already have the engines warmed up as our black SUV pulls into a parking space and all four of us exit the vehicle.

Once again, we say our hellos to these two FBI pilots that are now dear friends of ours, before we all take our seats. Marty sarcastically asks, "So where to this time?" I smile because I already know the flight plan.

That's when Cash says, "We're taking you to your new home. Sidney hasn't told you yet?" The look on Marty's face said it all.

With a broad smile she asks, "WELL!?" I smile back...but I say nothing.

*   *   *

Chapter 28

Master Chief O'Malley and his team have boarded an MC-130J Commando II at an airbase somewhere in Virginia. This airplane flies all sorts of clandestine operations and can easily handle everything from low visibility to low-level infiltration, exfiltration and resupply for special operations forces. It intrudes into politically sensitive or hostile territories primarily on night missions with single or multiple aircraft.

With four Turboprop Rolls-Royce AE 2100D3 engines and a range of 3,000 miles, the crew of this Commando II is heading west-southwest on a heading that will include two different drop zones along the Pacific Coast of Mexico.

This aircraft's crew consists of two pilots, one combat systems officer and two loadmasters — all are from the 160th Special Operations Aviation Regiment (Airborne). The Night Stalkers call Fort Campbell, Kentucky, home. The 160th SOAR possesses the best-qualified aviators, crew members and support personnel in the Army. The six SEALs try to relax and get some shut-eye during their six and a half-hour flight.

Buddha loves to witness the refueling process and had one of the loadmasters wake him up the second that these two aircraft began exchanging radio chat. With the Boeing KC-135 Stratotanker ten minutes out, Buddha was already on his way to the cockpit. The KC-135 was the United States Air Force's first jet-powered refueling tanker and was initially tasked with refueling strategic bombers. She can take off at a gross weight of 322,500 pounds.

The pilot and co-pilot both make room for Buddha to join them. Although some veteran pilots may be accustomed to the practice of jet fuel transference, it's never routine or easy. Aerial refueling remains one of the most difficult maneuvers in aviation, but it's also the key to many successful U.S. military operations.

No one knows why, but to Buddha there's something Zen-like to witnessing the transfer of aviation fuel from one aircraft to another. This transfer is done 30 minutes before the SEALs have to make their exit. This refueling will give the Commando II aircraft enough fuel for her return trip back to home base. When the transfer has concluded and Buddha has returned to join the team, Master Chief O'Malley is looking over at his brothers in arms as he says, "We've been over this plan many times. Once again, our country has asked us to take care of some unfinished business. This is what we do and we do it better than anyone. DJ and Oak will be out the door first with me. Buddha, you, Rags and Skids will be moving on to drop zone two. We get in and set up the lasers and then hump to our respective perches along the mountain range. Easy in and out...stay alert and watch your six!"

With that being said they all hear the crew chief yell, "Green light in five." All the SEALs stand and begin checking each other's equipment before the Master Chief takes his spot at the rear of the MC-130J and the senior airman loadmaster from the 160th Special Operations Aviation Regiment lowers the ramp. The light turns green and Charms, DJ and Oak walk the plank and drop into the darkness. Thirty minutes later Buddha, Rags and Skids take the same walk.

The first problem arises rather quickly. Skids experiences a parachute malfunction right out of the box and is immediately forced to separate himself from it. He keeps his cool and does his cutaway (the act of getting rid of the main canopy). He pulls the handle on the right of his belly and watches as the main chute swiftly disappears. He then pulls the left handle which deploys his reserve. Now he's on a different trajectory from Rags and Buddha. This was a HAHO jump (high altitude high opening) because the winds were perfect for the team to float and guide themselves to their targeted landing site. Skids knows he's way off track for that. He also knows he'll never hear the end of it from Buddha or Rags, but at least he'll be alive to tell the tale.

226

*   *   *

Two hours after takeoff, Marty's and my Gulfstream V is touching down 1,102 miles away at the Great Inagua Airport in Matthew Town, Bahamas. Inagua is the southernmost island in the Bahamas and actually consists of two separate islands, Great Inagua Island and Little Inagua Island. This is where Stacy Cellars and her HGTV Island Homes film crew were visiting when Marty was watching the show back at the safe-house in Anchorage, Alaska. On that particular show, some folks from North Carolina were making the move to this 596 square mile island. I wasn't fond of the home they chose, but I was totally in love with the house they discarded. It was on the ocean, beautifully landscaped and right in my price range. Marty thought she was in a dream when Stacy Cellars met our airplane. However, there were no cameras and no film crew allowed... just tranquility! Ms. Cellars smiled at Marty and said, "Hello Marty. It's a pleasure to finally meet you. Your house is fully furnished, as per your request. I believe you're going to love your new home. I am so grateful that you've given me the chance to do all the furnishing for you." Marty, of course, has no idea what Ms. Cellars is talking about. All of this was taken care of by Caitlin, Madam President's private secretary, who's always been into interior design and conspired with me to take on this project.

Marty thanks Stacy and quickly walks over to me and with a wrinkle in her brow whispers, "Do you know what she's talking about?"

I smile and reply, "I sure do. I'll tell you later. Just play along and enjoy yourself. We're following her to our new home."

*   *   *

The second Skids' feet touch the ground, he instantly goes to his knees and kisses it. He then activates his secure comms to quickly communicate with Buddha, "Cozen one...this is Cozen three...you copy?"

227

He hears, "One...go."

"Lost my main and had to improvise." Buddha smiles continuing, "Knew something went wrong when you blew past me. I've got your signal. It's strong... you're about a mile north on the opposite side of the target. Now put that gadabout gene of yours away and get over here posthaste."

"10-4...I've just picked up your signal. On my way!"

As Skids is burying his secondary chute, he hears kids talking and thinks to himself, "What kids are out at 2 AM and hanging around a drug filled warehouse?" He quietly sends a message to Buddha that he must go silent as he turns off his radio and stealthily heads in the direction of the voices. He's been trained not to assume anything but he thinks he's witnessing Mexican children possibly being used by the cartel to package drugs. That's when someone tugs on his uniform and asks, "¿Acabas de caer del cielo?" (Did you just fall from the sky?)

Skids replies, "Si!"

The young boy asks, "¿Eres americano, sí? ¿Viniste a salvarnos?"

Skids has to think about that question. *You are American...Yes? Did you come to save us?* Skids can't believe he didn't see this kid standing so close by. He's thinking to himself, *I could be dead right now.* Then he turns to this youngster and says, "Sí. Soy americano. ¿Hablas inglés?"

The young boy answers, "Yes, Mr. American. I study the English language at the orphanage. We all do."

Skids asks, "Are some of your friends from the orphanage inside this warehouse?"

228

"Si…I mean, yes Mr. American."

Skids asks his new friend, "What's your name?"

The young lad replies, "Pablo."

The SEAL responds, "My name is Skids. Come with me," as they both put 50 yards between themselves and the warehouse before Skids turns his comms back on, "Cozen-1 - we've got a problem!"

Once Skids explains the situation to Buddha all he hears is, "Shit!" then some deep thoughtful breathing before Cozen-1 continues, "Keep the kid, stay out of sight and I'll get back to you ASAP."

Skids replies, "10-4. Cozen-3 out."

Buddha (Cozen-1) immediately contacts Master Chief O'Malley (Delude-1) and lays open this brand new can of worms. Charms remarks, "Tell Skids to make his laser operational at his end of the warehouse. You stay on schedule and I'll get back to you after I contact Shockwave."

At the HQ JOC or Joint Command Center for this mission, the call from the Master Chief is put on speaker. When he's finished, Shockwave is shaking his head before loudly saying, "The intel on this mission left a lot to be desired. We're now in a new planning mode people and this clock is quickly ticking to zero. We have men in harm's way. We have approximately forty children working in our kill zone and we have an orphanage in play. This is a massive puzzle people and I need it put together quickly. Tick-tock…tick-tock."

Then the admiral (known on this mission as Shockwave) is back on secure comms, "Listen up Master Chief…you stay on your timeline. You leave Cozen-1, 2 and 3 in place for now. We're working the problem. Target package at both sites stays the same."

Charms responds with, "10-4 Shockwave."

With a CIA officer on staff and almost every major problem solver in the U.S. Government's arsenal in this room, they quickly get down to work. The CIA officer on staff was sent here specifically by Madam President. Her codename is "Maya" but her reputation as the best enigmatologist proceeds her. Ms. Alfreda Frances Bikowsky was part of the female team of CIA intelligence analysts dubbed "The Sisterhood" — better known as the ladies who took down Osama bin Laden. Knowing that time was of the essence, this team quickly and methodically laid out the problems and then worked each one toward a solution. In no specific order they put down. 1. Safety and or transport of everyone at the Guadalajara Orphanage. At the same time an intelligence analyst is given the job to quickly and systematically check out the Monsignor and his staff for any cartel involvement and how the orphanage is funded, etc., 2. One MH-47 Chinook must be on standby to retrieve the children working at the drug cartel's warehouse and where and when to move them for exfiltration. Another MH-47 is on standby in close proximity 3. When does the children's shift end? Who takes over for them? How do they arrive at this warehouse and at what time?

They all know that the warehouses are the second part of this SEAL team's mission and that they cannot show their hand to the cartel before phase one is complete. That would jeopardize the collective goals that have been set up by Madam President and the Joint Chiefs for this mission from its inception.

It is now 4 AM in Jalisco, Mexico, and the Global 8000 aircraft is due to land at this cartel's airfield in this sector of the Sierra Madre Occidental Mountain Range at approximately 9 AM. A five hour window means getting some assets in place immediately whether you use them or not. So, Ms. Bikowsky finds the Admiral and fills him in on the team's first decision, "We recommend deploying two MH-47 Chinook choppers on station at once and that both should employ SEAL teams."

The Admiral smiles and says, "That's kind of what I had in mind, only with slight modifications." The order is quickly given. Both the Admiral and Ms. Bikowsky know that each MH-47 can hold up to 100 people. No matter what — this should cover any and all EVAC situations. It will also put much needed firepower on the ground. Once this phase one is complete, they should (hopefully) have a variable window with which to work.

Charms, DJ and Oak have their lasers operational and have commandeered a vehicle from the city streets of Culiacan and are heading to their post in the Sierra Madre Occidental Mountains high above and a few miles away from Culiacan. This is where they will wait for phase one of the operation to begin.

Further south in Jalisco, Buddha and Rags have also reallocated some wheels but must wait for further orders from higher up the food chain. Buddha has already made sure Shockwave received the intel that the children are relieved at 9 AM. There are two adult supervisors watching these kids and there is usually no radio or phone contact during this shift, however, the supervisors do have access to both. Pablo also let Skids know that the next shift is adult males who arrive at 9 AM and are bussed in from Jalisco. That's when Buddha's radio comes back to life.

The specialized team at HQ JOC or Joint Command Center has come up with a number of solid mission recommendations, "Cozen-1 – this is Shockwave."

"Cozen-1 go."

"MH-47 with two teams will arrive soon, four clicks from your location. This MH will stay onsite and you'll have another one in your back pocket. Cozen-3 (Skids) must neutralize the two bogies before the backup arrives. When they arrive, you and Cozen-2 (Rags) fall back for phase one. Any questions?"

"Negative sir. Cozen-1 out."

As soon as Skids receives his orders from Buddha, he knows what has to be done before the team arrives, but he's also smiling as he thinks to himself, "Now at least I will have someone watching my six who's armed and over the age of nine."

*   *   *

Fifteen minutes later an MH-47 Chinook has landed four clicks from Buddha's position. The second the Crew Chief drops the exit ramp, out jumps six Christini AWD 450 custom military motorbikes followed closely by three Polaris MRZR 4 ATVs, each of these are equipped with an M240 belt-fed machine gun mounted on the rear. The six SEALs driving the Christinis are heading for the warehouses while the other six SEALs are in pairs of two (one driver and one gunner) on their way to secure the orphanage.

When the military motorbikes arrive, Buddha is on the comms to Skids."Cavalry has arrived. Is the coast clear on your end?

Skids responds, "10-4 all clear!"

Buddha advises Skids, "I'm sending you a special gift. You take good care of her. Use her wisely and may the force be you young Jedi."

Skids wonders what the hell Buddha's talking about and how can he change personalities from being Buddha to being Yoda? Still he answers back, "Thank you Jedi Master! All gifts are welcome."

232

Skids quickly becomes aware of the motorbikes closing in on his position and soon finds out what his gift is. Buddha has sent his Remmington custom-built M-40 rifle named Lulu along with a message, "You know what to do with her young Jedi!" Skids smiles while shaking his head.

While Skids is handing over the two adult supervisors from the warehouse, he explains to the newly arrived SEAL team leader Chief Petty Officer Carroll, "These two are full of information as he points to the two zip-tied adults who were watching the night shift kids. They are not really cartel members...just making enough money to feed their families. They may be way down on the cartel's food chain but they gave me these." As Skids is handing over two computers he continues, "All the warehouse comms are decommissioned. The kids are ready to move out and Pablo here (as he looks at his young friend and smiles) will take care of any language barriers as needed." As Skids is looking at his new ride he continues, "I need to borrow one of those."

As Skids slings Lulu over his shoulder, he hits the gas and is quickly changing gears as he speeds off just as the morning twilight is beginning the illumination process.

The captain of the MH-47 Chinook receives a radio call that the orphanage has been secured. Lieutenant Colonel Buckley gets on the internal comms and says, "New plan...stay alert. We're backing up the SEAL team at the orphanage and readying everyone for EXFIL." With that command, the MH-47 lifts off and banks to starboard.

* * *

Skids has orders to put fifteen miles between him and the warehouse. With his military motorcycle neatly camouflaged in the bushes, he knows his next orders were less direct...have a clear shot of one mile if possible...one shot and get out! His cover and concealment are more than adequate for this assignment and his target will soon be on approach. Skids is in the prone position and enjoys a clear line of sight, that is until two vehicles are approaching and neither one of them is a bus. Skids remembers that Pablo distinctly told him this road is rarely used by local traffic, so he stays in position and will let this play itself out.

Skids uses his Bespoke titanium 20X50X70mm scope to zoom in on the occupants of the two vehicles as they pass 40 yards to his right. He then keys his mic, "Cozen-1 this is three over."
"Go three."

"Two vehicles, four occupants each, all armed heading your way."

"10-4...stay on station."

"10-4."

Skids repositions himself just as he sees his target sauntering down the road in his direction. He readies himself quickly and readjusts his scope, chambers a 260 caliber Remington round loaded to 60,000 psi and takes aim. Two-seconds later, with the simple pull of the trigger, the radiator and engine block of the bus that was transporting the 9 AM cartel employees is engulfing the morning sky with hot steam. This engine will never run again.

With his mission complete, Skids folds up his tripod, rieslings his weapon and mounts his Christini AWD 450 custom military motorbike. Before he has time to start his engine he hears Buddha, "Cozen-3...this is one."

"Go one."

"Thanks for the heads up. All neutralized at the orphanage."

Skids smiles before keying his mic, "Bus negated. Lulu did her job."

Like a proud father Buddha says, "10-4...meet us at rendezvous point."

"10-4...Cozen-3 is en route."

With those words, Skids starts his motorbike, hits the gas and shifts the gears knowing that any loss of innocent life at the warehouses will be close to zero. He continues on his way to meet back up with Cozen one and two. Their destiny awaits atop the mountains of the Sierra Madre Occidental Mountain Range where Cozen 1, 2 and 3 will have a new call sign — Bombardier Two.

*   *   *

Chapter 29

Outside of the Mexican City of Culiacan, on the Pacific slopes of the Sierra Madre Occidental Mountain Range, lies a team of American frogmen. With their long distance, high-powered infrared telescope, they've been keeping a close eye on the members of the Sinaloa Cartel at the cartel's favorite drug smuggling landing site. It's a small and very well camouflaged runway they've created at the base of the mountain range. Things at the site have been buzzing over the past few hours and finally, these frogmen have the sighting they've been waiting for. The solid gold, custom built, four-door Mercedes belonging to the world's most wanted man, El Mayo, is sending up dust from the dirt road a few miles from his cartel's clandestine airfield. That's when the SEAL team's radio comes to life, "Bombardier one, this is bombardier two...are we a, go, over."

"10-4 bombardier two! Glad you could join the party. Globals are inbound shortly. Do you have eyes on El Mencho?"

"10-4 bombardier one! He's onsite."

About 427 miles south of bombardier one, on the same 700-mile-long mountain range, is bombardier two. That is the code name given to the other three members of this same Blue team. They are perched and neatly blending into the mountain-side quite a few miles outside of Jalisco, Mexico. Both teams know that 25,000 feet above them are two General Atomics MQ-9 Reaper drones. These remotely piloted aircraft employ 8 laser-guided (air-to-ground) AGM-114 Hellfire missiles that possess highly accurate, low collateral damage, anti-armor, anti-personnel, heavy blast fragmentation warheads.

The MQ-9 Reaper is a modified Predator drone that is 27 feet long with a wingspan of 49 feet. Updated with external fuel tanks, they are capable of holding 1,300 pounds of fuel. This provides for greater station time and further range. This modification also adds an extra blade to the propeller. The Reaper is employed primarily as an intelligence-collection asset and secondarily against dynamic execution targets. Given its significant loiter theme, wide-range sensors, multi-mode communications to her primary satellite link and precision weapons, this unmanned vehicle is perfect for today's mission.

*　　*　　*

Creech Air Force Base, in Clark County, Nevada, is the home of the United States Air Force (USAF) command and control facility of remotely piloted aircraft systems which fly missions across the globe. In addition, this military installation has the Unmanned Aerial Vehicle Battlelab, associated aerial warfare ground equipment and unmanned aerial vehicles.

Unmanned aircraft systems operators are trained intelligence specialists who provide information on enemy forces and battle areas. The basic crew consists of a rated pilot (officer) to control the aircraft and command the mission and an enlisted aircrew member to operate sensors and guide weapons. To meet combatant commanders' requirements, the Reaper delivers tailored capabilities using mission kits containing various weapons and sensor payload combinations. These men and women are also skilled in conducting air reconnaissance, surveillance, targeting missions and analyzing aerial photographs.

Before any mission begins, there is a concept of operations (CONOPS) which is the foundation upon which the United States military puts together a unifying strategy for aligning Operational Contract Support (OCS). These include joint, interagency, intergovernmental and multinational partners to improve the effectiveness, efficiency and use of contracts and all contractors during contingencies. They play key roles in ensuring the proper integration and synchronization of contracted support into all military operations.

From inside the command center at Creech Air Force Base, a USAF sergeant code-named Joy Stick takes the secure comms. "Joy Stick to bombardier one and two...do you read me over."

"10-4 one."

"10-4 two."

"One...your bird Jayhawk is hot. Two...your bird Hornet is hot. Globals are inbound to both locations — approximately five minutes out." Jayhawk and Hornet are the code-names for the two MQ-9s.

This mission had been on the drawing board for months. Madam President knew that President Xi of China had no plans to stop sending the fentanyl analogues to the cartels. She also knows that the Mexican President, Andrés Manuel López Obrador, though a decent man, has no control over the drug cartels operating within his borders. For that reason, she has America's Mexican Ambassador inside President Obrador's office as they both wait for a phone call that will only come when the AGM-114 Hellfire missiles are being launched.

*   *   *

While all this action is taking place in South America, back in the Bahamas, Bahamian real estate agent Stacy Cellars' vehicle stops near the anterior of a beautiful beach front home and she exits her car. As she is walking back to our vehicle, the smile on her face broadens. Biggin exits the passenger front seat and opens Marty's door. Special Agent Sanders never moves, so I guess I'll have to get my own door. The excitement on Marty's face says it all as Stacy calmly says, "I hope you'll like the clean lines, muted tones and the combination of natural and man-made materials. I used some of Frank Lloyd Wright's ideas and I hope you'll like them. They include vibrant colors, graphic shapes and integrating indoor and outdoor motifs. Your new home came without a name, so Sidney wanted to add character and show affection to the place you will now call home. So, to define its identity he named her ATLASTARCADIA." As Stacy is saying our new home's name, she's also pulling off the cover that displays the name over our new mid-century modern front door.

While Stacy and Marty are entering our new home, Biggin is walking me over to the car and signals for me to take Marty's old seat in the back. This is when Agent Sanders turns around and hands me a sealed manila envelope containing a box before he says, "Be very careful when you open this." I take the envelope and tear it open and let the box fall into my hand. It's taped shut and before I can say a word, Biggin is handing me a knife already opened. Then he says, "Hurry up already...we've been wanting to know what we've been carrying around these past few days. The FBI director gave this to Jennings with a smirk on his face saying it came from way up the food chain."

I cut the tape and lift the lid. My eyes begin to squint before going wide open with a look of disbelief. "What the hell is this? Are these diamonds?"

Inside the manila envelope is a note. I hand it to Special Agent Jennings Sanders and he begins reading..."These white diamonds were encrusted on the 5-liter bottle that was sent to you by Billionaire Vodka. We've had them counted and appraised. There are 3,000 white diamonds and each one is between 2 and 3 carats. Our government gemologist says the term 'white diamond' is used in the diamond jewelry industry when referring to standard transparent, colorless diamonds. This means that the presence of sub-microscopic inclusions will scatter the light passing through the diamond, giving it a translucent milky-white face-up appearance, sometimes described as "opalescent." Agent Sanders smiles at me as he continues..."None of these diamonds are blood diamonds and all of them were sent to you. As far as the United States government is concerned...*they* are yours. Our gemologist has appraised their value at anywhere from $5 to $8 million dollars!" With that, the three of us begin rocking the car with laughter.

*   *   *

While we're laughing and counting diamonds, 2,482 miles due west in the Sierra Madre Occidental Mountain Range, there are two Global 8000 private jets putting down their respective landing gears. It's "show time" for the Navy SEALs and their adrenaline is at its peak. "Bombardier one... has El Mayo arrived yet?"

"Negative two. However, vehicle is on approach."

"10-4."

"Bombardier one to Joy Stick..."

"Joy Stick...go"

"El Mayo's vehicle is on approach. Give us one minute."

"That's all you get Bombardier one. Window closes."

"10-4."

Within the 60 second window allotted, Bombardier one says, "We seem to have all bogies on site. The vehicle with El Mayo is hidden in trees, but believed to be inside the perimeter."

With that being said, from the HQ Joint Operations Center, an Air Force JAG officer radios the all clear to the Air Force Sergeant code-named Joy Stick who radios "Bombardier one and two...light em up as the MQ-9 Predator named Jayhawk sends one AGM-114 Hellfire missile on its way. Seconds later, outside of

Jalisco, the Predator named Hornet sends a single missile whose laser rangefinder quickly targets the laser guided munition. As soon as both missiles' cameras zoom in, it's only seconds before the SEALs witness catastrophic explosions at both locations. On the off chance the cartels didn't get the message — a second Hellfire missile from both drones is sent in. The second explosion, outside of Jalisco, sets off secondary explosions sending plumes of smoke high into the sky.

*   *   *

At this very same moment, U.S. Ambassador Petty receives a phone call from the White House and she quickly says, "Yes Ma'am" then hangs up the phone. She turns and looks at President Obrador before saying, "Mr. President I have an urgent message for you from Madam President."

*   *   *

Bombardier one states, "Zero movement on-site."

Bombardier two quickly chimes in, "Zero movement. Total devastation!"

"10-4 Bombardier one and two! We will redirect Jayhawk and Hornet to their secondary targets. Great job! Always nice working with you...safe travels."

Bombardier one quickly breaks in, "Hold one, Joy Stick. We have a single vehicle leaving site."

Joy Stick says, "10-4 Bombardier one, Jayhawk is tracking." Seconds later, "We've got 'em... a gold Mercedes kicking up lots of dust."

"10-4 Joy Stick! That's El Mayo's custom-built car!"

241

"10-4 Bombardier one! Just for your benefit, I want you to know that of the eight missiles on each Predator, only seven are HE high-explosive rounds. We added one R9X Hellfire to both drones just in case a situation like this arouse and we needed to make a very clear statement. Jayhawk has acquired the target and the R9X is inbound."

The R9X Hellfire is a variant with a kinetic warhead. Inside conventional warheads are high explosives, but this missile pierces and cuts its target rather than blowing it up. At 6 feet long and weighing 100 pounds, this missile has six 18-inch blades that pop out of its midsection seconds before impact. They can slice through most anything in their path. Its operational laser seeker is used against specific human targets and usually sends a very loud and clear message to whomever discovers the remains. The X was added to this missile's name during the experimental phase but the experiment ended when this missile worked just fine while taking out Ayman al-Zawahiri on the balcony of his safe-house in Kabul on August 2, 2022. Better known in military circles as the AGM-114 R9X, the Hellfire R9X is known to cause minimum collateral damage while engaging individual targets. The X stayed in place.

Joy Stick watches the video all the way to impact before cuing his mic, "Bombardier one and two...phase one complete. With a worldwide bounty of $15 million on his head, it seems that Mr. El Mayo has just been turned into ketchup. Moving on to target two."

With that information from Joy Stick, both teams remotely turn on their respective laser dots. These will guide the pilot and drones to their secondary targets.

At the warehouse locations, each three-member SEAL team had set up lasers. These missiles will only be looking for the exact color of light that their laser is using. By being blind to all other light, the laser reflection is extremely bright. The laser also sends a special pulse sequence and each missile understands which bright blinking light is theirs. At launch, they don't line up precisely. They must find their light and just steer in the general direction. As it gets closer it can resolve the dot a lot better. It probably never hits the dot directly but it never matters if it's an inch or two on either side...that's because the explosion is disastrous.

While Joy Stick is commanding Jayhawk and Hornet to their secondary targets, Bombardier one and two are quickly packing up their gear and disappearing down their respective mountainous western slopes. Each team will be swiftly moving to the Pacific shoreline. This is where their extraction out to sea will take place. The Special Activities Center (SAC) is a division of the United States CIA and they are responsible for covert and paramilitary operations. Two teams are on the Pacific coastline waiting to transport the SEALs out to a waiting SSN-774 class nuclear-powered fast attack submarine. The Virginia-class subs are designed for a broad spectrum of open-ocean and littoral missions, including anti-submarine warfare and intelligence gathering operations. Today they will be picking up "door kicking frogmen."

While the SEALs are in transit to the coast, the MQ-9 Predators named Jayhawk and Hornet are closing in on both cartels' processing warehouses. These warehouses aren't just where they process fentanyl for U.S. distribution, it's also where they process and package tons of cocaine. There will be no collateral damage (loss of life) at the Jalisco warehouses, thanks to Skid's single shot.

This is where Joy Stick has orders to fire all remaining missiles from both drones into these massive 200,000 square-foot warehouse complexes. It seems that Madam President wants to make it abundantly clear to all parties involved that if this is the game you want to play, then from now on, this will always be the outcome.

*　　*　　*

Chapter 30

Marty and I have spent thirty wonderful days turning ATLASTARCADIA into our home. That means I'm hanging pictures, as well as everything else that comes under the umbrella we men call "The Honey Do List." Taking out the recycling and garbage is just our added bonus that we all take for granted.

With a Captain Morgan and ginger beer in one hand, I answer the satellite phone with my other. "Well, hello Charms. I've been hoping to hear from you. It's my humble opinion that your team may have been responsible for a few explosions down Mexico way."

I can tell the Master Chief is all smiles by his remark, "I *could* tell you, but then I'd have to kill you and I certainly don't want to do that Mr. Krogh." We both laugh as he continues…"It took me quite some time to get permission to even acquire your sat-phone number. The network guarding you is more secure than those protecting the Hope diamond. Speaking of which…my men and I want to thank you for your generous donations into our newly acquired safety deposit boxes. What is this all about?"

I reply, "Do you remember back at the Machulishchy airbase as we were getting ready to land our Russian Ilyushin Il-112 V - Military Transport Aircraft and out of nowhere we received a radio message telling us which runway to use and then where to taxi? After we landed, I had one question for you. How the hell did you know we were heading here…and how we were getting here…or when we'd arrive? All you said to me was…'That's a story for another day.' Well, that sir is my answer to you now. That being said, I wanted each of you to have 20 diamonds. They were a gift to me and I wanted to spread them around to those I felt were the most deserving. They are yours free and clear…a gift for you and each of your teammates. Please tell Buddha, Oak, DJ, Rags and Skids it's been a pleasure doing business with them and I hope to join all of you someday soon for a cold green beer."

Charms replies, "Looks like you'll be able to tell them yourself. Did you get a call from Madam President's secretary Caitlin?"

"Yes, I have! We will all be on the flight to Belarus. Are you all able to join us?"

"We have been given orders from Joint Special Operations Command to report to Presidential Airlift Group at Andrews Air Force Base for a six day Temporary Duty (TDY). We look forward to some peaceful time together Mr. Krogh. See you all next week."

In the meantime, very secure packages of diamonds were also sent out to Hulk, Big Al, Pistol Pete and Cathy (Whoman's wife). They were hand-carried by Biggin, so I knew in advance they'd all arrive safely. Speaking of Biggin, he received eleven diamonds which is one more than I gave his half-brother Special Agent Jennings Sanders.

The extra diamond was for services rendered. Biggin had set up the safety deposit boxes for the SEALs as well as traveling to four different states to deliver boxes to my old PSYOP team members. He then made sure FBI pilots Drake and Cash received a couple each.

After those deliveries, Biggin made a trip back home to New Orleans transporting sparkling stones for Chucci and Captain Hal as well as Chucci's dad and gramps. More on that later...

Biggin also flew up to Anchorage, Alaska, to visit Ross Brown and Police Chief Wayne and his wife Nita. That trip was also a delivery mission. They've all been given our satellite phone number and have already called to say thanks! Chief Wayne and Nita will be coming to the island for a two week visit this summer.

Marty and I couldn't be happier about that. I'd made a phone call to Tony and Helen in Hawaii and told them Marty and I had moved to the island of Great Inagua in the Bahamas and that I'd purchased a wonderful bar on the beach of Matthew Town called Cepigel. (16)

At least when I bought it, that was its name — now it's called Hidden Gem. I made Tony and Helen an offer they couldn't refuse. They'd own half of the Hidden Gem and they'd be in charge of all the music. I'd purchase them a home and they'd have a deed for their house and the half ownership in the Hidden Gem.

They arrive next week.

(16) Book Series I - *Hypersomnolence.* Tony and Helen drove with me across the United States on my way to Whittier, Alaska. They later moved on to Hawaii where they rejoined the story.

Epilogue

Over the past six months, Tony and Helen have settled into the Bahamian lifestyle and their island music has the Hidden Gem packed and rocking every night. People come from all over Great Inagua to dine in the establishment. Word has gotten out to quite a few Miamians. It seems a lot of fishermen and women have spread the word that the Hidden Gem has the best cocktails, food and island music to be found anywhere in the Caribbean.

Though Marty and I have been sequestered on the island of Great Inagua, we've stayed in touch with the entire group we call family. Ms. Alfreda Frances Bikowsky, retired Special Agent Bennye Wolfe and Monica Wynnie are part of that family and though they had to be coaxed into visiting us on the island, the three women left with beautiful, sparkly bracelets designed by Marty. It seems "Designed by Marty" is the name of my gal's new jewelry store. She has quite a knack for stringing beads and seashells and then displaying them on beautiful selections of driftwood brought over from Little Inagua Island.

Chucci's grandfather (Gramps) came up with the idea of building a retirement and homeless veterans community shelter outside New Orleans. A local veteran's group in New Orleans is having the plans drawn up and the sparkling rocks that will be used to fund this project are in a safety deposit box at BankPlus Veterans Branch in Metairie, LA.

Hulk, Big Al and Pistol Pete will be joining us for a reunion this summer. All wives are included this time. They are proven warriors and we want to see how they are at fishing and drinking. Cathy (Whoman's wife) has promised to attend and we always look forward to spending time with her. Monica Wynnie didn't need coaxing back to the island to join us at this reunion. She was overwhelmed with joy knowing she'd be seeing all of us in one peaceful place in order to enjoy this awesome group.

It took us quite a while to get back in touch with Dolph Coley. He'd been out of the country disposing of bad guys, I guess. With some R&R coming up, he's promised to come spend a week with us and he can't wait to go fishing off of Great Inagua. He has no idea that he owns a house here and that his Hatteras GT45X is waiting for him at his dock.

Dmitry Utkin, the founder of Wagner Group, died very mysteriously when his aircraft fell from the sky.

Leon Verres, the pioneer mastermind behind Billionaire Vodka, Champagne and Cologne, was found to be nothing more than a billionaire businessman. His super-yacht Milliarder Vodka was used without his permission. The super-yacht had to be taken to dry dock at the North Florida Shipyard, Inc. in Mayport Naval Station for her screws (propeller system) to be de-slimed. The secretion from the hagfish coated the screws to prevent the super-yacht's propulsion system from scooping water which left her screws rotating uselessly in place. It took a couple of days for the shipyard workers, using a salt solution to remove all the slime, to get the super-yacht's propulsion system back into working order. It was then returned to its owner, Mr. Verres, who is presently in search of a new captain for his super-yacht.

Word got to me by way of the CIA director that Leon Verres was sending me a bottle of Billionaire Vodka, however there won't be any diamonds attached to the bottle. He just wanted me to be able to sit back and enjoy his creation. He'd heard from the CIA director that I'd received a poisoned bottle of his Billionaire Vodka which left a bad taste in his mouth. The bottle will be sent to the CIA director and then on to me. He was also very sorry to hear that his name had been brought into such a negative state.

Though sequestered, I'd received a call from Master Chief O'Malley to join the gang for some green beer. So Marty and I surreptitiously snuck off of Great Inagua and into Virginia Beach. There we made our way to the Young Veterans Brewery Company.

This is where we reminisced about our fabulous six days in Minsk, Belarus, a few weeks earlier. Flying on Air Force One is quite the experience. Having Marty, Kitty, Linda, Candy and Whoman's wife Cathy with us was out of this world. Talk about dreams...we were in one. All of the SEALs wives were able to join the party and Madam President made sure each and every one of us had everything we needed.

On the flight over, while all the ladies were bonding, Pistol Pete, Big Al, Hulk and I were able to hear some of the stories about the taking down of the two Mexican cartels and their fentanyl labs. Then we heard about the gun battle that went on when two vehicles loaded with cartel killers arrived at the Guadalajara Orphanage. The MH-47 was just touching down to remove the orphans along with the Monsignor and his staff when bullets started flying. The only American injured during this entire operation was Lieutenant Colonel Buckley, the pilot of the Chinook. He was hit in the left shoulder as he was landing the MH-47. This second team of SEALs had to be flown in because of intel received from Skids. This intel may have never happened had his parachute not malfunctioned. The reinforcement team of SEALs opened up with their M-240 belt-fed machine guns mounted on their jeeps and the battle was over in an instant...no enemy survivors. The Master Chief told us that while that battle was going on, he, DJ and Oak were packing their gear and traversing down the western slope of the Sierra Madre Occidental Mountain Range and heading for the coastline to their extraction point. The same exact thing was happening a few hundred miles to their south with Buddha, Skids and Rags.

Upon our arrival into Minsk National Airport, Air Force One was given the "Red Carpet" treatment. A Belarusian military band played *The Star Spangled Banner* as Madam President exited her aircraft. We were all still seated in the rear of the plane and watched as the two leaders shook hands and then embraced. As soon as their stretch limousines departed, we were escorted off and put into black SUVs and taken to the Minsk Marriott Hotel located on the beautiful Svislach River. This is also where the BYPOL freedom fighters were staying.

We quickly learned why the place seemed so empty. The entire hotel was all ours for the next few days. Our rooms included the Hospitality, Premium, Luxury and Presidential Suites. Guess which category Marty and I took? A note in each room stated that we must be ready at 6 pm MSK time and meet in the Fornello Restaurant.

It would be our first night with the Belarusian freedom fighters and our entire band of brothers. What a night it was! I hardly recognized Mira and Kira. They looked beautiful...as did all the ladies. To say we all enjoyed our time together would be an understatement.

The Spa would pamper the ladies with massages, stone therapy and beauty treatments (as if they needed that). We all enjoyed the Falcon Club Fitness Center, indoor swimming pool and 24 hour room service.

At our second evening's dinner party, we were joined by two Madam Presidents. We could tell ahead of time that something was happening because the security personnel at the hotel had tripled in size rather quickly. Both women gave wonderful speeches and handed out awards.

All in all, it was the most extraordinary time in my life and I'm sure I can speak for everyone there.

The flight back to Andrews Air Force Base was calm and mellow as we all seemed to be cherishing our memories.

Upon landing, we said our goodbyes. We hugged each other and knew we'd shared a special bond. Over the past week, each and every member of Blue Team had taken me aside and thanked me personally for their safety deposit box and its contents. In most cases, handing out sparkling rocks is a great way to make friends, but you can't buy *these* guys off. Our friendship is real and it's for life! The Master Chief has been invited to visit us at the island. He says there will come a day when he'll have to hang up his wetsuit and when that day comes, he'll be in touch.

The Monsignor and his staff at the Guadalajara Orphanage were cleared of any wrong doing. It seems they were under constant threat of death if they had resisted in letting the orphans do the slave labor for the cartel. We've since learned that over the past eight months of this slave labor, nine children died by overdosing on fentanyl. Biggin is working on a plan to help the orphanage with its food and water supply, medical staffing and general maintenance. Granite headstones are being constructed in Mexico for the nine dead children and a cemetery plot by the school has been purchased for the orphanage.

The ex-dictator of Belarus, Alexander Lukashenko, and Lieutenant General Alexander Volfovich were found guilty of war crimes and given life sentences by the International Court of Justice in the Hague.

Gray Cardinal released Paul Whelan, Marc Fogel and American journalist Evan Gershkovich. All three are back home in the United States of America.

China's President Xi has returned all property deeds to the U.S. and forgiven all debt owed. He's also granted Taiwan its independence and closed down the Wuhan Shuokang Biological Technology Company as well as the Suzhou Xiaoli Pharmatech chemical company. Both of those companies' CEOs have been imprisoned in China.

Before I forget, I surprised Marty with a mini Bernedoodle. She's beautiful and her name is Sparkles. They're inseparable!

In Memory

The sections of this book mentioning Jimmy Buffett and the Coral Reefer Band were written months before most of us even knew that Jimmy's time left on Earth was limited. To paraphrase Mr. Buffett – From me to you brother:

"I never used to miss the chance to listen to your many tales of life upon the sea. I'm growing older now, a little wiser with my years and I've come to understand the course your heart still steers."

Safe sailing brother...Bubbles Up!

In Memory of "The Hulk"

Before "Arcadia" was published, we lost another HB combat PSYOP team member. Ed Dulka was my first team leader in Vietnam and taught me how to stay alive in the mountains of the DMZ. I always thought he was too damn mean to die, but he lost his battle with cancer on February 1, 2024. You will be missed my friend!

"Arcadia" Credits

A super special THANKS goes out to Marty (Marlene Maria Tatham) for all her help with every endeavor I pursue. She has a knack for making sure I stay on track.

A special THANK YOU goes out to Joanne Welsh and Deb Thomas for their countless hours of proofreading and suggestions. They are always right on the money.

Thank you Pat Wiley for your mentoring and faith in me.

Many thanks to Jordan Kline for his professional work on all of my book covers. Another GREAT JOB my friend!

Thanks to my old and dear friend, Patrick Schlafly, for going to those dark places in service of our country. I always lean on Patrick for his knowledge of weapons in my writing.

A special thanks to my niece Amanda's husband, Stephen James, for his help with the Predator Drone sections of the book. Stephen is an Air Force Technical Sergeant "TSgt" with an MOS of 1N171. That job manages, supervises and performs intelligence activities and functions including exploitation, development and dissemination of multi-sensor imagery products to support war-fighting operations and other activities. We thank you for your continued service to our country.

My thanks always goes out to Sam and Seajay Milner for formatting my books and to their publishing company Sea Dunes Books for publishing them.

I must always thank Google and Google Earth for providing me with the research engines that help me find the many places around the world that I research to make my book more believable.

To Wikipedia for their treasure trove of information available at the touch of a finger.

My gratitude to my brothers in arms: Pistol Pete, Hulk, Big Al and Whoman. We may have lost Whoman a few years ago to brain cancer, but he's never far from our hearts. To our other brothers-in-arms from 7th PSYOP Bn. Company B that we lost in Vietnam: John Blanco, William Gearing, Jeremiah June, Gary Taylor and my dear friend James Pastore. You are with us always and my children and grandchildren know your stories and have visited with you all at the Vietnam Veterans Memorial in Washington, D.C.

And finally, a salute to all the men and women of the United States Armed Forces who watch over us all 24/7. It's their dedication and professionalism that keeps America safe. God bless you all!

Other Books by Stanley Michelsen

Fiction

Political Thrillers:

"Hypersomnolence?"

and

"Bedlamites"

Non-fiction

"Soaring...The Legacy of U.S. Aviator #23 Lieutenant Commander William Merrill Corry, Jr."
Co-Author: James Corry

Stanley Michelsen

A graduate of the U.S. Army
Psychological Operations
Special Warfare School
at Fort Bragg, NC.

In Vietnam he was with the 4th PSYOP Group
7th PSYOP Bn., Company B, Detachment 2
in direct support of the 3rd Marine Division at
Dong Ha Combat Base Northern I Corps
An HB Combat PSYOP Team Leader
Two tours in Vietnam.

Stanley is the proud father of two wonderful children and five
grandchildren.
He and his partner, Marlene Tatham,
reside in the mountains of Western North Carolina.